VISIONS FROM THE PHANTOM LINE

MORE TALES OF TERROR AND THE BIZARRE

B.A. RIES

CONTENTS

FOREWORD

Visions from the Phantom Line: More Tales of Terror and the Bizarre can be enjoyed as a standalone read. However, several of these stories continue the journeys of characters established in my prior book, *Friends, Lovers, & Other Gaslighters: 25 Tales of Terror and the Bizarre*. If you want a quick refresher on the characters and events from that book relevant to this one, please feel free to review the Continuity Refresher located near the end of this compilation.

The stories *Phantom Train of Roanoke Valley* and *The Rogue Trail* intentionally weave together fiction and reality. While many descriptions of their settings (and the histories of those settings) are based in reality, the legends that are the primary focus of these stories, as well as some corresponding details, derive from my imagination.

Once again, I can only hope that you enjoy reading these stories as much as I enjoyed creating them.

1

—————

RETURN TO OFFICE

Nationwide Mandatory Return to Office

The email subject line hit me like a punch to the gut.

Of course, there was no "return" involved, for me at least. I'd been hired, *pre-pandemic*, to a fully remote position. I recalled the countless hours I'd spent scouring for such a role and how ecstatic I'd been when I'd been selected for it. The job entailed hard work, but I'd excelled at it, and my husband and I had built our family around the flexibility it offered.

Now, my employer had the gall to suggest that its rescission of the promise it had made to me would improve "productivity," foster "increased collaboration," and instill a sense of "family" amongst our staff. *Nope, nope, and yuck,* I thought.

The email continued by declaring that "true success and experience" required a regular presence in the office. It all read like our CEO, in typical form, projecting his own uselessness and impotence onto his employees. I sighed. Why couldn't I – or, for that matter, anyone else on my team – be dumb, lazy, and shortsighted enough to climb the corporate ladder as high as he had?

My husband and I scrambled to make the necessary life changes as my applications to other jobs went nowhere. Realizing we could no longer give our dog the amount of exercise and attention she needed, we rehomed her to live with my mother-in-law. We staggered our work schedules to permit one of us to drop off our twins at daycare and the other to pick them up at the end of the day. My husband, who always fought to maintain a positive attitude, reminded me that we were still living a good life in the grand scheme of things, even if we were set to have less time together as a family.

"I know," I replied. "It's just that we all know that these changes aren't happening for good reasons. We're moving *backwards*, just because the dipshits who run these companies think they're a lot smarter than they really are." I shrugged, feeling defeated and exasperated. "But that's just the way it's always been, and always going to be, isn't it?"

~

Finding a parking space – driving was the only option, due to the lack of public transit – proved nightmarish. For over twenty minutes, I meandered through all nine floors of the garage hunting for a spot. Finally, I wedged my car into the only gap I could find, which lay between a support column and a truck left sloppily over the line by its driver, and escaped my vehicle by crawling out of the back seat.

As I hurried down a staircase and towards the main building, I wondered how anyone who arrived after me would be able to park. I was there relatively early, after all, and I hadn't seen any other available spaces.

Passing underneath the giant Abernathy Industries emblem, I entered the main lobby, where a young woman an azure jacket-and-skirt suit waved to me. "You must be Cora," she said, before introducing herself as Monica. "I'm with HR, and I'll be showing you the way to your office."

"Nice to meet you, Monica," I said. "I believe we've talked by email a few times."

"Indeed we have!" As we shook hands, a bright, beaming smile stretched across her face. "This is *such* an exciting day for me," she gushed, a tear in her eye. "For all of us, really. You've been a part of this company for years, but, now, it feels different. Like you're finally a part of our family."

This took me aback. Naturally, I did not see, and had no desire to ever see, the people I put up with to pay my mortgage as brothers or sisters. Or second cousins twice removed, for that matter. "Um, so, how do I find my office?" I asked, eager to change the subject.

"Oh, right," Monica responded, as if snapping out of a trance. "This way."

As she led me to the building's main elevator, we passed a set of closed double-doors labeled "Auditorium." "We do big events in there too," Monica explained. "In fact, we'll be doing a welcome celebration for you and all the other former remote workers in there this afternoon. Everyone will be in attendance. We're all *so* excited for it!"

Dear God, I thought, reflexively recoiling at the thought of an office social gathering. All I wanted from this company was a fucking paycheck, not a party to honor its latest efforts to torment me.

Inside the elevator, Monica pressed the button for "19." This confused me, as my supervisor had emailed me that my team's offices were on the 18th floor.

Monica, as if reading my mind, informed me that renovations were occurring in the 18th floor elevator lobby. "So, you'll have to go to the 19th floor, and then work your way down from there! I'll show you."

"Oh, okay," I mumbled, annoyed at the extra time it would take to reach my workspace.

The doors opened to reveal a gloomy hallway. Half the overhead lights seemed to be broken, and the other half flickered sporadically over a narrow patch of marble floor surrounded by a sea of carpet patterned in sickly shades of brown, grey, and dark green. "Accounting is that way," said Monica, motioning to the right, "And HR, including my office, is straight ahead. But for now, follow me this way through sales."

At this, Monica abruptly scurried into the darkness. I called out for her to slow down, but she ignored me. Seeing no other option, I doubled my speed to keep up with her.

We passed offices, cubicles, a run-down kitchen, and copy machines. I became disoriented as Monica turned sharply to the left, then to the left again at the next intersection, then right, then left once more.

As Monica took me past a corner office, I peeked through the window of its closed door. Inside, I glimpsed a well-dressed figure sitting behind a desk. He was frozen in place, as if deep in thought, and, bizarrely, his face seemed to have no features at all. No eyes, no nose, no mouth – just smooth skin bereft of any other qualities.

That can't be right, I thought to myself, as I continued to hurry after Monica. Surely the window was made of frosted glass, or my eyes were playing tricks on me in the low light.

Monica's voice emerged from the distant shadows. "You still there, Cora?"

"Yeah, yeah on my way," I panted as I jogged towards her.

Monica proceeded to lead me down a staircase. The floor below was just as gloomy as the floor above, and reaching my cubicle required transversing a maze of narrow corridors.

"And here it is – your very own workspace!" announced Monica as I examined the small area, which contained only a dingy chair facing a dusty computer on a plain desk. "If you have any concerns, just let me know! Otherwise, I'll be seeing you at the welcoming party later!"

"Actually, I do have a few questions," I said, as I took a seat. "About the lighting, and the route we took to get here. And the lack of space in the parking garage, and..." To my surprise, I looked back to find Monica gone.

"Monica?" I called. She didn't respond, and when I got up to search for her, she seemed to have vanished.

~

My computer slowly came to life, only to promptly turn itself off moments later. I groaned as the process repeated itself several times before the computer finally stayed on long enough for the 'log in' screen to appear. I hastily entered my credentials.

My computer's hard drive proceeded to heat up and emit a series of discordant noises, as if my mere act of logging into it was causing it to struggle under an intense strain. How was I going to get anything done with all these delays? If I were using my work laptop, which I'd been required to mail back several days ago, I'd have accomplished a considerable amount already.

Finally, after several minutes, everything appeared to have loaded. I opened two spreadsheets and was about to start working when an unfamiliar voice startled me.

"Cora! So good to see you."

I turned to find myself facing a Hispanic woman with long brown hair. Before I could react, she dashed up to me and wrapped her arms around me.

"Woah, woah, stop that!" I screamed as I angrily shoved her off me.

She backed up, her expression changing to a mixture of puzzlement and concern. "Is something wrong, Cora? Did I surprise you?"

"Who *are* you?" I asked.

"What? You know who I am. Don't be silly."

"Um, no."

She let out an irritated sigh. "Look, Cora, I'm not playing whatever game this is. It's me, Ava, your mentor and partner on *countless* projects. And you *know* that from the dozens and dozens of video calls we've had together. So why are you pretending not to?"

This left me dumfounded and bewildered. The person she was describing, the Ava I'd worked with for years, simply wasn't the woman standing at the entrance of my cubicle. That Ava – the correct one – was *Black* for starters, had a totally different voice, and was not the kind of person to surprise me with an unsolicited hug.

When I didn't respond – I didn't know *how* to, after all – fake-Ava chimed in. "It's probably just the lights – they sure keep it dim around here, don't they? But you'll get used to it! When management first removed most of the lights, it upset me. But I adjusted, and it stopped bothering me after a while." She continued, oblivious to the total disinterest I attempted to project. "Less electricity saves money and supports the bottom line, after all, and that's what matters most!

Anyway, did you hear the latest about Michael? His wife discovered the pictures – the ones with that flight attendant I told you about – and she's *furious*! Michael, meanwhile, keeps..."

As she spoke, my mind tried to wrap itself around what was happening. Who was this person, and why was she impersonating Ava? And why was everything at the office so goddamn weird?

"Anyway," continued fake-Ava, after several minutes of monologuing, "are you alright, Cora? You look tired."

"Yeah, I'm just feeling a little run-down," I answered, truthfully. James and Ella had woken up twice last night. I'd barely gotten any sleep.

"The twins keeping you up again?" she asked.

This bothered me. It felt like an invasion of my privacy. How the hell did this lady know about my family situation? I'd vented about family issues to Ava – the *real* Ava – many times, but *this* lady had no way of knowing any of that.

"Look, why don't we talk later?" I asked, eager to get rid of her. "I need to get back to work."

"Sure thing! I'll see you soon! Let's grab lunch sometime soon." At that, fake-Ava finally left me in peace.

I turned back to my computer. I thought about typing up a resignation letter and marching right out, assuming I could even find the building exit at this point. Everything that had happened thus far today left me deeply uncomfortable. I didn't want to work here anymore, consequences be damned.

I opened a blank Word document and began drafting an email to my supervisor explaining all the reasons why I was providing my two-week's notice. The thoughts I laid out were unfiltered and littered with pejoratives directed at company leadership. I knew I would water it down and clean it up prior to sending it, but, for now, it felt good to write how I honestly felt.

Before long, the words before me blurred together as the combination of minimal lighting and barely two hours of sleep sent me into a daze. *I'll close my eyes, just for a second,* I told myself as I leaned back and retreated into memories of happier times.

~

I awoke to the sound of a high-pitched whine. At first, I assumed it to be the nighttime cry of James or Ella signifying the need for a diaper change or feeding. But, as I regained my senses, I realized that I was still at work, and that I'd somehow managed to fall into a deep sleep in my cubicle's second-rate chair. Frantically, I checked my phone. It was 3:01 p.m. I'd slept nearly *all day*.

I chided myself for letting this happen. I'd never slept at work before, much less for so long. Though, in fairness to me, nearly all the lights were out, and the room was almost pitch-black.

Whatever, I thought. I'd made up my mind to quit this job anyway. Perhaps it was something of a conciliation prize that I'd managed to fall into the deepest nap since I gave birth to the twins on the same day I would provide my two-week's notice.

But why was it so damn dark, and what *was* the distant sound – which continued to wail through my work area – that had woken me?

I discerned something strange about my computer, too. When I placed my hands on the keyboard, the buttons felt different than usual. They didn't press down, or react at all to my touch.

When I shined my only source of light – my cell phone's flashlight function – on my computer, I saw that my computer had been replaced by *a paper replica of itself*, the kind of thing you'd (if you're old enough) see in a display at an office supplies store.

What the fuck? I thought. The weirdness of it alone bothered me plenty, but even worse was the implication that someone had switched out my functioning computer while I dozed right in front of it. *That's it, I'm getting out of here.*

The first thing I noticed as I entered the surrounding labyrinth of offices and cubicles is that they all appeared to be unoccupied. My flashlight revealed a few signs of life – a stray pen, a coffee mug, or a half-finished snack – but no people. Picture frames stood on some desks and hung on some walls, but they displayed only blank voids rather than images of smiling families.

I tried to retrace the route Monica had taken me on, but quickly found myself at a dead end. "Hello?" I hollered. "I'm a bit lost, can anybody help me?" There was no response.

As I wandered further, turning in different directions as I went, it dawned on me that I'd yet to see a single window to the outside world. Even as my surroundings seemed to stretch on unbelievably far, the lack of any glimpse of the sun or sky made me feel claustrophobic. I encountered two staircase doors, but, in what I assumed to be a serious fire hazard, each was locked. The handle to one of them – marked "Emergency Exit" – was even encumbered by layers of heavy metal chains.

The sound that woke me reverberated again. I was close to it, and I could now sense that it possessed a hollow, machine-like timbre. Lacking any better ideas, I headed down towards it.

The carpeted floor before me was damp. Some kind of puddle had formed on it and, while I couldn't get a good look at it, the wet substance on it did not appear to be water. Rather, it had a murky, greenish quality to it. Using my flashlight, I traced the liquid to its source, which appeared to be an air vent that steadily dripping a small stream of it onto the ground below.

I hopped over puddle, landing near the closed door to the room that appeared to be the source of the sound. When I opened the door, the blinding light inside forced me to shut my eyes.

As my vision slowly adjusted, I realized that the sound simply originated from the standard copy machine housed in this room, which appeared to be in the midst of a large printing job.

Examining it more closely, I realized that it seemed to be stuck in a peculiar loop. Each page in a large ream of paper entered it on one side, went through the machine, and exited without a single marking on it. Once the output tray reached a particular height, the sheets would slide down a ramp into the input tray, repeating the loud and pointless cycle. I placed a finger on the "Power" button and held it there until the machine turned off.

An eerie silence followed, broken only by the soft pats of my feet against the carpet as I re-entered the hallway. I walked, trying every door as I did so. Most were locked. Some led to vacant offices. Others led to empty closets, or break rooms with crumbs and pots half-filled with the remnants of last week's coffee.

As time passed, the darkness around me, still punctured only by my phone light, seemed to grow more opaque, more encompassing. Occasionally, I'd see what looked to be the same supply cabinet filled with purple highlighters, or the same translucent puddle of gunk, or the same cubicle with a running fan and a chair plopped on its side – hints that I was somehow traveling in a circle – but I took no discernible turns, and the order in which I came upon each landmark was inconsistent.

How do I get out of here? I realized I was becoming thirsty, and I knew my phone battery wouldn't last forever. When I tried calling my husband – to be followed, if he didn't answer, by a call to the front desk, and then 911 if necessary – the call failed, despite my phone displaying that it had service.

Distant sounds drew my attention. At first, they resembled high-pitched giggles, but as I approached, they erupted into the buoyant laughter of a crowd.

How anyone could feel compelled to express any feeling of joy in this hellhole perplexed me, but I attempted to track down the source all the same. *If I just follow the laughter, I'll find someone who can lead me out,* I told myself. But, deep down, what I wanted most was the simple reassurance that I wasn't stuck here all alone.

I ran down hallways. I climbed over cubicle walls. I yanked at stuck doorknobs and stormed from one side of a sticky, dingy kitchen to the exit on the other side. Finally, I found myself in a narrow corridor. At the opposite end, an overhead light blared over an open rectangular space. At least a dozen figures stood in it, but my eyes – having long ago adjusted to the dark – couldn't make out any distinguishing features on them. They just stood there, facing me.

Then, all at once, they were gone. Their laughter faded, too, leaving behind only the same sterile silence that had haunted me for so long.

Had they run away or gone somewhere else? I chased after them, calling out for help.

I found myself in exactly the place I was looking for: an elevator lobby. Contrary to Monica's warning, I see no evidence of renovations. The people assembled here must have just gone downstairs. I didn't ask myself what they were doing standing here and bellowing for so long. I didn't need to know that. I just needed to get the hell out – something I finally had a way to do.

Nervously, I held out my hand and prayed that the "Down" button. I held my breath as the floor display slowly reached my level – 12, 13, 14, 15, 16, 17… The doors then opened to reveal a clean, well-lit elevator cab. I rushed inside, hit the "Lobby" button, and watched with relief as the doors closed and the elevator began its descent.

I tapped my sweaty fingers impatiently against the wall as the floors steadily ticked down. Finally, "L" appeared, and the doors opened to the main lobby.

Only one thing stood between me and the exit: a pale woman with curly red hair, the first person I'd seen in ages, whose face lit up upon seeing me exit the elevator. "Girl, what took you so long?" she hollered in a nauseatingly excited voice. "You almost missed it, come on!"

"I, uh," I sped past her, my gaze focused on the way out.

She moved rapidly, her firm hand grabbing me around the wrist before I could react. I attempted to fling her off, but with surprising force, she easily held me in place.

"Cora, the party's *that* way," she said, gesturing towards the auditorium with the hand that wasn't restraining me. "I know how much you want to get home and see the twins, but you *have* to at least make an appearance."

"Let me go!" I cried.

She adopted a deadpan expression. "Cora, we're *not* doing that. First you pretend not to know me, next you zone out the *whole* time I'm filling you in about Michael, and now you try to skip your own welcome back party? You and me were like sisters, Cora. What happened to you?"

My jaw dropped. Was *this* person *also* pretending to be Ava?

I tried to pull away from her again, only for the second fake Ava to whirl around, restrain me, and, with remarkable strength, pull me towards the auditorium. I kept trying to fight her, to pull her off of me, but all succeeded in doing was exhausting myself even further.

Some of what followed passed in a blur. I recall Ava, or whatever she was, dragging me passed row after row of empty seats, across countless small puddles of rancid goo, and onto a stage covered in banners, streams, and balloons; an unnatural warmth drifting down from the air above; and the sense that I was being watched by something hostile and utterly evil. I remember spotting a loose balloon and watching it as it floated ever so slowly, up and above the auditorium stage. With a loud "pop," it burst upon making contact with a sight that still horrifies me to this day.

An amalgam of body parts stretched across the ceiling. A soup of limbs, torsos, lips, ears and, more than anything, faces. *So many* faces, all floating in an inverted pool, a hazy green substance occasionally dripping from their pained, open mouths onto the floor below.

A plethora of voices, one of which I recognized as Monica's, began speaking. "Welcome home." "We're happy to have you here with us." "We've been waiting for you for so long." "I knew you'd make it."

I felt paralyzed. For a moment, I stood there, speechless and stunned, as the faces – male and female, black and white, young and old – oozed into a new form held together by flabby patches of skin and bent tendons. They combined into a gigantic, monstrous face, with an open, hungry mouth lined by hundreds of lips, filled with teeth composed of thousands of teeth.

Out of its mouth slithered a long, slimy organ. It unfurled as it dropped, landing before me with a wet 'plop'. It was a tongue, stitched together from the tongues and various other organs that had once belonged to the marketers, janitors, supervisors, accountants, and secretaries of my company.

My captor pushed me closer to it. For a moment, I thought about giving up. About letting the sticky ligament wrap around me and pull me upwards into the gaping mouth. I wondered what it would be like to be digested by that thing, to become a part of it, to become one with everyone else. I imagined it swallowing up my anxieties, my student debt, and my bouts of insomnia, and replacing them with bottomless sleep.

The mouth above me emanated several words in a deep, slurred voice, but I wasn't paying attention to it. I knew I had to fight. Not just for myself, but also for the twins, my husband, and the life I wanted to live. James and Ella are counting on me, I told myself, as I mustered the kind of strength that courses through an animal protecting its young.

It caught fake-Ava off guard. At first, she managed to keep her grip on me, but the pain from the way I scratched and dug my nails into her arm eventually wore her down. With all my might, I pried her off of me and, without wasting a moment, took the opportunity to run.

I remember screaming. Loud, even deafening, screaming – from above, as if every face that made up that creature was shrieking its disapproval. But I didn't look up, nor did I glance back to see if fake-Ava was following me.

No, all I did was run. I sprinted across the auditorium, through the main lobby, and out the front door. I kept going for as long as I could, until my feet were blistered and my body could take me no further. I didn't care about my car – which, to this day, I assume remains where I left it between the support column and the truck. I just cared about putting as much distance as possible between me and my employer.

~

I still have nightmares about what I saw. More than anything, what frightens me is the knowledge that it's still out there, and that it's still hungry.

There was a strange email on my computer the next morning. It was from Monica, and it stated that my resignation email had been accepted. This struck me as weird, as I'd never finished writing, much less sent, that email. But I had no reason to pick a fight about it – Monica promised a good severance, after all, and even added that I wouldn't have to do anything more to collect it. No paperwork, no projects to finish up. It would be a clean break.

"Best wishes to you and your family!" she wrote at the end of the message. This made me uncomfortable, though it took me a moment to realize why.

Then it dawned on me. It was what the thing, the face on the ceiling, had said to me just as I made my move to escape. The words I have tried so very, very hard to block out of my mind ever since:

"Join us, Cora. Come, become a part of our family."

2

THE VISITOR

Uncle Wyatt spoke in a firm, commanding voice. "Patrick and Megan, please come over here. We have something important to discuss."

My little sister and I exchanged a nervous glance. Were we in trouble? Had mom's condition worsened?

Aunt Amy, perhaps sensing our reaction, used a more reassuring tone. "It's quite alright. You haven't done anything wrong. We just need to talk. Please, take a seat."

Feeling somewhat relieved, we did so.

Uncle Wyatt took a deep breath before talking again. "We've been tracking the road conditions nearby, and the flooding has only gotten worse. That means that neither your dad, nor anyone else for that matter, is likely going to be able to get here anytime soon. There's one route through the valley that may open up, but the authorities aren't optimistic. So, you're likely going to be stuck with us for at least a few days longer."

"Oh, that's okay with us," I replied. "We like it here. Right, sis?" Megan nodded. She tried to speak, but Aunt Amy quickly cut her off.

"No, no, that's not it – we like having you here, and we know that Robert and Gary feel the same way. It's just that, well, there's something rather *unusual* that could occur between now and when you leave, and it's very important that you be prepared for it. I want you to listen carefully to what we're about to tell you. Your lives may very well depend on it."

~

We'd always been close with our cousins. The blood relationship was through my mother, who was Uncle Wyatt's sister. They had two kids – Robert, who was a year older than Megan, and Gary, who was a year older than me.

They lived about three hours from us. Their home was massive, much larger than ours, and lavishly decorated. Reaching it required traversing many miles of windy roads up and down numerous heavily forested Appalachian hills.

We often visited each other, with my family housing theirs in the spring and their family housing ours around the holidays. Though, this year, they'd abruptly cancelled the planned Christmas gathering, citing Robert falling ill.

When my mom, Megan, and I visited a holiday market at a town near where our cousins lived, we asked if any of them wanted to join us. Uncle Wyatt and Gary did so, and we spent a nice afternoon with them perusing crafts displays and munching on snacks from food stands.

We were about to head home – eager to get ahead of a looming winter storm – when mom fell seriously ill. We weren't sure what it was, but we quickly realized that she was in no shape to drive, and there wasn't a good hospital anywhere nearby.

I never got the full details about what happened to her. I know that it started out as food poisoning, but became something worse that lingered for some time. I remember Uncle Wyatt and Aunt Amy helping mom into their house and setting her up in the guest bedroom. A doctor, or at least someone I assumed to be one, braved the downpour to take a look at her, and recommended several days of bedrest as her body fought off whatever affliction she faced. Meanwhile, our dad, who was across the country on a business obligation, scrambled to reach us as soon as he could.

Thus, for two days, Megan and I had been stranded with our cousins. As worried as we were about mom, we nonetheless enjoyed spending our days hanging out with Robert and Gary – the former of whom, strangely enough, did not seem sick at all. Naturally, we often paired off, with Megan and Robert playing with dolls or stuffed animals, and Gary and I watching the kinds of violent movies my parents wouldn't allow around our house on their large basement television.

The situation was a bit strange, but Megan and I were making the most of it and, honestly, we were having a pretty good time. That is, until Uncle Wyatt and Aunt Amy told us something we would never forget.

~

"Our *lives*?" I gasped. "What are you talking about?"

Aunt Amy reached out to me and Megan and gently took both of our hands, which she squeezed lightly before responding. "What we're about to tell you is going to sound, well, farfetched. But, please, *please* trust me that it's real. And, also, that if you listen to what we tell you, everything's going to be okay. Robert and Gary have been through it many times, and, as you can see, they're just fine."

"There's a man who visits us." Uncle Wyatt paused for a moment. He frowned and touched his forehead, as if pondering what he'd just said. "Well, he's...not quite a 'man', or a 'he', even, but that's how we refer to him. He comes once every year. We don't know when, but it's always when all of us are home together. There are rules about it... like, we can't all take an extended overseas vacation to try to avoid him. He'll punish us if we do that. We just have to live our lives here and, at some point...he shows up."

As Megan's face took on a concerned expression, a sense of panic ran through me. Had the cousins we'd grown up around all lost their minds?

Aunt Amy again seemed attuned to our reactions. "It's okay, Megan. And, I understand you being skeptical, Patrick." Once again, she read me perfectly. "But please, just hear us out."

Uncle Wyatt continued. "I can't, won't get into the details. I don't fully understand it myself. It's just that, well, it's December, and he hasn't arrived yet. So, he's due any day now. When he gets here, he'll knock five times. That's how we know it's him. Then, we have to let him inside, and, and...um..." He stopped, seemingly struggling to find the right words.

Sensing her husband's hesitation, Aunt Amy interjected. "You have to ignore him. Just ignore him. And, eventually, he'll go away, and then he won't bother us again. Until next year. Sometimes he stays for only ten minutes. Other times, close to an hour. He doesn't care about infants or the seriously ill - if your mom's still stuck in bed when he arrives, he'll probably ignore her altogether. But, the rest of us need to be on our best behavior, acting like a normal, happy family. The key is that no matter what he does, *do not acknowledge his presence*, at all costs. But don't freeze up, either. You need to act like he isn't there at all."

Aunt Amy looked at us sorrowfully. "We'd hoped to never have to tell you about this. We don't tell anyone, not if we can help it, but we see no choice here. Tonight, we're going to do a practice run, with Wyatt pretending to be the visitor. Before we get started with that, do you have any questions?"

At first, I couldn't say anything. Naturally, I did have questions - so many, in fact, that it was difficult for me to sort through them all. I had concerns, too. My mind fought to reconcile my past history with my cousins, family members I loved and trusted, with the utter insanity of what they were saying to me and Megan.

Megan turned to me. She was worried and confused, and she was looking to me for guidance. I croaked, "Um, uh, so, this man-" That's when it happened.

KNOCK. A heavy thud emanated from the front door.

Aunt Amy's face grew pale. "Shit. He doesn't usually come this late in the evening."

This bothered me. I'd never even heard Aunt Amy curse before. More importantly, neither she nor Wyatt seemed to be in control of the situation.

KNOCK

Uncle Wyatt hollered upstairs. "Robert, Gary, he's here! Get to your spots, now!" I heard shuffling as they made their way down the staircase that connects the bedrooms to the main level.

I wanted to leap into action. I wanted to do *something*. Was the person at the door as dangerous as my aunt and uncle had said? And, if so, why were they just letting him inside like this? Shouldn't they try to keep him out?

And, for that matter, should I grab Megan and try to flee outside with her? That would put distance between us and both the visitor and the family I was no longer sure I could trust. But, then I remembered the heavy storm and realized that the only option was to stay here.

KNOCK KNOCK

Aunt Amy turned to Megan and me. "We're out of time. Sit at the living room table with Robert and Gary and play whatever board game they've set up. We'll be in here making dinner. Focus on the game and don't make eye contact with him. Don't look at him at all, if you can help it, no matter how close he gets to you. Got it?"

Before we could respond, she nudged us towards the living room. Robert and Gary were already there, setting up a Monopoly board.

Too much was happening, too quickly. I decided that the best course of action, at least for the moment, was to follow my aunt and uncle's instructions. I gripped Megan's hand and told her that we were going to be okay, and we proceeded to join Robert and Gary at the table.

KNOCK

"Gary, what's up with all this?" I whispered, prompting Gary to raise a finger over his mouth while dealing us our starting amount of Monopoly money.

Uncle Wyatt, meanwhile, opened the door.

The visitor wasn't wearing a coat. Nor, despite the downpour outside, was he even wet. I began to wonder how he'd even gotten here at all, given the state of the roads nearby.

He had an aged, wrinkly face and wore a plaid button-down short-sleeved sport shirt tucked into a pair of khaki pants. What little remained of his thin, white hair combed over a large bald spot. He looked...totally innocuous, at least insofar as I managed to glimpse him in my periphery while keeping my eyes directed towards the board.

"Megan, you need to pick one of these," I said, gesturing to the dog, iron, and shoe pieces. I was doing my best to keep her attention on the game, rather than whatever was happening at the front door. She selected the shoe.

As the visitor stepped further into the house, Uncle Wyatt closed the door and retreated quietly to the kitchen, where I could hear the sink running and the clattering of dishes. Aunt Amy called out to us from there, her voice straining to sound casual. "Just a little while longer until dinner's ready!"

While Gary motioned for me to put my starting piece - the battleship - at "Go," I continued to observe the visitor out of the corner of my eye. He moved slowly, with a stilted and awkward gait, past our cousin's ornately-decorated Christmas tree. He lifted a family photo from the top of a cabinet and held it in front of his face, as if to examine it. Only, his eyes shifted in the other direction, peering curiously toward the four of us in the living room.

"I put together some snacks for you all," announced Uncle Wyatt as Robert rolled the die for his first turn. Uncle Wyatt proceeded to place a plate of cheese and crackers on the table next to the board.

He returned to the kitchen, leaving us alone with the visitor who sauntered slowly in our direction. He then turned and meandered around the living room couch until he was behind me and, thus, fully out of my sight.

Megan glanced up at me - no, behind me, and her eyes widened. "Hey, Megan, how about trying some of the food?" I suggested, trying to divert her attention from whatever the visitor was doing. Gary, catching on, handed her a cracker with a piece of cheese on it. She took a bite of it and, with great effort, tore her eyes from behind me.

I could sense the visitor getting closer to me. The first thing I noticed was the stench. It was like a mix of vomit, burning rubber, and the foul scent of a large pile of moldy, rotten garbage. The smell worsened as he crept closer until, finally, he was mere inches away. I felt hot, putrid breath on my neck, and a shadow appeared on the floor as he leaned over me.

It was my turn. So I rolled the dice. Snake eyes. I moved the battleship figurine two spaces.

That's when I heard the whispering. It was more like a chattering crowd - dozens of small, quiet voices trying to overtalk one another. One, which reminded me of one of the kids from the *Oliver!* musical Megan had recently been obsessed with, repeated the word "*trapped.*" Another, which resembled that of a middle-aged male chain smoker, moaned "*hungry.*" An wispy, androgenous voice emerged from the others. It giggled, and then articulated in an oddly playful manner, "*Wanna know how you're going to die? Wanna know? Wanna know? Wanna know?*"

Gary's voice drew my attention back to the game. "Patrick."

"Yeah? What?" I bit my lip, realizing I sounded a little too startled.

"It's still your turn. Doubles, you know?"

"Oh. Right."

The voice cackled, as if taking delight in the misery it was causing me. "*You'll live to see your sister die. I know how. I know when. But you don't want to know how. You don't want to know when.*"

Jesus fucking Christ, I thought. I wanted to bash this, this, thing's face in. I wanted to scream at it. I wanted to take Megan out of here.

But I realized by this point that my aunt and uncle's warnings were worth heeding. So, instead, I rolled the die again. Two fours. I moved the battleship eight spaces and limply announced that I was purchasing a railroad.

"*Wyatt. Wyatt. Wyatt. Wyatt will be quiet.*"

I rolled a third time. Two threes.

This prompted Robert to pipe up. "Speeding! Directly to jail!"

Ignoring the game, the visitor murmured in my ear. "*From a great height he'll fall. Years from now he'll hear the call.*" He then snickered obnoxiously.

Meanwhile, the other two voices repeated.

"*Trapped, trapped, trapped.*"

"Hungry, hungry, hungry."

"Trapped, trapped, trapped."

"Hungry, hungry, hungry."

As I moved the battleship to the 'jail' space, something dropped from where the man's head hovered over mine. It landed on the table with a wet 'plop.' It took me a moment to realize what it was.

It was a *tongue* - one that somehow stretched several feet. My jaw dropped as I realized that it wasn't just a single tongue - no, it was *dozens* of smaller, human-sized tongues sewn together into one giant appendage.

With a loud 'flump,' *another* massive tongue hit the table, followed by a third. All three then crawled towards the cheese tray, leaving behind a disgusting trail of saliva as they did so. Each wrapped around a portion of the food, only to then be retracted back into the visitor's mouth.

Somehow, Robert and Gary remained entirely unperturbed by this grotesquery. Megan, on the other hand, appeared on the brink of breaking down.

Gary tried to direct her attention back to the game. "It's your turn, Megan."

Megan ignored him, clearly panicking. I can't say I blamed her. A bead of sweat dripped down her face, and her body shook all over. Tears formed in her eyes, and I could tell she was applying all her strength to hold back a scream.

"Hey Megan, you need to go." I said. "How about I roll for you, okay?"

The visitor took notice of Megan's disintegrating mental state. He withdrew from me and hobbled over to her.

The die produced a four and a three. "Seven it is then. Why don't you move your piece, Megan?" I smiled and made an effort to sound as calm as possible. Yet, Megan remained frozen.

The visitor was immediately behind her now. I noticed bulges forming, and then deflating, in the skin on his head. First in his left cheek, then his forehead, then his right cheek. Megan's face formed a disgusted expression as she experienced the full impact of his repugnant smell.

"Patrick...I, I can't..."

The visitor emitted a muffled noise that sounded like a wild animal screeching through a tight muzzle. That's when his body started changing.

"You're going to be fine, Megan. Just play out your turn," I begged.

Meanwhile, the man's nose started to droop out of place. His eyeballs were next, followed by each remaining feature of his face. All of it drifted out of its place and down, lower, lower, until it tumbled down his shirt or fell onto the floor. Holes formed in the skin that remained, and out of those holes dripped several streams of blood that landed on Megan's pile of money of the one property she'd accumulated.

"One, two, three, four, five, six, seven," I counted as I moved her piece, desperate to get her attention. I gulped as, behind Megan, what remained of the visitor's face folded in on itself and collapsed, as if hollow at its core. Flaps of skin descended beneath his shirt, leaving only an empty void in their place.

"Community chest," I related. "How about drawing a card, huh?" I held out the yellow deck for her.

I maintained a supportive smile even as a series of horrors emerged from where the visitor's head had once been. A long, spherical shape came out of his neck, followed by another, then a third. Each loosely resembled the head of a snake, but with dozens of human-shaped eyes of various colors - brown, hazel, blue - surrounding its mouth. The heads hovered around my sister, with one above her and one on either side.

Simultaneously, each opened its mouth, revealing three circular layers of razor-sharp teeth inside. Their mouths kept opening further and further. I gasped as their size expanded to that large enough to swallow an orange, then a grapefruit, and then even a...

I lifted the top card for her. "Hey, sis, it says here that you got second place in a beauty contest! But that's not right, is it?" I forced a laugh. "I'll bet it originally said that you won first place, but it became second place because *I* picked up the card, and the game knew I'd never win a contest like that." I knew my comment didn't make a lot of sense, but I made myself laugh again anyway.

She smiled and then, even as tears streamed down her eyes, chuckled. "Yeah. That's what happened. I'll um, I'll uh, I'll..."

Gary completed her thought. "Collect the 10 dollar prize." He handed her the bill. She calmly took hold of it and added it to her hand.

Thankfully, the creatures - whatever existed within the visitor - took notice and slowly pulled away from Megan. Thank god, I thought.

That's when Aunt Amy arrived with the food. The sight of this *thing*, with its mouths seemingly poised to tear apart my little sister, caught her totally off guard.

Impulsively, she screamed. In doing so, she lost control of the platter she was holding. The plates on it fell, shattering loudly against the floor, which quickly became covered by bits of food and broken porcelain.

"Keep playing," mumbled Gary. Robert nodded and made his roll.

When I glanced back at the visitor, his body had reformed, albeit imperfectly. The skin around his face had returned, but his nose was tilted, and one eye dangled out of its socket.

He took a step towards Aunt Amy, who whimpered. "No, no, no. I'm sorry. I can't...I can't keep..."

The visitor let out the same animalist cry as before as it pinned her against the wall.

To my horror, Amy didn't fight back. Instead, she merely spoke in a desperate, pleading tone. "What do you say we go to the basement, away from the family?"

Robert began sobbing, prompting a "shh" from Gary as he performed his turn.

The visitor withdrew and gestured towards the door that led to the basement. Amy nodded and then briefly turned back to us. When she spoke, she attempted to interject her words with senses of calmness and normalcy, but her rushed delivery and panicked stuttering rendered these efforts utterly contrived. "I...uh, I, um, I'm just grabbing something from the freezer, and I'll, um, be back in just a moment."

Amy opened the door and began the descent. The visitor followed, closing the door behind him.

Robert called out for his father, prompting a pale-faced Uncle Wyatt to enter the room from where he'd been observing in the kitchen. "Dad, what do we do?"

"We can't do anything. We just can't."

"What the hell is wrong with you?" I yelled as Megan and Robert's sobbing became audible. "Aunt Amy is down there with that *monster*. We have to do *something*. All of us together can fight it. We have to try."

Wyatt stammered angrily in response. "No! No. That won't work. You need to get back to your game. If it comes back up here, and we're arguing like this-"

I cut him off. "So you're going to do *nothing* to protect your own wife?"

Wyatt, his face a deep red, shrieked his response. "Patrick, you don't know what you're talking about. You will do as I say, or the same thing that's happening to her will happen to us. It's too late for Amy. All we can do is save ourselves."

"That's total bullshit," I retorted.

Gary, to my disdain, took Wyatt's side. "Dad's right. We need to keep playing like nothing happened. It's the only way. Please, if not for yourself, for us, and for your sister."

Wyatt waved his finger at me and Megan, as if disciplining us. He snarled, "If you two had just never showed up in the first place-"

This time, Gary, game to our defense. "Dad! It's not their fault. Like you said, we have to calm down."

~

Several minutes later, the basement door slowly opened. To my relief, Aunt Amy emerged from it and stepped into the kitchen. But where was the visitor? And what had happened down there?

"One hotel on Mediterranean," I said, handing cash to Gary.

Gary shot me a disdainful glare. "Really? You know, statistically-"

"Just give me the goddamn hotel," I snapped.

Aunt Amy began walking slowly across the room. A sense of dread fell over me as I got a better view of her. She moved awkwardly, lurching from side to side. Her skin drooped and shook with each step. When she reached the front door, she turned back towards us.

A wide, dilapidated smile grew on her face. She stood there like that for several moments. As she did so, saliva spilled out of her mouth and dripped over the pale, sagging skin on her neck and chin. She then spoke in a rough, gravely voice. "It's been a pleasure. But most of you won't be seeing me again." She then opened the door and stepped outside.

Uncle Wyatt was the first to express relief. "I think it's over. Jesus Christ, I think it's over." Megan burst into the tears she'd been holding back. I hurried over to her and hugged her.

That's when there was another knock at the door.

"Mom, she's back!" cried Robert. Before anyone could stop him, he sprinted over to it.

Gary wailed for his brother to stop. "Robert, stop!"

Ignoring him, Robert pulled open the door, revealing someone I did not expect to see.

~

My dad would later explain how, using the car he'd rented from the airport, he'd followed a series of detours along backroads throughout the valley south of my cousin's house. There was no phone service, but, with the assistance of an atlas, he managed to find a safe route there. His wife was sick, after all. He had to get to her.

Upon his arrival, Wyatt rushed mom, Megan and I out to dad's car. When we tried babbling to our dad about what had happened, Wyatt interrupted and overtalked us. "They watched some scary movie. I shouldn't have let them see it, but there's only so much I can do when Amy's stuck at her mother's place." Gary and Robert joined in, insisting that they had watched a movie with us about a terrifying monster who snuck into a family's home.

"Thank you so much for caring for my family, Wyatt," my dad

responded. He then turned to Megan and me, "And, kids, enough with the horror stories. You're too old for this. Especially you, Patrick."

~

Dad brought mom to a hospital that gave her the treatment she needed. In the years that followed, Wyatt, Robert, and Gary did everything they could to convince me and Megan that our memories of what occurred that night were incorrect.

Gary would insist that Wyatt and Amy had had a loud fight, and that we'd mixed up our memories of it with a movie we'd watched.

It was never very convincing. Gary couldn't identify the movie, nor could he explain how we missed all the signs that led to the divorce that was supposedly responsible for us never seeing Aunt Amy again.

Megan and I tried to make sense of what we'd seen. The lack of answers weighed on us. Who was the visitor, why did our cousins let him in, and what happened in the basement?

Nightmares haunted us both for years. In my dreams, I'd watch, helplessly, as the visitor ripped apart my poor, lovely aunt. I'd stare, paralyzed, as he carved out long strips of her skin and placed it on top of his own.

Megan and I had little desire to be around our cousins again. In fact, we hardly saw Robert and Gary until Wyatt's funeral service. By that point, I was nearly thirty, and Megan had recently married a classmate she'd met in medical school.

We knew better than to argue again about what we'd witnessed at their house so many years ago, nor to ask why Amy wasn't in attendance. "I just don't know why he did it," cried a pale-faced Robert after the service. "He just wasn't the same ever since..." His voice drifted off.

On a photo display, I recognized the old man in a plaid, button-down shirt who stood in the backdrop of a photo of Wyatt and Amy's wedding. According to the caption, he was Amy's father, and he'd passed away when I was an infant.

~

It took decades, but the events of that night finally faded from my mind. They existed only as an inexplicable childhood memory, and Gary and Robert's theory that we'd imagined what occurred began to feel more plausible.

When I visit Megan, who has three kids of her own now, we don't talk about it anymore. I'm old enough, now, to know that monsters don't exist, much less bizarre shapeshifters who smell like trash and devour those who react to them.

All that changed when my phone rang this evening. Megan spoke in a rushed, panicked tone. *"She's back."*

"What? Who's back?"

"It's Aunt Amy. Patrick, she hasn't aged a day from when we last saw her, and she just knocked five times at the front door."

3

PHANTOM TRAIN OF ROANOKE VALLEY

I was grumbling my way through yard work yesterday afternoon, trying to finish up the chores I'd been forced to do. The sun was hot, and I was tired of pulling weeds, so I wandered into the woods just beyond our backyard fence. It was a part of our property I never really went to, but something I couldn't explain just told me to go in. I noticed a small patch of dirt that looked oddly loose. Out of curiosity, I started to dig with a stick. A few inches down, I hit something hard. It was an iPhone. I brushed the dirt off the screen and powered it up. The phone was unlocked, and when it connected to our Wi-Fi, it began downloading a series of audio recordings from an iCloud account.

Recording 1 – May 25, 2019, at 10:31 a.m.

Young man [later identified as Ryan]: Well, my second year of college flew by. Once again, I overcommitted a bit and ended up having to back out of a few obligations.

But I'm glad I stuck it out with *The Cavalier Daily*. They needed the help, and the reporting I did for them led me to attend all sorts of interesting events. It's remarkable how much goes on in an average week on campus that most of the university doesn't pay any attention to.

Normally, only seniors get selected as editors. They get significant control over content, as well as a small salary. Melissa told me if I wanted to stand a chance at getting an editor position as a junior, I'd need to return from the summer with something to show for it. "Write something about Roanoke," she'd said. "We get new students from your area every year, but most people here hardly know anything about it."

So, what can I write about my small hometown that will interest people on a campus two hours away? I suppose I could churn out a multipage description of how it gets regularly mistaken for the *other* Roanoke, the one that colonists disappeared from in North Carolina. But I'm sure there's a better subject out there.

I'll have to come up with an idea soon if I'm going to have time to produce something good. Whatever I do, I'll record my progress and any interviews on my phone like I'm doing now, and I can transcribe it all when I've gathered enough material. A friend of mine just started a true-crime podcast. The format seems perfect for this kind of story, and it'll let me share my own process, too.

Recording 2 – May 29, 2019, at 11:30 p.m.

Ryan: I have a lead! I went on a run by River's Edge this evening. When I came upon the abandoned railroad tracks by the bridge over the Roanoke River, I remembered those stories I grew up hearing. The stories differed in the details, but they all involved a ghostly train traveling through the city on a derelict Norfolk-Southern line.

I did a little research. As it turns out, phantom train legends are quite common. Trains are still in regular use throughout the country, but they were obviously a more central form of passenger transportation in the past than they are now, nowhere more so than in a formerly prominent rail hub like Roanoke. People who mourn a loved one may imagine their ghost rising out of a grave. It's not too different from how, in the minds of those who miss the era they represent, long-retired steam locomotives pass over miles of abandoned, moss-covered tracks.

The legends differ, though, as to the trains' destinations. Most of the time, the witnesses simply relate seeing a train pass mysteriously in the night in an area where the tracks are no longer in use, and that'll be the end of the story.

On the rare occasion that one of these trains stops, some of the witnesses will go on board to investigate. It's a common story for the witness to see a loved one, step off (or be ushered off for not having a ticket), and learn the next day that the person they saw had died during the night, the implication being that the train ride consisted of their soul passing on into the next life.

Other tales involve a train stuck in time reenacting a famous event, like the doomed souls heading into Nashville on every anniversary of the Great Train Wreck of 1918, or a mourning train forever bringing the body of the assassinated President Lincoln to grieving citizens between Washington D.C. and Springfield, Illinois.

What's remarkable, though, is that, despite the dozens of renditions of the local legend I heard growing up in Roanoke, I can't find any mention of our own phantom train story online today. I've gone through the obvious search engines as well as multiple social media pages dedicated to local history. Nowhere have I found even a murmur about the subject.

I sense that there's a story here – a folk tale waiting to be gathered. These tales have existed orally throughout the region for decades, at least, and they are waiting for someone to write them up formally. That someone will be me, and this will make for a great article when I return – one that condenses rumors into a coherent piece while also touching on Roanoke's past and present as a railroad town.

Unrelatedly, I met a sweet girl while working at the Grandin. Jennifer's a year older than me and lives in Raleigh Court. When we finished our shifts, she joined me in the back of the theatre to catch the second half of *Brightburn*. It wasn't quite a date, but I did agree to hang out with her and a few of her friends next weekend. Something tells me it's an audition for her friends' approval. If I do well enough, maybe I'll get a date with her after that. I'm keeping my fingers crossed.

Recording 3 – June 3, 2019, at 9:55 a.m.

Ryan: I am currently approaching the Roanoke City Historical

Society to ask a few questions about local ghost train lore. Depending on the response I get, I may or may not bring up that I'm making an audio recording of all this, as I'm technically not obligated to mention it. Okay, here I am.

Excuse me, sir, do you mind if I ask you a few questions about local history?

Society Member: Of course. It's nice to see a young person take an interest in the subject. What can I help you with?

Ryan: I have questions about trains, one train in particular. My name's Ryan, by the way.

Society Member: You can call me Eric. And, that's a subject I know plenty about. What do you want to know?

Ryan: Well, you see, I grew up hearing stories about a ghost train-

Eric: Let me stop you right there. Did you really come here to talk to me about 'ghost trains'?

Ryan: It's not that I think they're real. Don't get me wrong, I'm not crazy or anything. It's just that, I'm trying to write about the stories themselves – what they consist of and how they evolved. You see, as a kid, I-

Eric: You heard a story that spooked you, right? The thing is, most people *outgrow* their childhood fears and move on with their lives. I suggest you do the same.

Ryan: So, you don't know any stories about a ghost train in this area?

Eric: I *know* that there are no rumors, no legends, nothing. If anything like that existed, I'd know about it. Do yourself a favor by finding something else to write about. Now, if there's nothing else I can do for you, I'd like to get on with my day, and I'd like you to leave.

Recording 4 – June 3, 2019 at 10:45 a.m.

Woman: Right this way!

[knocking]

Woman: Mr. Thompson, you have a visitor.

Mr. Thompson: Do come in! Take a seat. We don't get too many reporters coming around the train museum these days. You with the Roanoke Times?

Ryan: No, no, I'm just writing for a college paper. I was wondering if I could ask you a few questions about local history? That's quite a model you've got on your desk.

Mr. Thompson: Yes, yes, I'm building an exact replica of one of the old trains – Class A number 1218. I'm painting the pilot right now.

Ryan: Pilot? I thought it was an engineer who operated the train, and a conductor who ran it and called the shots.

Mr. Thompson: [laughs] No, no, son, the pilot isn't a person. It's this v-shaped structure here, underneath the circular front of the smokebox. It's for knocking away anything in the train's path. Do you know what they called it in the old days?

Ryan: No.

Mr. Thompson: A cowcatcher! I assume you can guess why. Now, even the dumbest cow is bright enough to try to get out of the way of a moving train. But, sometimes they'd get stuck on the tracks. Now, what in particular are you wondering about?

Ryan: The history of the railroads in Roanoke. It's hard to imagine what the city was like as a major hub, the sound of the steam engines constantly at work. I was hoping you could tell me about the engineers, the people who ran the trains. What was their world like?

Mr. Thompson: Mr. Ah, yes. The railroad was the lifeblood of this city. You had your engineers, your firemen, your conductors, your brakemen. It was a close-knit group. The engineers, they were the kings. The ones with their hands on the throttle. There's nothing like it, that power. You feel the whole train rumbling underneath you, a thousand tons of steel and fire, and you're the one in control. You see the country pass by from a perspective no one else gets. It was like that for the others, too - they all had their own distinct identities and experiences.

Ryan: What about the abandoned tracks? You can still find them out in the woods, covered in moss. Why do some lines get left to rot like that?

Mr. Thompson: Progress, son. She moves on. Once upon a time, you couldn't imagine a world without the rail, but then came the trucks and the highways. It's a shame. It's like the world just decided to forget a part of its own body. A lot of people hated to see it go. A lot of people still miss it.

Ryan: I can see why. It's a rich history. Do you get a lot of people asking about the old legends? The folklore that cropped up around the railroads?

Mr. Thompson: If that's what you're looking for, you've come to the right place. We've got plenty of stories. The old timers used to say the ghost of a conductor, one who never punched a ticket, would ride the last passenger car of every train. But that's just a harmless tale, a bit of fun. What kind of story are you hoping to find?

Ryan: Well, it's a bit more specific. I grew up hearing about a ghost train. One that's still supposed to appear every now and then on some of the old, abandoned tracks nearby.

[A long pause. The soft scraping of Mr. Thompson's brush against the model stops.]

Mr. Thompson: You're talking about the Kilpatrick train.

Ryan: Yes! That's it. My sister and I were taught a little about it in school, but I can't find anything online. I was hoping you could tell me more about the story.

Mr. Thompson: [In a quieter voice] Son, there's a reason you can't find anything online. There's a reason people stopped talking about it.

Ryan: I don't understand.

Mr. Thompson: You don't have to. You just have to leave it alone. Now listen to me, and listen closely. Don't go around asking about any ghost trains. Whatever you think you know, forget about it before the people you know forget about you.

[Pause]

Mr. Thompson: Nancy, please escort this young man out of my office.

Recording 5 – June 3, 2019, at 3:15 p.m.

Ryan: Excuse me, ma'am, do you mind if I ask your daughter something?

Woman: What about?

Ryan: Does your daughter attend the school down the street? I know she'd be on summer break now but I'm asking about during the school year.

Woman: Yes, she attends Crystal Spring.

Ryan: Well, you see, I graduated from there. Finished fifth grade in 2009. I'm doing a report on a subject I first learned about when I was a student there. I'm wondering if it's still taught the same way. Do you mind if I ask your daughter a couple questions?

Woman: Samantha, will you answer a few questions for this young man?

Samantha: Yes!

Ryan: Thank you, Samantha. Can you tell me what grade you are in?

Samantha: I just finished the second grade, and in August, I'll be a third grader!

Ryan: And how old are you?

Samantha: Eight!

Ryan: Wow, eight! That's great. I remember being eight. That was a long time ago. I'm all grown up now. Samantha, have you learned anything about trains in your classes?

Samantha: Yes! Trains used to be everywhere here. I got to ride one at the zoo!

Ryan: Ah, yes, the 'zoo-choo'. I remember riding that at your age! Now, let me ask you, have you learned anything about ghost trains?

Samantha: Huh?

Woman: I'm sorry, did you say 'ghost trains'?

Ryan: Yes! It's an old legend. When I was Samantha's age, my teacher told us that there was a train from many, many years ago that would still pass through town every now and then at night. It would appear long after bedtime, and nobody knew where it came from or where it was going. Now, Samantha, have you learned about this?

Woman: That's quite enough. Can't you see that you're upsetting her?

Ryan: I'm just trying to do some research-

Woman: Next time you want to talk about ghosts with a nine-year-old, ask a parent's permission in advance.

Ryan: I'm sorry, I just...

Samantha: Mom, I thought ghosts weren't real.

Woman: They aren't, dear.

Samantha: But he says his teachers told him that they were-

Woman: He's wrong. No teacher would ever say that, because teachers don't say things that aren't true. Goodbye, sir!

Recording 6 – June 3, 2019, at 6:11 p.m.

Ryan: By the way, I'm going to record this, Ariel.

Ariel: Why would you do that?

Ryan: Because, we're talking about the train legend, and I'm trying to record every conversation I have on that subject.

Ariel: Shouldn't you be getting back to your yard work?

Ryan: Shouldn't you be offering to help? Dad always makes me do it alone. Just because I'm your older brother doesn't mean I should have to do all the chores on my own.

Ariel: It's not that you're my older brother. It's that mom and dad aren't charging you any rent. It's only fair for you to help out around here.

Ryan: It's not like you pay rent either!

Ariel: I don't have to! It doesn't count because I'm still in high school.

Ryan: Oh, whatever Ariel. Look, I want you to tell me what you remember about the train legend like we talked about earlier. The whole thing.

Ariel: I can. I even looked it up last night after you texted me about it. It was a really fuzzy memory, and I wanted to make sure I got all the details right for you. Well, Mrs. Pendleton talked about it a little bit in second grade history. According to her, it started with a *different* ghost train. Mrs. Pendleton said that her grandfather had worked on the line that heads east to Lynchburg. According to her grandfather, on one dark, rainy night, his own train's engineer, John Kilpatrick, had to slam on the brakes to avoid hitting something - *another* train that had appeared before them. It was older than any train in operation should be, and it moved at a slow speed.

Mrs. Pendleton said that her grandfather's train managed to stop itself just in time to avoid a collision. Kilpatrick and Mrs. Pendleton's grandfather reported what they'd seen, but no one took them seriously, as no other train should have been on the line at that time.

Mrs. Pendleton's grandfather only saw the vague outline of the second train. Kilpatrick, though, was much closer and claimed to have seen men and women onboard. They were dressed formally – the way people dressed when they travelled a long time ago. Kilpatrick remembered the blank looks on their faces. They were oblivious to all that was around them. Once Kilpatrick got his own train moving again, neither he nor Mrs. Pendleton's grandfather saw any trace of the second train again.

Kilpatrick did some research after that. He learned that, in 1889, there'd been an accident in Thaxton, a little west of Bedford, close to where they'd spotted the second train. A heavy storm had disrupted the tracks, causing a passenger car to crash. Nearly twenty people died and many more were hurt.

Mrs. Pendleton's grandfather truly believed he'd seen a ghost train. It spooked him. But, he moved on with his life. Kilpatrick, though, was never the same. He spent years obsessing over it – particularly the way he'd seen so many people unknowingly heading to their own deaths. On the locomotives Kilpatrick helped operate, the other crew members claimed that Kilpatrick constantly peered outside, as if he was wondering if he'd catch sight of the ill-fated train again. He told them that he wanted to warn its passengers about what was going to happen and somehow stop the disaster from occurring in the first place.

The legend we were taught was that this ghostly encounter made Kilpatrick go mad. He raved constantly of lost spirits wandering in the night. After three more instances of him bringing a train to a stop unnecessarily – allegedly to avoid hitting an obstacle that, upon further investigation, was found to not actually exist – he lost his job.

He didn't take it well. Only a few days went by before he threw himself in front of the same train he'd spent his career operating.

Soon after, the sightings began. Every few months, someone would report seeing a train traveling in areas where one should not be present. Mrs. Pendleton's grandfather saw it once, and he swears that John Kilpatrick was operating it from the locomotive cab. Kilpatrick searches for lost souls like the ghost passengers he saw during his own life, stopping when he sees any to let them onboard to join him in perpetual purgatory. Or, at least, that's how the legend goes. How did I do?

Ryan: Great, you did just great. It's a quality story, isn't it?

Ariel: I suppose.

Ryan: It's odd, you know. So far, nobody else I've talked to knows anything about it. I don't think teachers bring it up anymore. It's like the town has collective amnesia.

Ariel: I think we were one of the last classes to learn about it. The state probably just updated the curriculum. I can't say I blame them for removing 'wacky ghost stories' from the list.

Ryan: I just don't get why even the man I talked to at the historical society didn't seem to know about it. The legend is a major part of our town's history, and I can't write about it if the only other source of information is my sister's memory from grade school.

Ariel: Aren't you hanging out with some friends this weekend? Maybe you can ask them what they know.

Ryan: I've got an even better idea.

Recording 7 – June 7, 2019, at 10:15 p.m.

Ryan: I'm present tonight with an esteemed group of local residents: Jennifer, Alice, and Trevor. The former is the star employee of the Grandin Theatre and the latter two...I just met tonight.

Alice: Hello, future Ryan! How's transcribing all these recordings going? Let me guess: It's lots of fun, and you're having no doubts that your ghost train article was a *great* use of your summer.

Trevor: How much farther do we have to go?

Ryan: We're practically there. Just follow me off the pavement to the tracks. They'll lead us to where we need to go.

Jennifer: How long have these train tracks been out of use? Everything's covered by grass.

Ryan: Thirty, forty years probably.

Alice: I can't believe I let you talk us into this.

Ryan: It's like we agreed. I brought a handle of vodka, and in return you guys agreed to come out with me to the site of Kilpatrick's death so I can do another set of interviews on location. Heck, with all the recordings I'm making, maybe I'll create a podcast instead of a written article.

Jennifer: Aren't you the only one of us who isn't 21? Funny how you're the one contributing the liquor.

Ryan: [laughs] I suppose it is. Come along, just a little further. These tracks will lead us close to the outskirts of the cemetery.

Alice: That's a convenient place for him to commit suicide. They probably didn't have to take him far to bury him.

Jennifer: Is the cemetery that old?

Ryan: I think that it is. Anyway, we've made it.

Trevor: This is where he jumped in front of the train?

Ryan: Yep. If you look here, there's a tiny historical marker by the side of the tracks.

Jennifer: 'Here died John Kilpatrick of Salem, Virginia, following over 25 years of distinguished service as an engineer.' It doesn't even mention the suicide.

Alice: It's an unpleasant subject.

Ryan: So, did any of you hear anything about this guy, or the legend surrounding him, growing up?

Alice: Yeah, I learned about it. My grandfather told me that he sold his soul to the devil, and that he travels around in a bright red train that transports the sinful to hell.

Ryan: What? I've never heard that. Plus, everyone I talked to said it was a standard looking black train, just like the ones he operated during life.

Trevor: I heard the devil thing too, but not that the train was red. My uncle told me that the train is supposed to have a green glow. He never saw it, but he swears that he heard it whistle.

Ryan: How did your uncle know the whistle came from Kilpatrick's train?

Trevor: He didn't know for sure. But he was out late one night when he saw billowing smoke coming from the woods. He was worried it was a fire, so he ran over to it to investigate. When he got there, he found only overgrown tracks that had long been out of use, like where we're standing now. But in the distance, he heard a steam train whistling pattern. Two long, one short, and one long blast. He had no doubt a train had just been there, and, given the poor condition of the tracks, it wasn't a train from our reality. Any real train would have instantly derailed.

Jennifer: I learned a little about it in school. The teacher didn't tell us anything about a deal with the devil, or about it being red or green. What she said more-or-less matches what Ryan's been telling us. She did mention that people could sometimes hear it whistling in the night.

[light whistle sound repeats]

Ryan: Do you all hear that?

Jennifer: Hear what?

Trevor: Ryan's just messing with us.

Ryan: [laughs] Yes, I gotcha. But what do you say we sit here for a moment and just listen?

Trevor: I don't know about that. In school I was shown some PSA video about people being run over after lying down on a track they wrongly thought was out of use.

Ryan: I think we're safe. I'll turn this thing off, and we can enjoy the moment while looking out for any spooky ghost trains. And, for Trevor's sake, I'll watch out for any real trains as well.

Alice: Trevor, stop hogging the joint.

Recording 8 – June 7, 2019, at 11:01 p.m.

Old Man: If I see you here again after hours, I'm calling the authorities!

Trevor: Calm down, mister. We're not causing any trouble.

Old Man: You're trespassing on park grounds after dark. And I may be old but I haven't lost my sense of smell. I know what you're up to! Now scram!

Jennifer: Alright, alright, we're going.

Ryan: Is that geezer holding a shotgun?

Alice: Can we walk faster? I want to get out of here.

Jennifer: I do think it was a shotgun. He came from the graveyard, of all places, just to shoo us away.

Ryan: The trail's just ahead. We can get out of the park in no time.

Alice: Y'all didn't leave the weed, did you?

Trevor: Of course not! I've got what's left on me.

Ryan: I'll edit out that part of the recording.

Jennifer: You're still recording?

Ryan: I turned it back on a moment ago.

Trevor: I'm glad our potential deaths gave you some good material for your podcast debut.

Ryan: It's not like that! I was just creating some evidence in case he shot at us.

Alice: There's the parking lot up ahead. It's only a short walk back to my place from here.

<a high-pitched sound repeats in the distance>

Trevor: What the hell?

Alice: It's just like...

Jennifer: It can't be.

Trevor: The sound...Two long, one short, one long...

Ryan: That's a common pattern for signaling that a train is approaching a grade crossing, you know. There are real trains around here, after all. That's probably all that it is.

Jennifer: But the area it came from...it's been out of use for ages, right?

Ryan: Hmm. Honestly, I'm not sure.

Trevor: Let's just get out of here.

Recording 9 – June 11, 2019, at 11:58 a.m.

Ryan: I'm driving towards the home of Mrs. Pendleton, who taught both me and my sister at Crystal Spring Elementary. A couple teachers mentioned the ghost train rumors, but she was the only one who really expanded on them. I sense that she knew more than she let on. There may be some details that were too scary to share with second graders. And, maybe she'll even have an explanation regarding why the students aren't taught about it anymore.

Oh, nice, I just got a text message from Jennifer. 'Are you free tonight?' This sounds like the one-on-one date I've been hoping for. Somehow, her friends seem to have vouched for me even after my plan resulted in an old man chasing us out of the park with a firearm. She held my hand when we returned from taking the trash out at the end of our shift at the theatre Monday night, and we kissed before driving home. I can't wait to see her again this evening.

Well, here I am. Out of respect for Mrs. Pendleton, I'm going to turn this off until she agrees to let me record an interview.

Recording 10 – June 11, 2019, at 12:15 p.m.

Ryan: Alright, I just turned it on. Can you please state your name and how long you've lived in the area?

Mrs. Pendleton: Mary Pendleton. I've been here my whole life.

Ryan: And what's your connection to me?

Mrs. Pendleton: I had the *delightful* experience of teaching you in second grade! And a few years later I taught your little sister as well.

Ryan: Which one of us was more trouble?

Mrs. Pendleton: [laughs] You both had your moments when you got on my nerves. But overall you were lovely children. I'm not about to pick favorites between you two. I never do that with my kids.

Ryan: I still remember a lot about what you taught me about local history. For example, Roanoke's original name "Big Lick" and its early growth as a train hub.

Mrs. Pendleton: I'm glad my lessons stuck with you over all these years!

Ryan: They really did. There was one in particular I haven't forgotten. You told me, and my sister's class, about John Kilpatrick's ghost train.

[silence]

Ryan: Mrs. Pendleton, do you still teach that story today? And if not, why did you stop?

Mrs. Pendleton: Don't do this.

Ryan: Don't do what?

Mrs. Pendleton: Don't bring it back.

Ryan: Bring *what* back?

Mrs. Pendleton: My classes kept getting smaller. I didn't know why. I'd start the year with a layout to accommodate the students who I'd be teaching. I'd tell students about the legend. We'd arrange field trips to the site; Cub Scouts would do campouts nearby. At the end of the year, there'd be a whole table of empty seats. How is that possible? I kept asking myself. Why are there empty seats now, but not before?

Ryan: I don't follow you. Did some students transfer out?

Mrs. Pendleton: That's just it. I figured that, surely, some students had just switched schools. But, i had no memory of that happening. I checked my files, and there was no record of additional students anywhere. The students still in my class – you, your sister, others – were the only ones listed. And it's not like I specifically remembered any other students, or anyone else did either.

Ryan: It's been *really* a long time, but I don't remember anyone leaving my class that year.

Mrs. Pendleton: No, you wouldn't. No one does. Ryan, how many students were in your class?

Ryan: I dunno, I think there were just over forty in my whole grade.

Mrs. Pendleton: That's what the records reflect. But every year, I arranged the room on the assumption that there were close to fifty in the grade; sixteen or seventeen in each class. But as the year went on, suddenly one student was sitting at an otherwise empty table.

Ryan: But how is that possible?

Mrs. Pendleton: We got a directive a few years after I taught your sister never to mention the Kilpatrick train again. I resisted at first, as I enjoyed sharing the story due to my own grandfather's role in it. But, the school board was firm, so I changed my lessons accordingly. Suddenly, my classes started with the same number of students that they ended with.

Ryan: So, are you suggesting that knowledge of the train caused... people to disappear? But, how did nobody even remember them?

Mrs. Pendleton: I used to have nightmares, too. They were terrible, Ryan. They were so terrible. But when I stopped teaching the lessons, the nightmares stopped.

Ryan: Were the nightmares related to the train?

Mrs. Pendleton: Oh, Ryan, I haven't thought about them in years. Why are you making me remember them?

Ryan: Mrs. Pendleton, I didn't mean to upset you.

Mrs. Pendleton: [crying] I've seen it, Ryan. I've seen it in my dreams. I've woken up outside in the cold air. I didn't know how I got there but I knew where I was going. I was going to *it*.

Ryan: To the train?

Mrs. Pendleton: It's no *train*, Ryan. That's the thing. It *was* a train, once. But now...now...

Ryan: Mrs. Pendleton, are you okay? Do you need me to call an ambulance?

Mrs. Pendleton: [stammering] It was once black iron. It was once black iron...

Man: What's going on in here? What are you doing with my wife?

Ryan: I don't know! I was just asking her a few questions!

Man: Turn that thing off before I-

Recording 11 – June 12, 2019, at 8:45 a.m.

Ryan: Ryan here. It's Wednesday morning. I've got the day off work. This recording may sound a bit like an audio diary at first. But it is relevant to the article.

I'm driving back home from Jennifer's apartment. Yes, you heard that right. It's been an eventful last twenty-four hours with some downs but also some ups.

Let me recap. First, I managed, for the third time this summer, to start an interview that ended with me being thrown out of a building. If you add the old man with the shotgun, it's the fourth time I've been driven away from somewhere by force lately. So, I don't exactly feel like Mr. Popular these days.

On the bright side, my date with Jennifer was everything I'd hoped for. We only made it ten minutes into the rom-com we were watching together before we started making out, and then...I guess I'm the only one who'll ever listen to this, but I'll spare the details all the same.

Hopefully Ariel won't be too awkward about things when I get home. Heck, maybe she'll high-five me; she's the one who keeps saying I need a girlfriend, after all.

Is that what Jennifer and I are now? I may have that conversation with her the next time we're alone together. Or maybe I should wait a little longer? She knows I have to return to school at the end of the summer; maybe I shouldn't even address that subject at all.

Anyway, now for the gloomier stuff. I think my conversation with Mrs. Pendleton got to me. It sure escalated quickly. One minute, she was as composed as ever; the next, she was sweating, crying, and bright red in the face. By the time I left, she had her head down and was yelling in anguish. I somehow feel responsible for what happened to her...but I can't be, right? I'm concerned that she has some buried mental condition that I triggered. But how could I have known that bringing up the legend of the ghost train would do that?

Her emotional disintegration struck at my subconscious. That's my working theory, at least, for the terrible dream I had last night. I was standing at the site of Kilpatrick's suicide. But it wasn't located amidst dense woods like it is now; instead, it was by a proper train platform. It was early morning and the sun had yet to rise. Several people stood with me, presumably waiting for the train to arrive.

In the distance, an eerie green glow approached through thick fog. A sickening feeling took hold of me. I knew that I didn't want to be on the platform when the source of the glow arrived. I wanted to leave. But when I tried to go, the other people grabbed me and held me in place. So I waited, helplessly.

As the locomotive emerged from the gloom, it looked different from what I expected. It was a murky black-red hue, and its iron structure was deformed and misshapen. The upper-half of a face, its skin stretched and strained, covered the front of the engine's smoke box. The screeching of the train's breaks emerged as a scream from a gaping mouth that extended across the pilot. I felt weightless, and then slowly realized that I was in pain.

Jennifer woke me from where I'd fallen. I'd sleepwalked away from the couch where I'd drifted off with her, out the door, and to the staircase that led from her floor to her building's lobby level. I'd stumbled down at least several stairs and landed on the hard floor. Luckily, I emerged from it with only a few minor bruises.

Jennifer gave me some weird looks. I don't blame her. I told her that I've sleepwalked a few times before, and that it usually happened when I was in a new place. In truth, I've never done something like this before in my life. It freaked me out. But it was a good lie and did the trick. Jennifer calmed down.

I held her the rest of the night as she went back to sleep. I lay wide awake, however, as my mind fixated on the grotesque image from my dream. I couldn't shake the sensation that the train wasn't some figment of my imagination – that it was out there calling for me and drawing me nearer.

Recording 12 – June 12, 2019, at 11:12 a.m.

Ryan: Mrs. Trout, it's me, Ryan. Do you remember me? I waited for the school bus in your front yard every morning for ten years.

Mrs. Trout: No.

Ryan: Well, Mrs. Trout, I live next door-

Mrs. Trout: Leave me alone. Can't an old woman step outside without being harassed?

Ryan: Look, Mrs. Trout, I was just wondering if you could answer a question of mine. You knew a lot of people who worked on the old railroads, and I was wondering if you heard any stories from them about the Kilpatrick ghost train-

Mrs. Trout: You cut that out right now, you hear me!

Ryan: I was just wondering-

Mrs. Trout: No more of that crap. No more, I tell you! Next thing you know, you're gonna rope me, or someone you care about, into what's coming to you. Drop this, now, if you care about the people around you!

Recording 13 – June 12, 2019, at 1:08 p.m.

[baby cries in the background]

Woman: Isabel, dear, please quiet down!

Ryan: If you need to take care of your baby, I can wait, or I can come back later.

Woman: Oh, don't worry. Isabel will get over it. What'd you want to ask me about?

Ryan: About some local legends. Am I correct that your grandfather worked on the railroads?

Woman: Yeah, that's right. Granddad loved telling me stories about his decades as a conductor.

Ryan: Did he know John Kilpatrick?

[baby continues crying]

Woman: Hush already, Isabel! Dear Lord, what's wrong with her?

Ryan: I really can wait if you need some time with Isabel.

[baby cries louder]

Woman: SHUT THE FUCK UP!

[baby continues crying]

Ryan: Maybe another time? I-I think I'll be going.

Woman: Not so fast. I heard your question. I just needed a moment to process it. ISABEL SHUT UP ALREADY!

Ryan: Miss, I think Isabel-

Woman: You're here about the ghost train aren't you? You want to bring those nightmares back?

Ryan: No, I don't know what you're talking about-

Woman: You're with him, aren't you? Tryna' fetch me to bring me to it? Well I'm not going. I'm not letting you invade my mind again either.

Ryan: Ma'am, what are you doing with that knife?

[Woman screams]

Ryan: Jesus! Oh god! Oh god!

[baby continues crying]

Recording 14 – June 12, 2019, at 4:50 p.m.

This is Ryan. The police have finally let me go. Early this afternoon, Margaret Potter killed herself. Twisted a long kitchen knife across her neck. I'm lucky the police believed my story. There was blood all over my face when they arrived. I can't stop thinking about what happened. At least poor Isabel is in the care of her uncle now.

I-I...I need to let this go. I was stubborn, and I ignored all the signs. Who needs a stupid journal position a year early anyway? Some things are best left forgotten.

Recording 15 – June 13, 2019, at 6:46 p.m.

I want to go back to night-before-last when I went to sleep next to Jennifer on the couch. Before the first nightmare. It's hard to count how many nightmares there've been now. Two in dreams, and more in reality.

When I got home, I walked past my concerned sister and parents and went straight to the bathroom where I stripped and showered and scrubbed every drop of Margaret Potter's blood off my body. I thought I was clean, but when I opened the shower curtain, the reflection in the mirror for a moment displayed the stretched face of detached skin that covered the front of the train in my dreams, and blood oozed down from its eyes. I grabbed a towel and hurried out of the room.

I locked the door to my room, dried myself off, and buried myself in sheets. I heard knocks and yelled that I would be fine in the morning but that I needed to rest.

I slept but I didn't rest. In my dreams, I found myself back at the platform. In my hand were two tickets. The first said "Single Ride – 11:59 p.m. 6/13/2019". It was still the 12th at the time; it meant I had until...tonight before it left. The second said "Round Trip – 11:59 p.m. 6/14/2019".

A pale man waiting to my left saw me examining it. He had a top hat and a thick mustache. "I see you've got yourself a round trip in two nights," he said. "The funny thing about a circle is that it never ends."

The train approached through the thick fog. It whistled four times – long, long, short, long.

Its outline slowly moved closer. Its screech throbbed through my head.

To my right, images from my memories unfolded. I watched Jennifer take my hand behind the theatre. I watched our kiss and the smiles that followed. I watched us hike out with her friends; flee the man with the shotgun; cuddle up on her couch; and spend the night that followed together.

I tried to move, to ask them for help, but my feet were frozen in place as the train came to a stop. A thick layer of fog obscured all but the green glow that surrounded it and the demented face that covered the front of the locomotive.

"This ride's not for you," said the pale man. "Not all of you, at least." He politely tipped his hat and approached the train. He disappeared into the mist.

I remained immobilized as I watched an image of myself and Jennifer, their hands clasped together, cross from my memories onto the platform, where they followed the pale man's path until the dense grey vapor consumed them.

"All aboard!" yelled a voice. I heard the thuds of shutting doors, followed by the train starting up again.

I awoke at the edge of the park. It took me nearly an hour to make it back to my house. I found the window to my bedroom wide open. How could I have done all of this while asleep? It wasn't possible. When I crawled back in bed, it was nearly 4 a.m.

I awoke only a few minutes before my shift began. I threw on some clothes and headed to the theatre. All I wanted was to be with Jennifer again. I could tell her about all I'd been through once the morning set of screenings began and the crowd died down. She'd hug me and support me and I'd feel better.

Instead, when I arrived, she gave me nothing more than a half-hearted smile as she ran the popcorn machine.

When business died down, I asked her if she was okay. She shrugged and said she thought she was fine.

"Jennifer," I told her, "I don't understand what's going on with me. I feel like I'm losing my mind. I just...it made me really happy to be with you the other night."

A sour expression spread over her face. She told me she didn't know what I was talking about. After a few minutes, I realized that she had no memory of us going on a date, me taking her out to the park with her friends, or even us holding hands and kissing behind the theatre. She told me to see a doctor and proceeded to avoid me.

Something tells me this isn't simply 'ghosting' me, as it's typically called. She seemed so serious, so genuine in her conviction that none of what I told her really happened. But I have proof. I have my recordings, including the recordings of her when we went out to the park.

I wish I'd thought of that at the time. But I suppose the terrifying dreams, the sleepwalking, and Ms. Potter's suicide shook me up too much already to think rationally. Jennifer forgetting about the time we spent together was just too much. I abandoned my shift, stormed out of work, and went home.

My boss has called me three times, but I haven't answered. I'm all out of ideas. Something terrible is happening to me, and I don't know what to do. Should I go back to Jennifer? Should I leave town? I can't shake the feeling that if I don't find a way to stop what's happening to me, my disappearance will end up a part of the local folklore.

Recording 16 – June 13, 2019, at 9:04 p.m.

I don't deserve a sister as caring as Ariel. She could tell that I was upset and insisted on spending time with me to make me feel better.

She didn't pry when I told her that I didn't want to talk. I don't want to drag her into this any more than I have already. Same goes for anyone else I've interviewed over the last few weeks.

I started to relax after we turned on the television. For a few minutes, I managed not to think of the tickets or the sense of impending doom I'd felt about whatever will happen at 11:59 p.m. tonight.

Towards the end of the show we were watching, the images started to scramble. When I complained about it, Ariel looked at me blankly.

She flipped the channel to some competition show. Contestants sang on a stage.

At first, the stage was clear. But, as the show progressed, crimson puddles formed on it. The puddles grew in size and depth until the contestants, who took no notice, waded in knee-deep pools as they performed.

"Is this some kind of Halloween-themed special?" I asked, even as I realized how little sense that made.

"Huh?" said Ariel.

The liquid kept rising as the image cut to a host who was judging the contest. Blood poured rapidly from the elongated eyes and stretched mouth of his massive and deformed face, feeding the red pool that now flooded the set.

I freaked out. Ariel tried to calm me and asked me if I needed to go to a hospital. When I looked back at the television, it displayed nothing other than a mundane singing show with no deformed faces or contestants caked in blood.

I told her that I needed to go and sprang to my car. There's no point in trying to calm myself anymore. Something's happening to me, and I need to take action.

I'm driving as I record this. I don't have much of a plan. Only a hunch. There's one person I can think of who may have answers. If my instincts are correct, he may be the only one who can help me.

Recording 17 – June 13, 2019, at 9:55 p.m.

[loud car horn beeps]

[train whistles]

Ryan: [shouting] What's your problem?

[loud car horn repeats]

Ryan: [shouting] I can't go now! There's a train passing ahead for Christ's sake!

Man: [shouting] Christ's got nothin' to do with what's coming for you! A Baptism of blood's headin' your way! Your rebirth won't be as a child of God!

[car horn continues beeping]

Ryan: The fuck is wrong with this guy? Finally, the train's about through. I'm going to pull over and let this asshole pass me.

[car engine starts]

Man: [passing] Baptism of blood's comin' your way!

Ryan: [shouting] Fuck off, you fundamentalist freak!

Recording 18 – June 13, 2019, at 10:25 p.m.

[knocks]

Ryan: Hello! I know you're in there!

[knocks continue]

Old man: Come on in.

[door opens]

Ryan: Look, sir, I'm so sorry to bother you, it's just...

Old man: You've been seeing it in your dreams, haven't you? And you've got a train ticket for tonight.

Ryan: Yes, how did you-

Old man: I've seen it before. Too many times. Name's Charles, by the way. Hold still.

[camera shutter sound]

Ryan: Jesus, what was that for? I can't see anything.

Charles: You'll be fine in a moment. I know the flash on my old camera is a bit harsh.

Ryan: Look, I have so many questions.

Charles: Sit down and relax a bit. I'll make some tea.

Ryan: It's hard to relax when I have-

Charles: About an hour and a half, right?

Ryan: ...right.

[water pours]

Charles: I see you eying my shotgun. Don't worry. I don't even own any shells. It's just for show.

Ryan: It scared the hell out of me and my friends the other night.

Charles: I thought you might have been one of them, but I wasn't sure. My eyesight isn't what it used to be.

Ryan: What's it like living on cemetery grounds? Surely you're not required to be here.

Charles: My family's cared for this graveyard since it was first established. The city gave us the deed for this patch of land within it. We could have given it up ages ago, but we've always preferred to live on the property we care for. It also helps me with another duty. One that concerns you.

Ryan: I had a feeling you knew something about all this – about

Kilpatrick's phantom train. It was just a hunch but I had no other leads. You weren't just chasing me and my friends away because we were out late in the park, were you?

Charles: No, no. My house overlooks the sight of Kilpatrick's suicide. His train – 'phantom train', as you call it, stops there. And, kids like you chasing after ghost stories will often be there for him to pick up. It happened much more in the past than it does these days, but I still keep a lookout. If it weren't for me, you'd be there on the train at this very moment, and you wouldn't be getting off anytime soon.

Ryan: You said it used to happen more in the past. Why is that?

Charles: Kilpatrick's phantom train had a hold on this city for decades. Eventually it left a mark so black that it was impossible not to notice. I led an effort to stop teaching about it, stop talking about it, stop sharing information about it. Dozens and dozens of people used to go missing. That number is much smaller now.

Ryan: I haven't seen records of that many missing persons.

Charles: You wouldn't have. Kilpatrick's train doesn't just lure victims from this world into the next. It takes the memories of the victims with it. It sucks everything out of this world about them. Even, gradually, every physical record of each victim's existence. Let me show you something.

Ryan: Do you need help with that?

Charles: No, no, I got it, and the box isn't heavy. Here we go. Now, tell me, what do you see inside?

Ryan: There's...hundreds of scraps of paper. Most are newspaper articles. This one is about a missing Scout troop. Disappeared around Dixie Caverns in 1968. There are dozens of photos in here, too. Taken from your camera, I assume.

Charles: And here's one more to add to the collection. I should have asked you to smile.

Ryan: Why are you putting my photo in there?

Charles: Nobody's gonna remember you otherwise.

Ryan: If this thing...this train erases everyone's memories of those who go onboard – and even erases all records about them, then how do you still have everything in this box?

Charles: I can't explain the science of it to you, if science is even a thing that matters here. But I can tell you that the process is gradual. It can be combatted. I cherish this box. I go through it every morning and every night. That hampers the erasure, at least for a while. It once had even more pictures and articles. I used to know every name in here. But by looking through it every day, I can keep some memory of these people alive. It may not do the victims any good, but it's something, and I think it matters.

[boiling water hisses]

Charles: I'll let that steep for a minute. You see, I didn't always live here alone. The train got my son. I recite everything I know about him every morning and every evening. I tell myself that maybe my memory tethers him to the realm of the living. Maybe it will give him strength to escape from purgatory. But the train's power is strong. A few weeks ago, I realized that I didn't know his name any more. All I have now is this picture.

Ryan: I'm so sorry.

Charles: It's taken from you, hasn't it?

Ryan: Yes. I had been dating a girl. In my dream, the two of us got onboard. Now, it's like she barely knows me. What about you? Has it appeared in your dreams like it has in mine?

Charles: For a while, I'd see it. The train would always be obscured by something, like fog or a tree line. But I'd sense it approaching where I waited at a platform. And I'd wake up with it closer to me every night. One day, I drove five hours south and went to sleep in a hotel in North Carolina. When I woke up, I was in grass in the park not three yards from the site of Kilpatrick's suicide. I called the hotel, and my car was still in its lot. I don't know how it was possible. I don't think you can run away from it. Eventually, I taught myself to have dreamless sleep. It kept it at bay. Over time, I think it lost interest in me.

Ryan: Can you help me? I can go a few days without sleeping. Maybe I can learn the same thing you learned.

Charles: Maybe. Maybe. I can try to help you. I don't know if you can learn it that fast, but we can fight it together.

Ryan: I can't believe I got myself into all this trouble. All for a stupid article.

Charles: Article?

Ryan: Yeah. I've talked to people all over town about the train. You're the first to give me some answers.

Charles: I see. I think the tea's ready. Let me add some milk to it.

Ryan: It's terrifying to me, that it erases people from existence. Your poor son.

Charles: Here you go.

Ryan: It has a funny taste.

Charles: Don't worry. It's just a strong flavor.

Ryan: How do you think Kilpatrick chooses whose dreams to haunt? Lots of people who used to know about the legend haven't disappeared.

Charles: He goes after those who come to him. Not just in a physical sense, but in their minds. The train feeds on a specific kind of curiosity. People who talk about the legend casually? He leaves them be, usually. But you...there's something more to what you're doing.

Ryan: So, if...excuse me... [Pause] [Ryan taking a deep breath] So, if I just lose interest, and stop, then maybe he'd leave me alone?

Charles: It's too late for that. The train knows you've found it. You've looked into the abyss, and now the abyss is looking back at you. That's why I keep an eye out here. Kilpatrick uses the legend to draw people in, to pull them closer. And once they're close enough, their dreams become his hunting grounds.

Ryan: It's...uh...I'm feeling...

Charles: Weak? Dizzy?

[several minutes pass without speaking]

[crickets and scraping]

Ryan: Hey...Charles...what happened? Why are we on the old track?

Charles: I hoped I could help you, but reporters don't keep secrets. I doubt it'll come after anyone just for reading something posted about it online. But the curious will come here to investigate for themselves. For their sakes, I can't let you go.

Ryan: Wait! I've already decided to stop! I've canceled the whole project, and I'll delete the recordings. Please, untie me.

Charles: I'm sorry. But you have a train to catch.

[departing footsteps]

Recording 19 – June 14, 2019, at 7:08 a.m.

Ryan: I don't know where to begin. I...I...need to recount what I've been through. I don't know what good it will do, since I'm convinced that I need to erase every recording I've made. But I'm going to spell it all out anyway. I'm going to complete my research.

I lost consciousness after Charles left me by the tracks. I awoke to find Mrs. Pendleton, of all people, undoing my bindings. She explained that she didn't know how she ended up there.

"You were given a ticket, weren't you?" I asked. "In your dream?"

"Round trip." Her face looked pale. "Let's get out of here."

But it was too late. Figures surrounded and subdued us.

"You have a train to catch, young man," said the pale man from my dreams.

Fog descended. Phosphorescent green approached from the distance. A whistle bellowed four times.

"I want to leave! Let me go!" cried Mrs. Pendleton.

A tear ran down my cheek as I realized that I was responsible for her fate.

The face emerged. A familiar, chilling scream howled out of its elongated mouth as the train slowed.

The mist faded after it stopped.

It was once black iron. But it wasn't anymore.

It was a *blood* train. Its structure consisted largely of human skin, flesh, and organs. Bone formed its pistons, valves, and coupling rods. Hundreds of skulls lined its walls.

The pale man turned to me. I shuddered. His long face was gone. Behind his dangling tongue and beneath his veiny eyes dripped blood and mucous from where his nose and mouth should have been. I understood where his features had gone when he pointed to the stretched skin that covered the front of the train engine.

He and the others dragged me and Mrs. Pendleton to an entrance to a train car. My heart beat rapidly. "No, no, no," muttered my old teacher. I wanted, so badly, not to see what was behind the door.

All at once, it swung open. A cascade of blood crashed upon us. Mrs. Pendleton screamed. I probably did the same. We would have been swept away but for the others holding us in place.

There was so much of it, and it just kept pouring. I felt like the whole world had turned into a sea of red.

Finally, the wave receded. The pale man pushed me and Mrs. Pendleton inside.

Pink tissue lined the inner walls and ceiling. As we plodded through puddles of red, I noticed that the room contained seats, like it had once been a passenger car. Upon closer inspection, I realized that the seats were made of portions of ribcages melded together. Bits of flesh clung to the bones, one set of which connected to a torn neck and battered head that faintly pulsated and breathed.

We crossed from this car to the next, moving towards the engine.

To my surprise, the next car was dry and well-kept. The blood that dripped off of me stained the white carpet as I walked, but the dozens of resigned, empty-looking passengers sitting around me did not seem to care.

A uniformed man approached and asked for my ticket.

At first, I was too dazed to respond.

"Your ticket?" he repeated.

"No ticket," I said. Maybe he would throw me off?

The man sighed and removed a pad of paper. He flipped through it before reading from it: "Ryan Grove. Single Ride. You may sit anywhere on this car. Make sure to get off at the next stop."

He left me alone after that. The train started up.

I examined the other passenger. Six children in Scout uniforms sat together. A woman in a pinner apron and a mobcap leaned on a man in an old military uniform. Many of the passengers were missing limbs or chunks of their bodies.

The door to our compartment from the next car opened, revealing a figure obscured by shadow. "This way."

I froze. The other passengers slowly turned their faces towards me. I sensed anger at my hesitation.

"Now," said the shadowy figure.

We followed him until we reached the locomotive. The figure stayed just out of sight, but I discerned that he wore a thick coat, gloves and a dirty cap.

"Do you see how it fades?" he asked, motioning to a long gap in the metallic structure of the car's ceiling.

With surprising deftness, he reached out a tattered arm of discolored, exposed bone. He grabbed Mrs. Pendleton and tore off a portion of the side of her chest with his bare hand. She screamed and collapsed as he smoothed her detached flesh over the gap. A green glow emanated from wherever the flesh met the train's metal. The flesh hardened and settled into place as it joined the train's structure.

"That's enough from you for today," said the man. He turned to me while Mrs. Pendleton whimpered.

"You-you're him, aren't you?" I stuttered. "What do you want with me?"

He didn't acknowledge me at first. Instead, faded memories flashed before me as translucent images of my infancy, my home, my family, my friends. With a flick of Kilpatrick's wrist, each image floated into the boiler, which lit up. The train accelerated as my memories powered it like coal once did.

"I don't want to be here," I said.

"There is a way out," said Kilpatrick. "I want you to think something over: I'll let you go, and return all that I've taken, if you publish the article. There are so many repairs that need to be done, after all."

"No," I said.

"If that's what you decide, then I'll see you tomorrow night," responded Kilpatrick. "We'll have so long to get to know each other."

I woke up in my house. I was sweaty and dirty, and everything about my room was off. It was empty. No clothes, no pictures, nothing but the bed I lay in.

I checked my pockets. My wallet was gone. I still had my phone, on its last bit of power, and the ticket from my dream. "Round Trip – 11:59 p.m. 6/14/2019". Tonight. I remembered what the pale man said: "The funny thing about a circle is that it never ends."

I stepped into the hallway. My family's house felt foreign. Ariel, mom, and dad smiled together in pictures on the wall. I didn't belong there anymore.

I'm in the backyard now. As soon as I finish this recording, I'm deleting everything on my phone and burying it in the woods. Hopefully it'll disappear soon, just like everything else I once owned. Just like I will tonight. All that will remain of me soon will be a photo in Charles' shoebox. It's probably best that way.

I'm more than a little tempted to publish the article. But I've made up my mind. Maybe, someday, this will all stop. Maybe enough people will forget about the legend that Kilpatrick's train, and all those trapped onboard, will fade away.

Mom, Dad, Ariel – our life together was real, even if I suspect that you're going to forget that it ever happened. I love you all and I always will.

The recordings end here. What's described in them – it can't be real, can it? I look now at the empty room in our house. The one that's always been there. I never thought about it much, but why did we never do anything with it? And how is it that I heard my own name and voice in these recordings?

I find myself replaying the events that led to me finding this phone. It's not like me to wander off and dig up loose dirt. It's almost like something... compelled me into discovering something I wish had stayed buried.

I woke up this morning from a terrible dream of an old train. It stopped in front of me and, through thick fog, I identified a young man with my mother's face and my father's green eyes reaching out to me with a maimed hand through a half-open window.

4

LIFE OF LILY: PART 1

"You should make a move!" teased Mae. "She's been eyeing you all night."

"No, she hasn't," I retorted, feigning annoyance. I had a natural tendency to retreat into isolated complacency, and Mae had a natural tendency to try to nudge me out of it. I loved her for it, though I made a game of trying not to show it.

She was right. The girl in a long flannel button-down, opened to reveal a t-shirt that displayed a cartoonish image of a crowd of zombified kittens munching on a hapless human victim, had been glancing my way throughout the concert. Sure, she hadn't been outright staring as Mae suggested, but she had cast more than a few looks my way, to the point that even *I'd* caught onto it.

The crowd cheered as the band revved up for their next song. Casey, Mae's boyfriend, played bass in it. They were the opening act, and Mae and I were among the few attendees there for them rather than the headliner.

Mae hollered excitedly a few moments in as a guitar riff confirmed they were playing a track she particularly liked, which took inspiration from a short-lived Japanese band called Pasteboard. The echoing guitar, which drowned out the vocals, reverberated through the venue. Though I'd developed an appreciation for their shoegaze style, it was still much louder and messier than the music that I usually preferred.

I shot a glance over to the girl. She was at least a few years younger than me, and she had short, messy brown hair with blonde highlights. When she made eye contact with me, I abruptly looked away.

When the song concluded, Mae leaned into me and shouted into my ear. "I could use another drink. Wanna come with me?"

"I'll get one for you," I replied. "I know you don't want to miss any of the show, and I could use a break from all the noise."

"Sure, I'll pay you back later." She didn't need to specify what she wanted – from the many years we'd lived together, I was well aware of what she'd order.

I slowly made my way through the crowd and to the bar at the other end of the venue. The wall that separated it from the main auditorium absorbed much of the cacophony. When I ordered a sidecar, I relished the feeling of being able to hear my own voice and talk without shouting.

As I picked up the drink, a mellow voice with a slight Tennessee accent spoke from behind me. "You're not here for the Undead Housecats, are you?"

I whirled around, surprised. It was *her*. Had she followed me? As I struggled to respond in my flustered state, she ordered a PBR from the bartender.

"Um, no," I said, as she sipped it. "My housemate's, er, friend's, I mean, well both – her boyfriend's in the band playing now."

She nodded. Her expression was reserved, but there was a twinkle to the edge of her thin smile, like she was holding back some sly observation. She took another gulp.

"How did you know?" I asked.

She shrugged. "You stand out a bit. Like you're trying to make yourself enjoy being here. You seem *so* much more at home back here where it's quieter."

"Sounds like you've been watching me closely."

"Sorry. I people-watch sometimes when I'm alone. And that was hardly a one-way thing, was it?" I felt myself blush as she motioned to an unoccupied booth. "Wanna sit down a second?"

"Alright," I said. I could feel my heart beat with excitement. She – it occurred to me that I didn't even know her name – was growing on me. I hardly ever went along with this kind of thing, assuming I was reading the situation correctly. Though, that was mostly because I so rarely put myself in social situations where I might meet someone new. Yet, here I was, on a rare night out, getting a drink with a girl I just met. A cute girl, at that. "Let me just text my friend real quick."

She's here, I typed out. *Mind waiting a minute on your drink?*

Shortly after, my buzzed with a "Fire" reaction, followed by, *"The drink's all yours. Have fun :)"*

~

We talked for a bit. She introduced herself as Lily. She was from a small town two hours east and had moved to the city 10 months ago. While applying to entry level jobs in the music industry, she'd been bartending down the street at the Velvet Prism.

"You familiar with it?"

I nodded as I sipped the last of the mixed drink. "Kind of place I went when I was younger."

Lily scoffed at this. "Age isn't the reason you stopped going. And you're still plenty young. You just feel older."

"Maybe."

She finished her beer, placed the empty can on the table, and reached both of her hands out toward me. "Come on. I'm going to see that you lose that feeling tonight."

I took them, and she led me back to the concert.

~

Casey's band was on its last song as we returned. Our plan had been to leave after they finished, as tomorrow was a workday for both Mae and Casey, but Lily enticed me to stay behind with her for the main show.

"So, um, is this band loud?" I asked her after waving goodbye to my housemate.

I realized that I deserved the incredulous look she gave me. A band with the name *Undead Housecats* wouldn't be playing quiet and contemplative ballads, after all.

~

I danced more in the two hours that followed than I had in the last few years combined. I ignored the soreness, the exhaustion, and the lingering sense of dread that had haunted me since my doctor had mentioned a need for "follow-up tests" that morning. Instead, I embraced the clamor of the music, the rush of fast tempos, and the dizzying energy that surged through the room.

By the end, Lily, who by this point had tied her flannel shirt around her waist, was as caked in sweat as I was. She'd pushed me along and gave me moves and gestures to mimic, all the while occasionally holding one or both of my hands.

It was after midnight when we finally stepped into the welcome chill of the cool night air. She hopped to the top of a cobblestone wall that looked over an empty section of the parking lot. I climbed up after her. When I took a seat next to her, I understood why she liked the spot. It provided a pristine view of the city's downtown. The lights that covered the tall buildings cast a striking glow amidst the darkness of the late night.

"It's a nice spot, isn't it?" she asked.

"Absolutely," I said as I held her hand. "I love it." I leaned my head back and embraced the pleasant breeze. Despite the ache forming in the back of my head, I felt remarkably at ease.

She gave my hand a short squeeze. "Can I tell you something?"

"Only if you let me tell you something first," I replied.

"No," she retorted, playfully. "Me first."

"Fine."

"You just attended my birthday party."

"*What?*"

"I mean, not really. But today's my birthday. The ticket was a treat for myself.

"Well, happy birthday! I wish you'd told me."

She giggled. "It's okay. I debated whether to tell you. It's just that now you know I did something all alone on my birthday. Most people would find that sad. It's because I haven't made any serious friends since I moved here. Both people I asked about joining me were busy, or at least said that they were."

"It's okay. And you're not alone anymore."

She put her arm around my shoulder. "You gonna guess about my age?"

"Do you want me to?

"Sure."

I used the opportunity to look her over, which prompted her to giggle again. "24."

"You would have been correct yesterday," Lily said through a smile.

"So I was close!"

"Yep. And you...28?"

"Hey, you gave me permission to guess *your* age, but I didn't give you permission to guess mine!"

"Fair enough. But aren't you a bit on the young side to be so sensitive?"

I sighed, thought for a moment, and decided to fess up. "You're guess was almost as close as mine, but in the other direction."

She nodded as she removed her long-sleeved shirt from her waist and put it on, the low temperature having finally caught up to her overheated body. "So, the thing you wanted to tell me?"

"Oh, right," I said. I felt myself shiver, though I wasn't sure if it was from nervousness or the same frigid air. I took a deep breath before speaking. "I really want to kiss you. I've wanted to for a while, actually."

Her face formed a surprised expression as my words sunk in. I realized that, for the first time that night, I'd caught her off-guard. A twinge of panic shot through me. Had I overplayed my hand?

But the feeling quickly dissipated as she leaned in and placed her lips against mine. I kissed back, hard, for several long seconds. When she finally withdrew, my heart swooned at the sight of the deep smile spread across her face and the sense of affection that glimmered in her warm, hazel eyes.

~

I collapsed into bed shortly after my Lyft driver dropped me off. Exhaustion took hold and deep, heated dreams starring the girl I'd just kissed set in.

When I awoke, it was after 11 a.m. Mae sat in her usual spot at the kitchen table, already back from her morning lectures. She held a red pen over a stack of papers. She took a break from grading to look up at me as I began heating up some water for the French press. "So, am I getting a 'thank-you' before or after you get your coffee?"

"For what?"

"For setting you up with the person I assume you were out so late with."

"You didn't set us up," I rejoined.

"When I saw her heading to the bar, I got the idea to drag you there and encourage you to talk to her. When you volunteered to go there on your own, I thought, all the better."

"No way," I gasped in disbelief. Was Mae ever *not* scheming on my behalf?

"*Yes* way. And I'm so glad it worked out. Can you tell me about her? Because that sounds a lot more fun than critiquing the latest batch of student papers."

I did. For several minutes, I recounted all that enthralled me about Lily and the evening we'd had together. "We even made plans to hang out again tonight."

"Tonight? You guys really made a connection."

"Oh gosh, I want to see her again so badly that tonight feels like an eternity away, even though it's just a matter of hours. We're going to a place close to where she lives. I just wish I had time to get her something for her birthday first."

Mae thought for a moment before speaking up. "You know, I have an idea about that."

~

I arrived at the bowling alley brimming with anticipation. *Just dress casually*, I'd told myself, but I'd nonetheless fretted over what casual clothes to wear, ultimately settling on a pair of worn-in black jeans and a denim jacket over an old, slightly faded Blondie t-shirt.

Lily arrived a couple minutes after me. I felt my pulse quicken at the sight of her. She wore a fitted blue knit top and a pair of grey jeans, and I watched her face light up when she saw me.

We gave each other a tight hug and proceeded to purchase a lane. It quickly became apparent that she knew her way around here, as she'd brought her own shoes and immediately selected a bowling ball a few pounds heavier than I would be comfortable using.

"I did this during college," she told me. "The women's bowling team was one of the few places where I felt like I fit in."

"You're going to *destroy* me then," I whined. "I've never been very good at bowling."

"You'll be fine," Lily assured me. "I'm not as good as I used to be. I haven't trained for two years, and, back then, I had a lot of muscle that I don't really have anymore."

The opening round did little to reassure me. Lily bowled a spare; my first ball guttered and my second barely managed to knock down two pins.

She made an effort to teach me proper form, showing me just how to grip the ball and just when to release it. It helped, and I started to catch up on the scoreboard, but I eventually grew too weak to keep it up, with my last few rolls wobbling awkwardly before falling into the gutter.

It was no matter. We paid less and less attention to the game as it progressed, immersed instead in conversation. I told her all about my old corporate job and, in an abbreviated fashion, the lawsuit I'd won against my employer. I described the consulting work I'd been doing part-time the last few months. I explained how I'd lived with Mae since college; how Casey first moved in with her a few years ago; and the unique situation Casey had with our neighbors Emma, April, and their infant daughter Harper.

"You're so far ahead of me in life," Lily interjected. "I feel like I'm going to be stuck bartending forever."

"You have plenty of time to figure things out, Lily."

"I hope you're right. But it's hard to feel that way sometimes. I can hardly afford my studio apartment, much less save up for anything better. Still, it beats going back home, by a long shot."

I sympathized with how she felt. The job market was brutal, and she was all on her own. Meanwhile, I had a support group and a career, as strange of one as it had been. As the final round began with her score 40 points higher than mine, I wondered if she'd brought me here, of all places, for a first formal date as a way of compensating for those insecurities.

"Let me ask you a question," I said as she bowled a perfect strike. "If you could do whatever you wanted, instead of subsisting like you're describing, what would you do?"

"I've always wanted to help people," said Lily. "Kids who need help, especially. I'd devote myself to find a way to do that. But, like, if you're asking about what I'd do for fun, just for myself, then, I dunno. Part of me wants to write a book. Another part of me wants to travel. I've barely left the state, and there's a whole host of places around the country I've always wanted to see. What about you? Is there something you've always wanted to do, but never been able?"

"Oh, I dunno. I probably should have had an answer of my own before I asked you that question, but I honestly haven't thought much about that kind of thing." I stepped forward and released my last ball of the game. It curbed awkwardly from the far right to the far left. I held out hope that it would at least bump into the back-left pin, but it tottered into the gutter at the last moment.

~

"So, what's next?" I asked her coyly as I changed back to my regular shoes.

She paused, glanced down for a second, then looked back at me. "You promise you won't be judgy about it?"

"About what?" I sensed she was nervous.

"Sorry, I'm getting ahead of myself. My place. It's just a short walk from here. It's just that it's small, you know, and it's a bit messy too."

"Lily," I replied, placing my hand gently on her shoulder, "Please don't worry. I couldn't care less about those things. I just want to be there with you."

~

Two hours later, I lay on my side with my arms wrapped around her bare back. The room around us was, indeed, messy, with unwashed dishes in the sink and clothes, including all that we'd been wearing, scattered all around the floor, but the vintage posters, one of Audrey Hepburn and another for the movie *Bound*, added some charm to it.

"Lily," I croaked in exhaustion, "that was, wow, um, Jesus..."

She rolled over so that she faced me. A loving glow emanated from her satisfied face. "Olivia, I've given this some thought...and I think we're compatible."

We both laughed hard at this. I kissed her on her forehead and held her against me.

She was fully correct. We'd only met last night; yet, it was as if we'd known and understood each other forever, to the point that we'd just shared one of the most physically satisfying experiences of my life.

She'd let me take the lead throughout. At first, I wasn't sure what to make of that, but I gradually inferred that she needed me to because she wasn't as experienced as I'd assumed. That placed me in an unusual situation – in my sporadic intimate encounters over the years, it was typically the other way around – but I'd risen to the occasion, and Lily had shown herself to be a fast and eager learner, with a seemingly endless supply of energy.

"You still have a spark in you," I told her. "I may look like I have my act together. But I often feel like life's passing me by, leaving me with little to show for it. All those years working the kind of dreary office job you want so badly snuffed out a lot of who I once was. There's a passion I used to have for life that's gradually faded."

She shook her head. "It doesn't look like that from my perspective. Not with how good you were at all that we just did."

I felt a bit of pride at that. "I guess I picked up a few things over the years."

"You've had some serious girlfriends in the past?"

"Oh, um..."

"Sorry," she interrupted. "We don't have to talk about exes, not now especially."

"No, it's okay," I clarified. "I never actually had any serious romantic partner. Just, less serious things, sometimes for a few weeks, sometimes for longer. Ten or so people, scattered across the years. Men included."

"Oh, really?" she said, sounding slightly perturbed by the last bit.

"Yeah. Including Ray, the most recent person I was involved with. He was a musician, a friend of Casey's, and we'd meet up, if you want to call it that, whenever he was in town. Couple months ago, he called me and told me he was getting serious with someone else. I haven't talked to him since. Last I heard, he and her are engaged."

"Well, that sucks for you."

"No, it's fine. And I'm happy for him. We had a lot of good times, but I always knew something like that was bound to occur eventually. What about you?"

She took a deep breath, a little red appearing on her face as she spoke. "Where I'm from, you know, like in a lot of places, it's really not okay to be the way I am. For a long time, because of that, I wasn't okay with the way I was either. In high school, I tried dating a guy – the most alpha, jock kind of guy who'd take me – because I thought it would prove something to myself, or at least to everyone else. But we never did anything serious – I never let us – and it went nowhere. College was a little better – it was a religious school, but not one of those that's super crazy about it, and I, like, grew more at peace with myself there, away from home. My third year, I got involved with a girl on the bowling team. We stuck it out for a while. We tried to keep things going long distance after we graduated, but, um, it didn't work out. I thought moving here and bartending where I bartend would help, but I'm still a bit too shy to talk to many people. And then I saw you at the concert, and, well, you know the rest."

"Yes, I do." We kissed gently until I remembered the necklace. "Oh, by the way Lily, I got you a belated birthday gift."

"Seriously? You don't have to do that."

"No, no, I wanted to, and you'll love it." I got up and tiptoed around the various items strewn across the floor until I found my purse. I removed the necklace and brought it over to Lily, who'd sat up against the bed's headboard.

Her eyes widened as she examined its ornate blue opal pendant, which was encased in a thin layer of silver. "It's *beautiful*, Olivia. But I feel uncomfortable accepting something like this, so soon especially. It must be incredibly valuable."

"You don't have to accept it if you don't want to," I assured her. "But it didn't cost me anything. Sorry if this is a little morose, but Mae and I have a friend, a good friend, who did a lot for us in the past, and who collected unusual items. He sadly passed away a few years ago. When he did, he left a box of items for us to use as we pleased. It's just been sitting in our basement. I wish I could take full credit, but it was Mae's idea to give you something from it, and we picked this out together." I omitted the parts about how our friend, Jean, had been disintegrated by a shapeshifting demon, or how he'd initially left the box for Emma, who'd in turn passed it along to Mae and me. *Those* details could wait for another time.

"Okay," she said as she lifted it over her head and placed it around her neck. "How does it look?"

"Absolutely gorgeous," I replied.

"Good," she said, her face beaming. "I plan to wear it all the time."

We resumed cuddling and eventually returned to the same position with me wrapped around her. Part of me wanted to keep talking – to fill her in on Mae and me's bizarre adventures, and even to confide in her about the stress I was feeling about my upcoming second round of medical screenings. But everything felt so perfect, so right, that I didn't want to disrupt the moment we were sharing.

She'd told me that she generally slept well and, indeed, her breathing soon settled into a relaxed rhythm as she drifted away into a soothing slumber that I followed her into shortly thereafter.

~

A neighbor's alarm woke me up early, its harsh sound barely muffled by the walls.

Geez, I thought. If this person's alarm could be heard this well in Lily's apartment, then how many people had heard the two of us last night? I decided not to dwell on it. Lord knows I'd put up with a *lot* of similar experiences over the years.

Sensing that I wasn't going to go back to sleep, I found and put on my clothes. Seeing that it was still early, and that Lily remained snoozing, I elected to make myself useful.

When Lily finally awoke, I'd cooked breakfast, folded a pile of her clean clothes, and started a load of laundry.

"How are you real?" she asked, bewildered.

"I could ask myself the same question about you," I responded cheerfully. "Take a seat, I cleared a spot for you."

~

When we finally parted, I decided to walk back home. In my joyful state, something felt perfect about reflecting on the past night while absorbing the early morning light.

To make up for the time she'd recently taken off, Lily would have to work many shifts over the next few days. We made a firm plan to meet up again in a week – she'd come over to my place this time, in the evening – with the hope that we'd find other opportunities in the interim to hang out as both of our schedules became clearer.

As I skipped and strolled down a residential street, a chubby man in a bathrobe collecting his newspaper looked me over, undoubtedly taking note of my messy hair and clothing from last evening. "Well, someone certainly had a good time," he observed.

"Believe me," I replied, "you have no idea."

~

That night, it all fell apart.

At first I couldn't believe it. It just couldn't be true. Things like that don't happen. Not to people I know. And especially not to people I care about.

I remember Casey calling Mae downstairs, followed by the murmurs of serious conversation; Mae's sorrowful expression as she told me she needed to speak with me; and the news reports she showed me.

No, no. This was a mistake. The stories had it wrong. It was someone else with the same name.

If I call, she'll answer, right? It won't go to voicemail again, will it? The fourth time, it'll be different, won't it?

I sobbed like I'd never sobbed before. I cried loudly enough to wake baby Harper next door. Mae sat with me all night listening to me moan and letting me rest my head on her shoulder. She stayed there with me the next day, bringing me food and water and doing everything she could to comfort me. Casey, April, and Emma periodically joined us as well.

It all passed in a blur. I felt my reality spin and fade away. I wanted no part of this cruel, sick world anymore. And, yet, here I was, stuck, empty, and miserable, but at least not alone.

"Mae," I moaned before finally going to sleep that second night, "why the fuck are people like this? Why did this have to happen?"

"I don't know, Olivia. I don't know. I'm so sorry."

~

When I woke up the next morning, Mae told me about the service. When I announced that I was attending, she insisted on going with me, emphasizing that I was in no shape to make a drive like that alone.

We set out two days later with Mae at the wheel of her old sedan. "I appreciate all you're doing for me," I told her. "As always."

"Don't worry about it. This is...really fucked up, beyond anything either of us have had to deal with. Of course I'm here for you. I wouldn't be anywhere else."

~

Upon entering the Baptist church, I was greeted by a memorial photo display. Lily looked very different in these images from how I remembered her, and not just for the obvious reason that she was younger in them, as they all predated her move to the city. She often wore traditional floral or pastel colored dresses, and her hair was long, straight, and sleek. In one photo, she, age eight or nine, looked over a newborn baby girl who I figured to be the little sister named Abigail she'd briefly mentioned to me.

In one, she, as a teen, posed with a well-built boy in a baseball uniform. Another had her, as a child, in a Girl Scout troop. Several more featured her as part of a church-affiliated youth group. She donned her high school gap-and-gown in three, and just one featured her at her college graduation.

As the service commenced, I realized I should have taken Mae up on her offer to attend it with me. I'd worried that I was taxing her too much already and didn't want her to have to sit in on a service for someone she'd hardly met. But, now, I felt self-consciously alone, especially as everyone else here seemed to know each other.

A pastor spoke first, followed by Lily's distraught mother. The Lily she described – church-going, obedient, and with her life cut short soon before she could find a husband and become a mother herself – overlapped little with the Lily I'd known for two nights.

A girl, late high school age, spoke next. I quickly realized this was Abigail. She spoke her heart directly in a way that the previous speakers had not. She talked about all the skills Lily had taught her, from tying her shoes to brushing her teeth, and about how Lily had always come to her side when she'd suffered from childhood night-mares. "I try to tell myself that she's still out there, watching over me," Abigail continued, "but, the truth is, that she's gone now, and the void she left behind will never be filled."

By the end of it, I was struggling to fight off yet another wave of tears. Not wanting to draw attention to myself, I snuck outside and sat on the sanctuary steps where I finally let it all out.

I heard the main door open and sensed someone approaching me from behind. A hand reached out with a tissue, which I took and used to wipe my face.

I looked up. The man was tall and muscular, and similar in age to Lily. He might have been the same person who'd posed with Lily in the baseball uniform, but my teary eyes struggled to get a good enough look at him for me to be certain, especially as the blinding overhead sunlight covered much of his face. "Thanks," I said.

"You're not from around here, are you?" he asked while lighting a cigarette.

I shook my head. "Just, um, a friend from the city."

"Know her long?"

"No, not long," I blurted out as I continued to dab my wet eyes and nose.

I watched him withdraw the cigarette and slowly blow out the smoke. "Real good friend," he said, his voice strangely menacing. "Just met her, and now you're all the way out here crying your eyes out. Quite a friendship you and her struck up. If you stick around, her folks may have a few questions about it. They blame others for her being where she was when it happened, you know. Just sayin'."

I didn't know how to respond to that, so I just sat there, silently wishing he'd leave me alone. Eventually, he tossed his cigarette and returned inside.

I didn't follow him. Instead, I texted Mae, who swooped by from the coffee shop where she'd been waiting and drove me back home.

~

I cooked an early dinner for Mae and Casey the next night. It was the least I could do after they'd both taken time off work to be with me. After Mae retired to her room and Casey headed next door to spend time with Harper, I booted up my work laptop to begin the process of rescheduling the appointments I'd cancelled.

That's life, isn't it? I said to myself as the loading screen appeared. *Horrible crimes happen to people we care about, and we all just have to move on.*

I still had plenty to be thankful for, though recognizing this didn't make me any less bitter. I had friends who cared about me and a job that permitted me at least some time off to grieve. I was just one of many people who had to find a way to compartmentalize the emotional impact of a tragedy while continuing to pay the bills.

No. I shut my computer. I was *devastated.* I needed more time to deal with this.

That's when I heard a knock at the door. I opened it to find myself facing an impossibility, something so beyond my realm of understanding that I struggled to process it.

As she registered my shock, her expression shifted from excitement to concern. "Olivia, what's wrong?" asked the girl whose life I'd accepted had ended. Whose future was stolen by the cowardly perpetrator of a stupid, senseless act of violence. "You didn't forget about the plan we made, did you?" asked the girl in the bartender uniform whose blue pendant necklace shone in the early moonlight.

I could only muster the strength to spit out one word. "Lily," I said, as I lurched towards her and held her warm body tightly, as if the tiniest breeze would send her flying away.

5

A BETTER SIBLING

We had been searching for three hours when Sean finally figured it out. I'm not sure if it was our hushed tone or our hesitation at the trail intersections we came across that gave it away.

"Are we lost?" he asked. I shuddered at his worried voice. This weekend was supposed to be an opportunity for me to bond with my younger brother, and he had begun the overnight hike with such excitement and exuberance. Now, we were deep in the woods, far into our phones' no-coverage zone, and my father and I had to break the bad news – bad news for which I was responsible.

Dad crouched down to Sean's height. "Yes," he said. "I didn't want to get you worried, because I've been to these woods before and I thought I could find a way out of them. But, I'm afraid your sister and I don't really know where we are." Sean's eyes grew wide. He was, after all, still at an age where he viewed his father as infallible and his much older sister – the ten-year age gap had made me almost a replacement for our long-absent mother. Now, I feared that my mistake had shattered this image.

"But it's okay, son," my dad continued, "We packed for an overnight trip, and we'll be fine. If we still can't find any of the main trails, I have an idea that I'm sure will bring us to safety. We'll be back at home tomorrow night just like we planned.

"But what about the map?" asked Sean, looking up at me.

I felt the color drain from my face. "I...I..." I stuttered, ashamed.

"Your sister seems to have lost our map," said dad. He shot me a stern glance. "But it's okay. You don't need to worry. We'll figure this out together, as a family."

I don't know how it happened. When we parked in Rich Valley near the trail entrance, Dad had put me in charge of the map. Everything had gone so smoothly at first. I led us down a half-mile dirt path that, like the rest of the Appalachian woods that stretched through much of Southwest Virginia, was lined on both sides with the vibrant colors of early fall leaves that decorated oak, maple, and birch trees. We arrived at the swimming hole at the base of a long cascade, a common stop for families looking for an easy outing, and proceeded to spend time playing in the water and then picnicking with food we had packed.

After we had dried off and changed back into our hiking clothes, we began the much longer trek to a prominent deep-woods campsite, where we planned to spend a night before returning home the next day. The coolness of the morning air faded into a strong midday sun. Dad and I sweated under the weight of the two tents and camping equipment we lugged on our backs, but the trail was mostly flat and we quickly got used to the burden.

Dad directed us at first. We split from the prominent trail onto a smaller, less well-maintained dirt path, and then onto another, even narrower one filled with rugged small rocks. It was barely a path at all as, from any distance, it was hard to distinguish from the surrounding woods. After a few hours of this, Dad commented that the territory we were going through looked unfamiliar to him, so we'd better take a look at the map.

We rested in a clearing. While Sean was climbing up a large stump, proclaiming it a throne upon which he sat as king of the woods, I fished through the items I was carrying to find the map. My dad stood over me, patiently. "You alright, there?" he said, noting the worried expression on my face.

"It's not here," I whispered, not wanting to worry my brother unnecessarily. Surely, it would turn up before long.

But it didn't. My dad and I looked through our respective backpacks and even Sean's small knapsack. The map was nowhere to be found.

"When was the last time you saw it?" asked my father.

I responded that it had been at the swimming hole, right as we were packing up our belongings again. We exchanged a concerned glance.

"Don't worry," said my father, reassuringly. "We'll figure this out."

That was six hours ago. We tried, of course, going back the way that we came. My father had always had a good sense of direction, so we followed his lead through several windy paths. Occasionally, I would feel like I recognized our surroundings, only to second-guess myself – was that the same set of spruce trees we had passed before, or a different one?

It got dark only a few hours after Sean caught on. "Dad," I said. "I'm so sorry."

He sighed. I felt the pain of all the times I had disappointed him run through me. Even worse was realizing that I was letting down my kid brother.

"It's alright – you didn't do it on purpose," dad said.

I asked him about his other idea. He took out his compass and explained that we had generally been heading southeast all morning and early afternoon. All we needed to do was go the opposite direction – northwest – and before long, we'd be close to where we started. At the very least, we'd come across a few peaks from which we'd be able to see the surrounding valleys and determine our location.

We trudged along this way for another hour before evening started to fall. The only sounds were those of the woods: insects buzzing around and gentle breezes swaying branches.

Realizing we only had a little natural light left, we kept our eyes out for a place to camp for the night, eventually identifying a patch of dirt largely unobstructed by trees or roots. Dad and I set up the two tents, one for Sean and me and one for him, and lined a space with rocks where we started a small fire with wood we had gathered nearby.

Dad exchanged pleasant words with us, telling us we would be back at home this time tomorrow night, as we cooked and ate the food we had packed for dinner. Eventually, Sean and I retired to our tent. Sean was worried but also exhausted from the day of intense hiking, and before long I heard the rhythmic breathing of him in deep sleep.

I, on the other hand, tossed and turned with discontent. Today's events triggered other painful memories. I remember sifting through mom's wallet, back when she and my dad's marriage had descended to the point of regular screaming matches, and using what I stole to procure the pills I craved for, pills that brought me a much-needed sense of contentment. The look of disappointment dad had given me earlier today had been the same as when he caught me taking more money, this time from my own brother's funds for a field trip, to feed my addiction. Now, I wanted so badly to be a better sister, but here I was again letting him down.

Unable to sleep, I emerged from the tent and returned to the fire. It was dying out, with only a few embers emitting light, and in this half-darkness I could see my father sitting there, leaning against his heavy backpack and whittling a stick with his hunting knife.

"Can't sleep?" he whispered.

I shook my head.

"I understand," he said. "Don't be too hard on yourself. I'm proud of you, honey." I must have continued looking downcast, because he continued trying to cheer me up and even apologized for his many work-related weekend absences from home.

We sat together quietly, staring into the fire, for a few moments before he got to his feet. "I'm going to see if I can get some rest for tomorrow. You should do the same, when you're ready. Just make sure to put out the fire when you go." With that, he entered his tent and left me alone.

I sat for a minute, observing how the woods seemed ominous and foreboding at night. Glancing at the opening of dad's backpack, I glimpsed the lid of a prescription box in a flicker of light from the dying fire.

In other circumstances, I would have left it alone as my youth rehab program had taught me. But I was so distraught at the dire situation in which I had placed my family that I guiltily reached for it, hoping to find something that could improve my mood. I didn't imagine that the box would contain the painkillers I craved for, but maybe it would have something that could help me relax.

I held the label in front of my eyes. Allergy pills. I sighed, disappointed in the contents and in myself, and reached into dad's backpack to return the container. My hand felt a thick, folded piece of paper. My heart sank as I realized what it was. I quickly pulled it out of the backpack.

It was the map. The same one I had used to guide us to the swimming hole this morning. The guide to the entire region of woods in which we had found ourselves lost.

My mind ran in circles. Sean and I had spent the last ten hours distressed at our situation, and dad had had the map on him all along. I felt dizzy thinking of all the implications. Had dad taken the map out of my backpack when I wasn't paying attention, and then pretended not to find it when I realized it was missing? I recalled a point when I had been in the water with Sean while dad prepared our picnic. He would have had a perfect opportunity to remove it then. But why would he do that?

Dad had also been the one to assure us we didn't need to check the map for the first several miles, stopping me from noting its absence until we were already deep into the forest.

What was going on? Where was dad leading us, and why was he tricking us into thinking we were lost?

I thought about using the map to run away. With the compass, which I also found in dad's pack, I could surely return to the main trail and call for help. But could I leave Sean? Would he come with me voluntarily without waking up dad?

I grew angry, too, at all the blame dad had allowed me to assign to myself. That *bastard*. He had watched me become overcome with guilt, while all along he was the one leading Sean and I astray. Why was he doing this?

I turned on my cellphone, which, predictably, had no signal, and used its flashlight feature to find and pick up dad's knife, and also to find our location on the map. I noticed a ranger's station listed a bit north of us and decided to set off there and get help. Hopefully, I would find someone tonight who would return here and help figure out what was going on. And, hopefully, we would get back before dad realized I was gone.

I sat silently for a bit, trying to discern if dad was asleep. I had a nightmarish image of him rushing out of his tent to find me in possession of the map, and I could only imagine what would happen next. For now, dad didn't realize that I was on to him, and that gave me some advantage in trying to thwart whatever he was trying to accomplish.

Moving as quietly as I could, I set out into the woods.

The initially flat route developed gradually into a steep ascent. I quickened my pace as I got further away from our makeshift camp-site. Beyond every crooked set of branches I saw a visage of my dad in the shadows, a man I had thought I could trust. In the distance I heard the faint sound of running water mixed with hoots from owls and mating calls from insects. My legs began to ache as I continued up the hill, but adrenaline pushed me forward.

Finally, as the perfect darkness of midnight settled around me, I reached the peak of the mountain and saw the outline of a dilapidated shack before me.

I walked slowly up to the entrance, my mind somehow more nervous than before. I was a young woman alone in the woods, after all – what if what I found inside was worse than my crazed father?

Hesitantly, I knocked quietly at the rusted door, then louder when I heard no response. Finally, I pushed at the door. It creaked open, apparently unlocked.

At first, I saw nothing inside but darkness. The floors were wooden, the ceiling was low, and the room before me appeared barren. Using my phone's flashlight once more, I made out a long, oval-shaped mirror at the other end. Stepping closer, I gazed into the reflection of my own distraught form. My thin frame shook with worry. My long, disheveled chestnut hair at least somewhat obscured my panicked and sweaty face.

In the reflection, I began to notice something floating over my left shoulder. I froze, too afraid to turn around and see it directly. A translucent, wispy shape appeared behind me. For a moment, I saw its murky textures swirl together to form a barren face that consisted only of eyes and a nose. Then, a mouth grew into it, and the entity let out an inhuman moan.

I panicked at this, stumbling to the corner of the room and tripping over an old piece of carpet. I felt myself fall to the ground, and then through the floor onto the dirt below.

I drew dad's knife and held it out towards the gap above me, prepared to swipe it at anything I saw. But nothing came, so I looked around and examined my surroundings.

What I found there shocked me even more than the shape that had appeared a moment earlier. I found myself surrounded on all sides by bones. Human bones. Hundreds of them.

I felt like I was about to pass out from the stench and from the horror coursing through my body. But even what I had seen so far did nothing to prepare me for what I was about to witness.

There was one body that consisted of more than bones. It was still lined with decomposing flesh, and it smelled the worst of all. I dropped the knife and vomited immediately after my phone's light gave me a better look at it.

It was my dad. His head and torso lay a few feet from me, and I saw a leg about a yard away. The dirt underneath was stained a deep auburn red.

At last, I heard footsteps creeping close to the hole in the floor where I had dropped down. Frantically, I shined my phone's light around the room, noticing a small gap in the wall. Crawling as fast as I could over the remains that littered the area underneath the floor of the shack, I slid through the hole and found myself back outside.

I took a brief moment to get my bearings, and then I sprinted down the hill as fast as I could, heading in the direction of the campsite and never looking back.

When I was close to the bottom of the hill, long out of sight of the building, I finally stopped. I hadn't realized how out-of-breath the journey up and down that hill had made me. Panting, I sat down against the back of a tree and noticed the first glimmers of morning light appearing on the horizon.

I went through it all in my mind. The mirror. The shape that formed behind me. The area between the floor and the dirt – not really a basement and more like a crawlspace – littered with human bones and my dad's decomposing body.

Of course, if *that* was my dad, then who was leading Sean and I into the woods? This person, who had shown such love and affection towards us – this couldn't be our real dad. Our real father was dead, and had been for some time, judging by the body I had seen, and this imposter had taken his place. Our real dad would never pretend to be lost like this, much less falsely place the blame on me for it. But how was any of this possible? I didn't have time to grieve. I knew at that moment that I had to stop the man in the campsite from achieving his goal. I didn't know what that goal was, but I knew it involved Sean and me.

I crept slowly back to where we had set up our tents. It was still early in the morning, and hopefully both my dad and Sean had not noticed my absence. Dad's tent was shut and looked no different from when I had left it. I returned the map and compass to dad's backpack and threw water on the last few embers of the fire, which I had forgotten to put out in my earlier panic. I carefully unzipped the door to my tent and crawled inside of it.

Thankfully, Sean was still asleep. Quietly, I pulled a towel from my backpack and wiped off sweat from all over my body. If the thing pretending to be dad came along, I wanted it to think I had been asleep in the tent, not running through the woods all night.

I lay down on my pillow and tried to think of a plan, of some way to lead my brother and me out of this nightmare. Quickly, I decided the best thing to do was to wake up Sean, tell him some story to convince him to follow me, and take him in the woods with me, as far away from dad's imposter as we could get. I could use the compass and map to find our way back to civilization. From there, I could convince the authorities to check out the abandoned ranger station in the woods. Upon finding the bodies, they'd know I was telling the truth. It wasn't a great plan, but it was all I could come up with.

No sooner had I resolved on this course of action than I heard footsteps approaching the tent. I braced myself, not sure what was outside. A moment later, the thing that was pretending to be my father shouted, "Good morning, kids, rise and shine! Sorry to wake you so soon, but we need to get an early start if we're going to find our way out of here." Sean stirred as I realized that I had missed my chance.

Within a half hour, we had eaten a light breakfast and packed up our belongings. Sean and *it* both noticed my unease, and both assured me that I didn't need to beat myself up for losing the map. "We'll figure this out soon," said dad, patting me on the back. He was being so unusually kind and sincere that I nearly bought into the act. "After a couple miles hiking in the direction of the road, I guarantee we'll find our way back to the main trail."

The forest looked so much more welcoming in the daylight, and my father was being supportive. He optimistically insisted that our trip would end up being the same overnight camping experience it would have been had nothing gone wrong. Sean even returned to his more typical jovial mood.

That's when I started second-guessing myself. I thought about how I was lying in the tent, right where I had tried to go to sleep only a few hours earlier, when dad had called out for us to get up. The things I'd seen were simply impossible. Had I simply awoken from a vivid dream?

As we began hiking up a steeper incline, Sean and I both struggling to keep up with dad, a terrible image ran through my head, of me running off with Sean when, in fact, nothing was wrong, and me pointlessly putting him in more danger in the process.

"You okay, Laura?" said dad, looking back at me. "You don't seem yourself."

"I'm fine, dad," I said. I looked him over carefully, trying to find some discrepancy that could validate my imposter theory. But he perfectly resembled the same dad I had known, and depended on, for 17 years. He shrugged and moved on.

We climbed higher and higher. Sean, unburdened by any heavy camping gear, was just able to keep up. But I felt so tired, tired enough to feel like I had been out moving all of last night, not sleeping soundly as I was beginning to hope.

Then we reached the summit. All around us on either side were green valleys surrounded by thick forest. Then, ahead and by a steep cliff side, was a building.

Was this man an imposter, taking us to that horrible place, so that our bodies would be added to the many underneath it? Or was this a different place entirely?

The building before us now had a second floor, which I hadn't seen in the structure I visited last night. But it also conveyed a sense of familiarity that sent a deep chill down my spine.

"Maybe there is someone inside!" said Sean, excitedly.

I walked to the rocky cliff side. There was water running down it.

"Laura, come on!" called dad. "We need to check this place out! It looks like a ranger station. If anyone is here, they can help us!" He was by the building's entrance, Sean at his side.

I didn't budge.

"Wait here," I heard my dad say, followed by the sounds of his footsteps approaching me.

The stream below formed a waterfall, a cascade. At the bottom of the steep decline, I saw the shallow swimming pool where we had started the previous day. We were less than a mile from where we had parked, and if this man was really my father, he would have noticed and said that. It was entirely possible that I had been this close to the road last night and just didn't realize it – I had, after all, had plenty to distract me from carefully examining the map.

"Laura, you need to come over to us," said dad. He was right behind me now. I felt his hand grab me and nudge me in the direction of the building. "We need to see if there's anyone here who can help us. We can admire the view later." I resisted and continued to stare at the water below. He stepped in front of me, smiling and waving his hand around. "You okay, honey? You seem like you're in some kind of trance."

"Do you have your knife?" I asked, remembering that I had dropped it in the building the night before. If my dad didn't have it, then what I experienced had to be real.

"What?" said dad.

"If you have it, show it to me," I said.

"Well," said dad, pausing to think, "I don't remember where it is."

"I know where you keep it," I said.

My dad shot me a concerned look, something that seemed of a different character. "And where is that?" he asked.

"In your backpack," I said, "with the map *you* said *I* lost."

Dad's expression shifted. "Honey," he said, calmly, "I don't know what you're talking about. I don't have any map. You had the only one."

"You said we were far away from where we started," I said. My dad's eyes now cast an insidious glare. "But look down there. Don't you recognize it?"

Dad turned and looked down the precipice. "Oh, it's nothing!" he said. "There are all sorts of waterfalls in these woods, it's not the same one at al-"

He never finished the sentence. Seeing my chance, I slammed all my body weight into his back. Before he knew what was happening, he was flying off the edge and through the air. Adrenaline again pumped through my whole body as I realized what I had done. I watched as he skidded off the side of the cliffs before landing on a rocky alcove hundreds of feet below. It goes without saying that his body didn't move again.

I stepped back, slowly. *What have I done? What if I was wrong?*

Every thought in my mind now turned to Sean. I looked to see him backing away from me, understandably horrified. There were tears in his eyes.

"Sean, it's okay," I said, approaching him. "It's not what it looks like. It wasn't really dad. You have to believe me."

Sean now backed into the door of the building, which nudged open behind him.

A form stood inside, encased in a layer of shadow. Was it a park ranger? Was I mad? Did I just kill my father and traumatize my brother for life over nothing?

The figure stepped forward, reaching out for my brother. Emerging from the darkness, I recognized the figure: it was...me.

The other me grabbed Sean's shoulder and pulled. Sean screamed. I ran to the door as fast as I could.

The amorphous face from last night – that had been me, a new me, forming just like dad's replacement must have months ago. And it came into existence immediately after I looked into that mirror.

Sean bit into the hand of the other me, causing her to loosen her grip, and stumbled backwards outside. "Wait out here!" I hollered at him as I sprinted by, unsure if he would listen. I darted forward and dove at the other me, knocking us both to the ground.

The other me had my same circular face and green eyes, but she lacked the fright, stress, and horror that I remembered seeing in the mirror the previous night. I tried to grab her hands to restrain her, but she slammed her head into mine and knocked me onto the brittle floor, where I lay, stunned, near the hole I had formed last night. Remembering the knife I had left, I rolled close to the hole and reached down to find it.

"Looking for this?" I heard my own voice ring out. Turning, I saw her charge at me, knife in hand. I screamed as incredible pain coursed through my body as she jabbed the knife into the left side of my stomach. I looked down and saw blood gushing out and spilling down my shirt. I collapsed, dizzy.

The other me bent down, her face inches from mine. She held the knife, a slick sheen of my own blood on the blade. "This could have been so much easier." My doppelgängers voice had an empty, flat tone. "Sean deserves better than you."

She pulled the knife from my stomach. I cried out amidst the flood of hot, fresh pain. Her face, a perfect copy of mine, remained eerily placid. Her eyes were clinical and calculating, betraying none of the judgment I expected. "I am the superior sister."

As she moved to strike again, I recognized her presence as something cold and alien, a creature that saw my humanity as nothing more than a weakness to be purged.

My right hand felt a strong, spherical object. Just as the other me began her next strike with the knife, I slammed a human skull from below into her face with all my remaining strength. The other me collapsed backwards, blood gushing down her forehead. "You bitch," she stammered, stunned.

But she didn't stay down. She didn't have to. The unholy thing recovered almost instantly. Her eyes, still filled with that cold, empty calm, zeroed in on me as she sprang up and pounced, knocking the wind from my lungs. She slammed her hands down on my shoulders, pinning me to the floor as the skull rolled away.

"What's happening?" Sean's terrified voice rang out from the doorway. He stood there, frozen, his eyes wide, taking in the scene: me, bloody and gasping, pinned to the floor by a copy of myself wielding a bloody knife.

The doppelgänger turned her head to face Sean, her expression shifting to one of caring concern. "Thank God you're okay," she said, her voice smooth and soothing. "This...thing tried to attack me. She's the one who killed dad. You need to help me restrain her."

Panic seized me. I knew what she was doing. I struggled against her grip, but my body was weak, and the pain almost unbearable. "Sean, no," I gasped. "Don't listen to her! She...she came from the mirror. I need you to break it."

Sean nervously glanced at the mirror as the doppelgänger spoke firmly. "Don't listen to her. Sean, she's trying to confuse you. You *know* me. You know that I've always been here for you, just like I'm here for you now. You can trust me."

Tears welled in my eyes as waves of guilt and desperation washed over me. "Sean, please," I choked out, ignoring the pain. "She's *wrong*. You *can't* trust me. I stole money meant for you. I've been a terrible older sister to you. For God's sake, just run and get away from here, from both of us."

Sean's eyes darted between the two of us. Then, his gaze settled upon the skull on the ground. Slowly, deliberately, he picked it up, drew back his arms, and threw it at the mirror.

The glass shattered on impact. With a high-pitched, inhuman scream, the other me convulsed. She didn't burn, bleed, or disintegrate...she just vanished. An eerie calm settled over the shack, broken only by my ragged breathing and the frantic flutter of my heart.

"Sean," I called, weakly. He approached me tentatively, unsure of what to think. I mustered my depleted energy to whisper into his ear to take a path down to the water hole below, to follow the trail there to the road, and to get help.

As I lay on the ground, pushing my hand against the gushing wound, I felt the life drain out of me. Yet, overshadowing the immense pain was a creeping, suffocating terror as I thought of what lay behind the mirror that had shattered into a thousand pieces. Did the other me simply return to wherever she had originated? Was she still out there, waiting for another chance to emerge into my reality?

The blurred form of my brother grew smaller in my swimming vision. Sean was running away, just as I had told him. I closed my eyes, praying that all the worst parts of me would bleed out in the cold dirt. And I hoped that the broken mirror had taken the rest of the monster with it, leaving a trail too faint for it to ever follow him again.

6

———

PLAYPEN

Mom noticed me staring at the PlayPlace. "Only once you finish your food, honey." Eagerly, I devoured the remainder of my Happy Meal.

As I placed my shoes in the purple storage cubby, I gazed at the tall spiral slide and imagined the thrilling ride it promised.

But, to my surprise, a girl who exited it seemed indifferent to the experience. When she approached her mother, she spoke in a flat, hollow voice: "Can we come back, soon, with Mary and Joanne?"

I took little notice as I ran past a Cheeseburglar cut-out and dived into a bright yellow tube. I crawled through corridors, threw myself onto a bouncy blue mat, and climbed a rope ladder until I reached the slide entrance.

Through a bubble-shaped window, I saw my mom waiting for me by the slide's exit. With an enthusiastic cry, I leapt in head-first.

When I emerged, I tumbled out not onto the soft rubber wearmat near my mother but, instead, into a pit of multicolored plastic balls still within the PlayPlace.

This confused me. But, I reasoned that there must simply be two slides. As I waded through the plastic balls, I told myself that I'd find the slide I was looking for soon.

However, the only route before me led me back to the same slide. As I traveled repeatedly from the ball pit through an array of tubes and ladders, I found myself trapped in an endless loop.

Where was the slide that led outside? And where was the opening I'd used to first enter the PlayPlace?

I panicked. I cried for help, but no one seemed to hear me, even as I could hear noise from the area outside.

As I waded through the ball pit for the fifth time, my legs felt something strange. I reached down, finding, to my horror, two long, white bones.

Before I could react, a ghastly figure emerged nearby. As it sat up, plastic balls rolled off of it to reveal a featureless face that lacked eyes, a nose, or a mouth.

I scrambled away, screaming. It followed me – through tubes, up alcoves, down the slide, and along the same route again. It took all my energy to stay ahead of it.

Soon, I was panting and tired. My clothes felt loose, and my reflection, when I glimpsed it, appeared emaciated. The figure, meanwhile, seemed to grow stronger, and more details steadily appeared on its face.

Finally, I collapsed by the slide entrance. Thankfully, I realized that the figure was no longer behind me.

My relief was short-lived. Through the bubble window, I watched, helplessly, as my pursuer emerged from the slide - *outside the Play-Place*. It looked exactly like me now, from my tousled brown hair to my Batman t-shirt.

As my mom took its hand, it spoke in a monotone voice. "Can we have my birthday party here?"

"If that's what you want, sweetie."

"Thank you mom. My friends are going to love it."

7

THE MIDNIGHT CLOCK

The banner over the store's entrance screams, *"Time Is Running Out on Our Winter Sale!"*

A dark-haired woman with a wiry frame and a name tag that reads *Maven* greets me when I step inside. "Looking for something in particular?"

"A gift for a friend. He's wealthy, with sophisticated taste."

She leads me past hundreds of clocks of all shapes and sizes. As we approach a room in the back, I note the thin glass frame above the handle to a door to the outside.

An array of cheap-looking clocks litters the room's front. They emit an ear-splitting cacophony of chimes.

"Ignore those, they still need to be fixed and synchronized," Maven explains before directing me to the room's far end, which houses dozens of fancy, elegant clocks, all in pristine condition.

Maven points to a floor clock with a minimalist design. "The moon dial on this one is studded with premium quality diamonds." She shows me several more with embedded rubies, a golden dial, and other ornate decorations. All exceedingly expensive.

"Can I see this?" I ask, motioning to a bulky structure covered by a blanket.

"No, that one's special, and not for sale."

Ignoring her, I remove the blanket, revealing an intimidatingly large antique grandfather clock. Its faded cherry finish has an ominous, blood-red hue, and I spot a sparkling ruby in the center of the decorative shell on its arched bonnet pediment.

When I reach for a slip of paper dangling from its ball-shaped finial, Maven slaps my hand away. "Leave, now," she demands.

~

My real business with the shop had nothing to do with making a purchase. When I return, it's several hours past the closing hours posted on the front door, and I'm carrying a glass cutter. Tiptoeing over the remnants of the door window I'd shattered, I approach the valuables Maven had shown me.

Ignoring the discordant sounds of the clocks by the room's entrance, I proceed to gather the items that will sell for the highest price. I take several of the smaller high-end clocks, and use the other tools I brought to pluck the diamonds and other expensive decorations from others.

I'm nearly ready to haul my loot outside when I return to the antique grandfather clock for the ultimate prize.

The words on the note attached to it strike me as nonsensical: "*If you're reading this in the late hours of the night/You'll want to stay far out of my sight.*" Scoffing, I let go of it and reach for the ruby.

I'm about to make contact with it when a piercing chime rings out from the clock. It is incredibly loud, and it causes a wave of pain that reverberates throughout my body. I wince as another, stronger, chime follows, then another. This continues, each chime hurting me more than the last.

The twelfth chime sends me collapsing in agony to the ground. To my horror, my limbs twist and bend unnaturally. With a sickening chorus of 'snaps,' they splinter, then harden into useless blocks of black walnut wood.

Meanwhile, I feel my face stretch and contort. In the reflection of the grandfather clock's glass lens, I watch, helplessly, as Roman numerals carve themselves onto my strained cheeks and forehead.

~

The next morning, Maven examines me with sigh. "Will you thieves ever learn? At least you'll fetch a decent price once I've fixed you up."

I want to ask her what's happened. To beg her to help me. But, when I try to speak, the only sound that emerges from my form is a shrill, high-pitched chime.

8

DR. KINNETTE'S KITCHEN SET

Mom promised me that middle school would improve, but I remain as friendless as when I showed up as the "new girl" four months ago. Many of my classmates have known each other since kindergarten, and there's no room for me in their social circles.

My mom tries to help. She befriends the mother of my classmate Claire.

If our school has a hierarchy, Claire's at the top of it. The girls who compete to sit next to Claire often share rumors about boys who like her. It's always a boy from the same pristine neighborhood as Claire. No one else is acceptable, even as gossip.

I rarely step foot in Claire's part of town. I know it to be filled with the lavish homes of parents who work as doctors or architects or lawyers who raise honor-roll students. You won't find people like my subsidy-dependent single mother and me living there, or an apartment filled with as-seen-on-TV junk like ours.

To my embarrassment, it's my mother who arranges my first social outing since the move.

I'm nervous. Making a good impression with Claire seems like my only shot at social acceptance, even as I fear that Claire has already made up her mind about me.

As our dilapidated minivan approaches Claire's house, I watch as overgrown grass and broken windows transition into picket fences that separate wide streets from manicured yards.

Mom asks if I want her to go to the door with me. I shake my head, grab my bag, and approach Claire's house.

Claire's mom greets me warmly. Like her daughter, she is pale and thin, with finely-combed red hair, though she lacks Claire's freckles. She leads me to the sunroom, where Claire is curled up on a couch underneath a fan with a large LED light. Behind Claire, the glass that spans the room's perimeter provides a stunning view of surrounding woodlands, and to her side, a door leads to a patio that connects to the backyard.

"Hey Claire," I say. "Thanks for having me over."

She looks up briefly, flashes me a hollow smile, and resumes typing a message on her cell phone. For several long moments, I wait awkwardly, unsure of what to do.

I breathe in the still, arid air as Claire continues to text. Cookware clanks in the adjacent kitchen as Claire's mother prepares food. An ornate grandfather clock ticks in the hallway behind me.

Finally, Claire puts her phone away. She asks if I want to watch a movie after dinner. Her voice is dreary and unexcited.

I understand by now. As I'd suspected, Claire's mother forced her into this sleepover. Watching a movie together probably struck Claire as the best way to pass the time.

I select *Matilda* from the VHS collection. She tells me she's seen it a million times. I ask her if she'd prefer something else. She doesn't respond.

Claire's dad joins us for dinner. Unlike the frozen meals mom heats up for me, the food is fresh and well-flavored. Afterwards, Clair and I head to the basement. Compared to the rest of the house, it is barren and undecorated. Claire tells me her family is remodeling the area.

We pass an open door to the garage and settle down in a small room lined by empty concrete walls. I sit on a bean bag that faces a large TV. Claire steps past me and takes a spot on a couch covered in pink pillows.

Before Claire inserts the VHS tape, I make a final attempt to salvage the visit. "So...do you want to talk or anything? Before starting the movie?"

She shakes her head.

I tell her that I see her at school every day, but I don't feel like I really know her.

She shrugs and asks me what I want to talk about.

Her eyes wander as I struggle to come up with an answer. "What did you think about that book we had to read in English? The one where the kids had to keep digging the holes in the desert? I thought it was interesting."

She tells me it was fine. The silence that follows confirms that I am getting nowhere.

I try a different approach. "What about the boys in our class? Do you like any of them?"

She rolls her eyes and starts the movie.

We watch in silence. Eventually, Claire's mom calls down to let us know that she is going to bed and that we shouldn't stay up too late. Claire yawns and yells back that she plans to go to sleep once it ends.

She doesn't stay awake even that long. As the credits roll, I find her sound asleep on the couch behind me.

I'm disappointed, but not surprised, at how the evening has passed. I never stood a chance.

I turn off the television, change into my night clothes, and set up my sleeping bag. I crawl inside and let the distant ticking of the clock lull me to sleep.

I don't know what time it is when a sharp light jolts me awake. I realize that the television is on again, though its sound is at a low volume. Its light interrupts the otherwise total darkness around me. My eyes adjust to the image of a buff, shirtless man pushing a wheeled device across a floor. Cheesy music plays as he advertises a discount on the 'Ab-Slider', describing it as a $170 value available for only three easy payments of $29.99.

Claire remains asleep on the couch behind me. How did the television turn back on?

I tap the 'Power' button on the remote to no effect. I approach the television itself, where I search for a way to turn it off.

As the infomercial continues to play, a banner runs across the screen. I only get a quick glance at it before it disappears, but I think it says "Sarah" and "keep watching."

My name isn't exactly uncommon. But in my drowsy state, its appearance there startles me. A little curious, I decide to obey.

The screen fades to black. A lighthearted tune announces the start of a new infomercial. An audience of several dozen people appear, and they clap excitedly. They occupy only the first of several rows of seats, as if the infomercial lacked the budget for enough extras to fill the room.

A deep voice introduces the host as Dr. Robert Kinnette. The crowd goes wild as a short, middle-aged man with a heavy comb-over and thick, overgrown eyebrows jogs onto the stage, where he stands in a mock kitchen complete with a sink, a stove, plates, knives, and other cutlery.

He thanks the studio audience, then those watching from home. He speaks with intense commitment, like his whole existence had built up to this one defining moment.

He presents his product: *Dr. Kinnette's Kitchen Set*. I wonder who buys a whole kitchen set, and what being a doctor has to do with selling one.

He mentions a special deal – a free stainless steel saucepan – for anyone who calls in the next twenty minutes. The phone number that flashes across the screen is...off. It has at least ten digits, and several of them have shapes that I don't recognize.

Dr. Kinnette proceeds to praise a supposedly "state-of-the-art" titanium stove. He says it can cook supper in less than half the time of a leading competitor. "That's right," he says. "It can cook your son in less than *half the time* of our leading competitor."

My heart jolts. I must have heard him wrong. Right?

He asks for a volunteer. The camera cuts to the audience. At first, they sit still. Then, all at once, every single person raises his or her hand.

The image creeps me out. Why would they all raise their hands simultaneously like this? No real audience would act this way. If this were scripted, as I assumed it was, why would they be told to do this?

Dr. Kinnette scans the audience before pointing at an older woman. He identifies her as Alexia and asks her to join him. As Alexia stands and shuffles towards the stage, I notice a burn mark that runs from her forehead down to her shoulders.

The clapping starts up again and grows louder as Alexia approaches the kitchen set. When she arrives, Dr. Kinnette directs her to lay her arm on the counter. She obeys.

My eyes widen as Dr. Kinnette draws a long butcher knife. Alexia watches, blankly, as he swings it into Alexia's arm. Blood spurts across the stage as it lands just below her elbow, splattering across Dr. Kinnette's face and the kitchen equipment around him.

My jaw drops. I don't understand what I'm watching. I just sense that it is very, very wrong.

Dr. Kinnette howls, as if making a war cry, as he strikes Alexia's arm with faster and faster swings. Alexia's face conveys terror and agony, but she makes no effort to move or resist. The audience, meanwhile, hoots and hollers with alarming intensity. The camera switches, briefly, to a closeup of a young man with an eyepatch who yells words of encouragement.

Finally, Alexia's forearm detaches from her body. Dr. Kinnette raises it over his head and tells Alexia that she's done enough for today.

Alexia trudges back to her seat, seemingly uninterested in the thick red trail that follows her with each step.

Dr. Kinnette pulls open the stove's door and places Alexia's bloody limb on a metal rack inside. He turns to the camera. "I've always seen meals as the centerpiece of family life," he says. "Dinner is the most important meal of all. That's why you need to cook quality food using quality ingredients. And you know the best tools to use for that, don't you? It's with…"

He gestures towards the audience, who shout the answer in unison: "Dr. Kinnette's Kitchen Set!"

I press every button I can find on the outside of the TV, but I can't stop the infomercial from continuing to play. Finally, I glance at the cord that connects to a power outlet in the wall.

Before I move to unplug it, my gaze returns to the television. To my surprise, the image now consists only of a close-up of Dr. Kinnette's face, which stretches across the entire screen. "Not so fast!" he says, as a thin line of blood drips down his left cheek. "Please wait, there's more!"

I freeze. It's like he's reading my mind. But that's impossible, right?

A series of black-and-white clips play. The first shows a man and a boy standing next to a small stove. "Is your kitchen equipment too small for your family's needs?" says Dr. Kinnette's voice. Then, in color, the man and child appear next to the much larger, titanium stove Dr. Kinnette is trying to sell. "Then Dr. Kinnette's Kitchen Set has you covered!" exclaims the same exuberant voice. I observe that the child is gagged, and his hands are bound behind his back. The man shoves the child closer to the stove.

I shut my eyes and cover my ears. When I look out again, the infomercial displays the stage from the beginning, where Dr. Kinnette coats Alexia's cooked forearm in salt, pepper, and some kind of sauce. He takes a deep bite, greedily tugging strands of its flesh into his mouth. He swallows and makes a satisfied nod.

"See?" he says. "With only a few easy steps, Dr. Kinnette's Kitchen Set creates a satisfying meal for the whole, complete family! Mother, father, *and* daughter!"

The audience members clap again as Dr. Kinnette requests another volunteer. This time, when the camera cuts to the audience, no one's hand is raised.

Dr. Kinnette's face fills the screen again. His eyes drift slowly until he's looking right at me. "Sarah," he says. "How about you, Sarah? How would you like to be the next volunteer?"

"No," I mumble. "No…" He has to be referring to someone else. Someone there, in the studio with him, like Alexia.

But the camera never cuts away. It remains, patiently, on Dr. Kinnette's face. Ten, twenty, thirty long seconds pass.

Dr. Kinnette repeats my name. He tells me not to be shy – to come up to the stage. "If you're as quiet as Alexia was," he says, "then I promise you won't even wake up Claire."

My brain shifts to panic mode. I pull at the power cord.

The screen fades, but it doesn't cut off entirely like I expected. Instead, the image of Dr. Kinnette's face jostles and contorts. His subsequent words sound garbled and distorted. "Saaaarrahhhh. Whyyyy so shyyyy?"

The shot finally changes to a fractured, discolored image of the stage. But it's eerily empty. Dr. Kinnette, and his entire audience, are gone. Somehow, the still image of the vacant set disturbs me more than watching the gruesome spectacle unfold within it did. Where did everyone go?

A banner crawls across the screen. Looking closely, I make out the garbled words: "Five easy steps for four servings of Sarah."

At long last, the television cuts off. I'm left alone in the darkness. The only sounds I can hear are the clock's distant ticking and Claire's rhythmic breathing.

For a moment, I feel relief. This wasn't real. I had to have been dreaming. I couldn't have really seen those things. And, Dr. Kinnette couldn't have really seen me. I was safe.

Then, a slow, creaking noise draws my attention. It's coming from nearby.

My body shakes as I realize that what I'm hearing is the sound of the garage door slowly lifting.

Dr. Kinnette's voice emanates from the neighboring room. He's calling my name.

I sprint upstairs. I realize that I'm leaving Claire behind, but Dr. Kinnette had never showed any interest in her. He was only after me.

Time flows fast as I reach the main floor. I'm in an unfamiliar environment – a huge house I never had the opportunity to explore beyond a few rooms, and I can barely see anything in the darkness. I think about hiding. I think, too, of waking Claire's parents. They're adults. They'll know what to do.

"Saarraah," calls Dr. Kinnette's voice. He's close now – at least halfway up the stairs. "Don't be shy, just give it a try! Where are you hiding Sarah?"

I stumble past the kitchen and clumsily knock over a wooden stool as I flee to a room lined with bookshelves. I crawl under a desk and wait. Footsteps approach. I hold my breath as dark shoes stop next to me, then pass by as the figure departs.

I climb to my feet and head back the way I came. I realize I'm in the kitchen, but everything is different. The oven had been off before, but now it's preheating to 400 degrees. All the drawers are open. On the counter, dozens of knives are arranged into neat rows.

I scamper quietly until I find myself in the sun room. If I can just locate the door to the patio, I can find my way out. I reach around until I find a light switch. I know the light will give away my position, so I plan to only turn it on briefly – just long enough to allow me to find the door.

With a click, the overhead light beams on.

"SARAH," rings out not just one voice, but a chorus.

The surrounding glass reveals a horrifying sight: Dr. Kinnette's entire sickly, deformed audience has assembled outside the room. Their faces press against the glass as they shout my name in unison. *"SARAH SARAH SARAH."*

I break. At the top of my lungs, I scream and scream and scream.

Before me a dark, shadowy figure approaches from the kitchen. Tears run down my defeated face. I think about running, but then realize I have nowhere to go. I cover my eyes, resigned, and await my end.

"Sarah!" says the voice of a young girl. "What's wrong?"

I peer out to find Claire's thin frame before me. Suddenly, everything is quiet. Behind her befuddled face is a normal-looking kitchen with no knives and no open drawers.

I try to stammer out an explanation, but Claire doesn't care. She mutters something under her breath. Probably 'freak' or 'weirdo'.

I sputter about an evil infomercial to Claire's mother. She says I awoke from a bad dream. The garage door is closed, after all.

They let me sleep in Claire's bed upstairs. Despite feeling doomed to permanent exile by my would-be friend, I find comfort and a sense of security in knowing Claire's parents are in the next room. Maybe it really was a dream, I manage to tell myself. I sleep.

Sunlight comforts me in the morning. Claire's mother serves us banana pancakes. Claire is in a good enough mood that, for a minute, she even chats with me without sounding like someone forced her to. Maybe she just feels sorry for me after the display I put on last night. But maybe I won't be the social outcast I feared I'd be.

"See you Monday," I tell Claire when mom's minivan pulls into the driveway.

"Yeah, see you Monday," Claire responds. For a second, I think she looks up at me and smiles.

As I exit, I notice a wooden stool sprawled across the floor in a nearby hallway.

I climb into the van and close the door. I look back at the house to give my hosts a final farewell gesture.

She's still on the porch, but now she's joined by her mother and father. All three of them stand perfectly still, each holding a pristine, brightly colored box. The boxes are identical, depicting a smiling Dr. Kinnette beside his titanium stove and array of gleaming cutlery.

They don't look concerned, or even awake. They simply stand, their faces unsettlingly calm, wearing those same hollow, unblinking smiles I saw on the infomercial audience.

My own wave is slow and tentative, reflecting the sudden fear gripping me. As mom obliviously drives off, I watch out the back window as each of them pulls from their box a long, gleaming butcher knife. They mimic my gesture, rotating their knives side-to-side in a grotesque, synchronized wave.

9

INTERMISSION

The Pumpkin Man

When, many years ago, a carnival fortune teller warned my teenage self to stay away from "the Pumpkin Man," I laughed incredulously.

As the cart carrying me and my family ascends the Halloween-themed roller coaster, I watch in horror as a support beam for a large, orange decoration that towers over the track suddenly breaks apart.

The Reopening

When the roller coaster finally reopens a year after the horrendous accident, I am the only customer willing to take a seat on its inaugural ride.

The new safety measures ensure that the ride goes smoothly, but I'm confused as to why the images at the exit photo booth display a whole family sharing the train with me.

The First Tour

As I led the dozen members of my first tour group through the castle, I stuttered nervously while expounding on the estate's legends of vengeful ghosts and mysterious disappearances.

Thankfully, I think my group still enjoyed the experience, as both members gave me a generous tip at the tour's end.

The Video

My friend sent me an ADORABLE video of his infant daughter Addison clambering awkwardly up a long staircase and hopping into his arms.

I'm just confused as to why I hear a woman's voice screaming "*Nosidda*" in the video's background.

The Parking Garage

Guilt over the car crash I caused, and successfully blamed on my wife, compelled me to finally visit the only surviving victim in the hospital where he lay in a coma.

After descending nine levels in the crowded parking garage in attempt to locate a space, I find myself stuck in a frozen hellscape with no way of escaping the winged beast at its center.

The Deluded Woman

"I know this sounds crazy," the frightened woman confided in her therapist, "but I'm convinced that my husband has been replaced by some kind of shapeshifting monster."

"Don't worry, I'm going to help you get to the root of this delusion," he responded as he dispersed a telepathic alert that he'd finally located the last remaining human on Earth.

The Gift

"Eternity here won't be too bad," I think, as I switch on the television Satan generously placed in my hot, uncomfortable cell to see a long list of tv shows and movies.

Only, when I begin operating the remote, I realize that every channel is the TV Guide Channel.

10

A SAPPHIRE AS BLUE AS THE SKY

Today's going to be different. I'm going to win. I can feel it.

"Three, two, one..." The shot rang out.

Mary cheers for me.

My long strides are measured and calculated. A handful of runners remain ahead of me. I let them exhaust themselves. It's only a matter of time before they run out of energy. Consistency is key. Consistency is how I win.

As I approach the trail into the woods, the distant roar of the crowd fades until only one voice remains. It's a voice that doesn't belong here.

~

"You got a girlfriend?" she asked last Saturday night. Her curly auburn hair drooped onto her olive green dress, which hugged her figure. My hand twitched with desire to push it away and feel the skin underneath.

"What makes you say that?" I responded as I sipped from a red plastic cup as dance music blared in the background.

"The way you look at me, and then look away," she said. "You've been doing it since you arrived. You like what you see, but it makes you feel guilty."

~

Branches obscure the cloudless, deep blue sky. The comparatively cool temperature of the forest soothes my overheated, trim body. I leave in my dust one hotshot who thought he could beat me, and then another. The one-mile marker lies nearby. By the time I get there, I will be where I belong: at the front of the pack.

~

"I do," I told her. My heart fluttered. I chanced another glance. She was attractive, as well as at least three years older than me.

"And you didn't bring her to the party?" she asked.

"No, no," I said. "She — I'm…I'm a prospective student here doing an overnight. We're high school seniors. I want to attend here on a running scholarship. She doesn't want to go here though."

"I thought you looked young," she said. She smiled slyly. She introduced herself as Rachel.

~

The striking heat hits me as I exit the tree line. Much of the crowd has shifted to the marker ahead.

Mary yells words of encouragement. I shoot her a quick smile. She's always supported me.

I'm in first place with just over two miles to go. The crowd goes wild for me. I strut. It's a great feeling. A natural high.

I spot Rachel. My mood sinks. I'd been right about hearing her voice. But why would she be here, at a high school cross country meet? The college I visited is over three hours away. It doesn't make any sense.

~

"Do you want to get out of here?" Rachel asked.

I felt like I'd only just arrived. But she was intoxicating.

But what about Mary? We were happy together, weren't we? I wasn't about to betray her after all this time.

But Rachel only asked me to leave the party with her. It didn't have to mean anything beyond that.

I agreed. The alcohol in my system no doubt played a role in my deci-sion. I texted my host not to worry about me and accompanied Rachel outside.

~

What is Rachel doing here? My mind searches for rational explanations. Maybe she has a younger sibling in the race.

I don't say anything as I pass her. I only pity her for what the scorching sun will do to her pale skin if she keeps standing in the open.

She doesn't acknowledge me either. I don't mind. With Mary around, it's best for Rachel and I to act like we don't know each other.

~

"So, have you and your girlfriend been together long?" Rachel asked as I followed her across the main campus lawn.

"Three years," I told her.

"Does she satisfy you?"

I told her I didn't know what she meant.

"You know what I meant," said Rachel. She flashed a mischievous smile.

"She's...she has strong beliefs about waiting on certain things, and I respect that," I said.

"That's admirable of you," said Rachel. She held the door for me as I entered her dormitory.

~

I'm all alone. The next runner is at least twenty seconds behind me. I pant as I keep up the pace I'd trained for three years to maintain.

I dart down the dirt path until I reach the lowest elevation of the route.

Someone emerges from behind a tree up ahead. Wait – how did she get here?

Rachel tilts her head, as if examining me. I want to say something. I want to tell her to go away – to leave me alone. But I can't spare the breath. I pass her again.

~

Her room was well-decorated. Items on her desk and table stood out: a deck of large, detailed cards; incense; candles; a knife with a black handle; a parchment displaying a jagged shape. What kind of stuff was she into?

I examined a mineral of deep blue on her dresser. "It's a star sapphire crystal," said Rachel. "They say that if you look into it, you can see a whole little world inside."

For a brief moment, its shade slightly altered such that I could discern a stretching, agonized human face stretching out across its side. Its mouth formed a long, anguished cry.

I felt alarmed. My senses started to return. My last wise thought occurred to me: I should leave.

That's when her dress, and then the rest of her clothes, formed a small pile on the floor. I looked up from it to her, and I liked what I saw.

~

I approach the hill. It's the most difficult part of the course.

I hear someone behind me. I remind myself that victory is not assured.

I breathe heavily, furiously, as Rachel emerges again from the trees. Suddenly, she's everywhere. There are dozens of her at once, forming a crowd of mocking, identical faces.

I wipe sweat from my eye. When my vision returns, she's still there. She – each of her – reaches behind her and starts to unzip her dress.

I can't handle this. Not now. I have a race to worry about. I close my eyes.

My foot slams into a rock. For a moment, I am weightless. When I open my eyes, I'm on the ground. My body aches. Kyle is ahead of me.

Kyle. That bastard. He used to be faster than me. He once thought he'd be the star of the team.

I get to my feet and sprint, ignoring the pain in my ankles and heels. I charge, eager to reclaim my proper place.

~

"Did it live up to your expectations?" she whispered to me afterwards.

I nodded enthusiastically. I'd been clumsy and quick, but she didn't seem to mind, and the rush of having her had been an intense, all-consuming joy.

"I'm happy to hear that," she said. "Hold out your hand, like this." The palm of her right hand faced the ceiling.

I did as instructed and mimicked her gesture.

She mumbled something indecipherable under her breath. I suddenly felt limp. Swiftly, she dug the knife into me until a gash stretched across my hand.

~

We emerge from the woods to the penultimate open area. The zig-zag pattern of the five kilometer course again takes us close to where we start and end the race. The crowd sees Kyle, then me. I am humiliated but undeterred.

I spot Mary. She isn't cheering for me. Not with Rachel whispering into her ear. Are those tears running down Mary's face?

This can't be happening. All at once, everything is going wrong.

I chase Kyle into the last stretch of woods. We are almost neck-and-neck.

I look around. Rachel is there, watching. She peers at me from behind every bush, every tree. But, no one else can see us. Each time I see her, I am reminded of what I did – of what I'd thought would stay three hours away where Mary would never find it.

At the top of a small hill, I shove Kyle to the side. He topples and rolls away. His cries and accusations resound behind me. But who will believe him?

~

"What are you doing?" I asked as I winced from the pain. I tried to react, but my body didn't respond even as my blood dripped into the glass jar.

"Don't try to resist," asked Rachel. It's far too late for that. You're in my control now."

My memories of the moments that followed are fractured and disjointed. In a terrifying blur, I found myself driving, speeding through pre-dawn darkness. A sense of conviction guided my movements: Rachel asked me to do this. And that was more than enough to quell my internal doubts.

I arrived at a familiar house. I grabbed a rock near the back porch. The sound of the window shattering felt distant, muffled, like listening to a crash underwater. I slipped inside, not even flinching at the sharp shards of glass I stepped over.

I moved through the house with a chilling, practiced ease, as if performing a task I'd rehearsed a hundred times. I found Kyle in his bed, stirring from the noise. His eyes blinked open, locking onto mine. There was a moment of recognition - not fear, but pure, confused disbelief - before I drove the knife into his heart.

A hot, metallic scent filled the room. Deftly, still only vaguely in control of my own actions, I unscrewed the lid of a glass jar I'd brought, filling it with Kyle's fresh blood. The warmth of it soaked through my fingers as I sealed it shut. I didn't speak. I didn't hesitate. I simply turned and retraced my steps, leaving the house, the shattered window, and Kyle's widening, sightless eyes behind me.

When I arrived back at the dorm, Rachel was waiting for me outside, a look of knowing satisfaction on her face. She led me to her room.

I watched, frozen in place, as Rachel drizzled my blood, then Kyle's, over the sapphire, which started to glow. The glow became brighter, and brighter. "Sustenance from the corrupted," said Rachel. "Sustenance from the innocent victim." She turned to me, flashing a devilish smile. "Only one ingredient left. A soul to feast on for years." The sky blue that emanated from the sapphire took hold of me, pulling my feet from the ground.

~

Rachel appears before me constantly. I pass her every ten seconds. "You deserve this," she taunts.

"No!" I stammer. "Leave me alone!"

But she doesn't. "Run!" she calls. "Run! Keep the energy flowing!"

I do run. I run as fast as I can. I'm going to make it, I tell myself. I'm going to win. Everything's going to be okay.

So what if Rachel told Mary that I cheated on her? I was going to break up with Mary soon anyway, and Rachel's as much at fault as I am. Not every high school romance is meant to last. Our relationship had run its course. Mary knew that, right?

I exit the woods and reach the final stretch of the course.

I expect applause. But the crowd is…silent. My friends, my coach, my girlfriend – they provide none of the fanfare I expected. Mary's teary look conveys judgment and betrayal.

Only a patch of dirt separates me from the finish line. I'm fatigued and drained, but I keep going.

I reach out. I can nearly touch the ribbon.

That's when I sink. The dirt is soft, sandy, and wet. My feet are instantly sucked under. The more I resist, the deeper I descend, the soil grasping at my ankles like cold, wet hands.

Kyle hurries past me. He extends his arms as he breaches the ribbon. Dozens follow him. They step over me and ignore me.

"Help!" I beg. "Please, help!"

I am pulled further down. The dirt consumes me up to my neck.

A shadow falls over me. My eyes drift up Mary's body, past the cross around her neck and to her face. "Mary, I'm sorry," I say. "I'm so sorry for what I did. Please, please forgive me."

Mary turns away as the dirt swallows me whole. The last thing I remember before my head is pulled underground is the lush blue of the sky, and the sense that Rachel is watching me from behind it as she feeds off of my misery.

I wake up. I'm at home, in my room. I decide to write down what happened, what I tell myself I must have dreamed.

I check the clock. The meet begins in an hour. I throw on my uniform and peer out the window. As always, not a single cloud mars the deep blue of the sky.

I repeat that today won't be like the others. I'm not going to lose the race. I'm not going to lose Mary. I'm going to run fast enough to finally break free. Today's going to be different. I'm going to win. I can feel it.

11

—————

A PERFECT TEN

My foot slips on the ice. I stumble, nearly falling, before balancing against a glass window. On the other side, a mannequin flaunting a retro outfit gazes vacantly at me.

Luckily, my misstep went unnoticed. Bret and Angela are too immersed in their shared affection. They remain oblivious as I continue to follow them down Cary Street.

Angela isn't clumsy like I am. The strength of her grip against Bret's hand is calculated and comfortable. He never pulls his hand away and says, "Ouch, ease up there, that hurt." Not to her.

He tosses his empty paper cup and leads her into a bookstore. I enter a moment later.

Inside, I position myself in a corner by a fire extinguisher. A tuxedo cat brushes against my leg as I watch them peruse the Sci-Fi & Fantasy section.

Bret used to do this with me, back when he loved me. Before he threw me out. Before he found a replacement.

They exchange a quick kiss. It makes me yearn for the feel of Bret's lips against mine.

The physicality of our bond – how Bret expressed his love for me – is what I miss the most. I know what he and Angela are up to after he closes the shades of his bedroom window around 9:15 p.m. every weeknight and before he opens the shades around 8:40 a.m. every weekend morning. It simply can't compare to what he and I once had.

Bret brings a book to the checkout counter. "She's a ten, isn't she now?" says the clerk through a smirk.

"Don't talk about her like that," snaps Bret.

They complete the sale. The clerk's eyes walk up and down her perfect, gorgeous frame as she steps back outside. She wears the same gray winter coat as me, but, on her, it appears freshly tailored.

At the Byrd Theatre, Bret buys two tickets to the matinee. I buy one.

I wait in the lobby. I'd seen how much coffee Bret had been drinking.

An hour later, Bret emerges for the men's room. Now's my chance.

Bret is a creature of habit. I find her quickly.

I scoot through the otherwise-empty back row where Angela watches the screen as blankly as the mannequin watched me.

Swiftly, I remove the fire extinguisher from inside my winter coat and swing it with all my might.

My swing is clumsy, but the fire extinguisher connects with cold, satisfying precision. A bright cascade of shorted wires flashes. Angela's head disengages and falls.

Her arms jostle protectively. I dodge them. My hand slips down the back of her neck and presses the button three times, feeling the faint mechanical click beneath the synthetic skin. Her torso powers down.

I stuff Angela's remains under the neighboring seats. Soon, my lover will return, and he shouldn't notice that his old Angela 9.0 has replaced his new Angela 10.0 until the movie ends.

They said that my model had defects. Defects like jealousy and clumsiness. That I should be shoved into a trash can while a replacement arrives. But Bret couldn't get rid of me that easily.

He returns. When I grip his hand, perhaps a little too tightly, suspicion flickers, then fades.

I relax. At long last, we are lovers once again.

12

THE INITIATION

"**S**caredy-cat," teased Carmen.

"It's the least frightening haunted house on the planet, and you're still too chicken to go in," hissed Michelle.

I glared at the pair of eighth graders. Ever since I arrived at James Garfield Middle School, they'd taken it upon themselves to bully me relentlessly.

It didn't matter that our classes didn't overlap, as I was two years their junior. They always found ways to harass me during school events and field trips, as well as after hours, during which they waited for me to be alone, or at least away from any adults. They generally stuck to insults and put-downs, but they weren't beneath going further when they could get away with it. I'd come home with plenty of cuts, bruises, and pain in my scalp from where they'd pulled my thin black hair.

They'd sized me up as soon as I'd entered the school bus. I was new. I read the wrong books, usually weird stuff about magic and the occult. I lived in the wrong area – one that was a substantial step down from the neighborhood with its own country club earlier on the bus route. I was late to hit puberty, rendering me smaller and less developed than my peers. And, I was deeply claustrophobic, as they learned when they locked me for several minutes in a supply closet, prompting me to scream my heart out.

My dad kept telling me that if I just ignored them, they'd eventually leave me alone. But it was advice that I gradually realized was naïve. Sure, *some* bullies will lose interest if you don't give them the reaction they want. But not these ones.

On this particular occasion, it was Halloween. Our school took the holiday relatively seriously, condensing the day's class schedule and reserving the final two hours for festivities.

Due to rain, the event largely transpired in the school gymnasium. The room was filled with seasonal activities – apple-bobbing barrels, pumpkin carving stations, and even a dunk tank with a target that resembled a spider web and a giant jack-o'-lantern shaped base. The vice principal and an elderly teacher, both remarkably good sports, took turns sitting inside. They were dressed as a pair of witches who, according to local lore, wreaked havoc on our Pennsylvania community centuries ago.

I wish I could have enjoyed the event as much as my peers. But the echoing noise and the prospect of being stuck in a room with a large crowd quickly sent me fleeing. Before long, I found myself in an adjacent corridor where a small number of students perused a few less popular attractions.

I walked to the end of the hallway, where I saw that the music room had been transformed into a makeshift haunted house. *Great*, I thought. There was virtually nothing I hated more than haunted houses. I didn't mind the spooky decorations – in fact, I had a soft spot for them. What I hated was the idea of not knowing where I was, of not being able to see, and of being stuck in confined spaces where, at any moment, someone in a costume might jump out at me.

Seeing nothing else to do, I sat against the wall and waited for the event to be over. That's when Carmen and Michelle came along.

~

They'd followed me there. At first, they pestered me for being alone. "What a surprise finding the class weirdo here all by herself," snickered Carmen.

"No, um, I just wanted to see what was over here," I lied.

Michelle's face formed a skeptical expression. "If that's the case, then why are you sitting down?" She glanced at the music room entrance, then back to me. "You know what I think? I think you're too afraid to go in there. Little miss *terrified-of-everything*."

"No, that's not it-"

"Michelle's right!" chimed in Carmen. "You're too scared!"

"You're, like, the biggest wimp I've *ever* seen in my life," jeered Carmen. "Just pathetic."

"Leave me alone," I whimpered.

"*Leave me alone*," mocked Carmen, adopting a comically high-pitched voice to mimic my own. "We're going to tell *everyone* that you're too much of a coward to go into the world's least-scary haunted house."

They carried on like this for several minutes. As they did so, three students emerged from the haunted room. They looked, well, happy. As they headed back towards the main event in the gym, they talked and giggled excitedly amongst each other. Certainly, they didn't seem the least bit bothered by what they'd encountered.

I let out an annoyed moan as I realized that the path of least resistance was just to give Carmen and Michelle one less thing to bully me about by walking through this stupid attraction. Even with all my phobias, how bad could it honestly be? "Look, I'll do it, okay?"

"Whatever," Michelle retorted. "Like we really give a shit what you do. Just know, though, that if you chicken out and try to leave, we'll be here waiting, and we'll see it."

"Same goes if you come running out screaming, or having one of your pitiful little panic attacks," hissed Carmen as she removed her phone from her pocket. "Everyone'll have a video of it by morning."

"I'll be fine," I muttered. And with that, I pushed open the door marked "Entrance."

~

Before me, a combination of boxes, music stands, and book-shelves formed a corridor adorned with plastic spiders positioned on fake webs. As haunted houses go, it was certainly mild and kid-friendly. I did my best to control my fear as I pressed onwards.

Ms. Jensen, the music teacher, had certainly put a lot of effort into the environment. Plastic ghosts dangled from the ceiling. Prop graves, complete with fake hands reaching out from in front of them, littered the ground. The overhead lights flickered dimly, and what visibility I had was impeded by the fog emanating from a mist machine. Some of the props moved or made noises (or both) when they sensed my approach.

The path continued to a "Halloween Tunnel" formed of canvas held up by arched PVC pipes. A giant clown face covered its entrance, such that entering it resembled crawling into its mouth. There was no way around it – at least, not without turning around, or shoving bulky furniture out of the way.

I shuddered. As if the poor visibility wasn't enough, I now needed to enter a confined space, just as I'd feared.

This will all be over soon, I told myself. I took a deep breath, dropped to the carpeted floor, and crawled inside.

I placed one hand before the other and steadily made my way forward. Some decorations – mostly skeletons and pumpkins, all placed above the tunnel – were visible through the translucent canvas. But as I made more progress, the light started to fade, to the point that I could only see a few inches in front of me.

I kept thinking that I was about to reach the exit. But, the exit never came, even as I was sure that I'd traversed the full length of the room. As my body started to tire, I struggled to imagine how a tunnel this long could even fit in the area where it had been located. Perhaps if it wrapped back onto itself in a snake-like form. But I hadn't sensed any turns. As far as I could tell, I was moving continuously in the same direction.

This kept going for a long time. Eventually, I realized I was sweating profusely, and not just because of physical exhaustion. Panic swept over me. What if I got stuck here, as impossible as that was to rationalize? What if no one found me? I imagined the walls, which I could barely see, closing in upon me, and the oxygen in the stale air I was breathing slowly disappearing, leaving me to suffocate. My mind started to drift away, and I grew dizzy.

That's when a thought belatedly occurred to me. I had my house keys in my pocket. It would take a little effort, but I could use them to cut a tear into the thin canvas and force my way out. If I was somehow wrong about all this – if I wasn't stuck in an impossibly endless tunnel – I could deal with the consequences of damaging Ms. Jensen's prop later.

It was at that moment that I first heard it: a shrill cackle that reverberated through the tunnel. As it repeated, my surroundings tremored, as if shivering in fear.

At first, I thought it was coming from behind me. I quickened my pace, only to hear it ahead of me, too. That's when I realized that it was coming from both directions at once.

"*Lyd-i-a,*" echoed the eerily high-pitched voice ahead of me, which stretched my name into three syllables.

"*Lyd-i-a,*" echoed an identical voice behind me.

At first, I wondered if it could be Carmen and Michelle playing tricks on me. But that thought faded when, ahead of me, two bright red eyes pierced the darkness. I gasped as the glow they cast revealed a face half-covered with ancient skin. No skin at all covered the other half, exposing the figure's chalky white bone underneath.

I looked backwards, only to see two similar eyes from a similarly decayed face glaring at me from several yards behind.

"*Why so afraid?*" they asked, in unison.

I shook all over. I tried to croak out a response to them, but I couldn't muster the words. Whatever these things were, I didn't want to be anywhere near them.

Then something miraculous happened. Or, at least, it seemed that way to me at the time. The tunnel split off, with a new pathway opening to my right. Without a moment's hesitation, I turned and crawled as fast as I could.

Obviously, none of this made any sense. But I was caught up in the moment as my survival instincts kicked in. In the distance, I spotted light. Could there be an exit ahead?

As I clambered forward, I imagined the hideous figures close behind me. I didn't know who they were or what they wanted. I just knew that I couldn't let them catch up to me.

Finally, an exit appeared. As I climbed to my feet amidst blinding light, I felt aches all over my back and legs.

As my eyes adjusted, I realized I was back in the corridor outside the music room. *Thank God*, I thought, feeling a sense of relief.

It was short lived. I shrieked as pain seared through my lower leg.

I turned to see a decrepit, veiny hand reaching out of the tunnel. It had long, sharp fingernails. Blood – *my blood* – dripped from one of them where it had cut me. For a brief moment, the two revolting faces peered up at me from the tunnel with looks of pure hatred and malice. *I wasn't safe, and they were still following me.*

As I sprinted away, I screamed for help. Only, there was no one to hear me. As I passed by the cafeteria and into the gymnasium, I encountered no students or teachers. The whole building was eerily vacant.

The only new feature was the dust. Layers upon layers of it, several inches deep in many places, that caused me to cough and sneeze as my feet kicked it up.

Finally, I reached the main door to the outside. I pushed frantically at it, but it wouldn't budge. I realized, to my frustration, that it was chained shut.

Another set of loud cackles rang out, their echoes resounding through the hallway. I grimaced as two figures appeared. Once again, they were on either side of me – both at a far end of the corridor – where I was stuck in between them.

Both figures were, or at least once were, women. But, now, both their clothes – a low-necked gown, on one, and a grey dress and petticoat on the other. Their bodies were tattered, revealing patches of bone and dry, sickly skin. They both had stringy, grey hair, and they both appeared to levitate a few inches off the ground.

I watched as the one to my left suddenly dived into the thick dust that covered the floor, disappearing from sight. I turned to my right to see that the other woman, too, was gone.

That's when the floor close to me rumbled. My heart sank as both figures emerged less than a yard from me, each wielding a sharp dagger with a wooden hilt and a double-edged blade. Dust covered their forms, and they both emitted what sounded like a furious attack cry.

I ran once again.

~

Before long, I found myself crouched in a small nook in the back corner of the library. I was caked in sweat and dust, and it took several minutes for me to fully catch my breath.

As far as I could tell, I'd managed to shake my pursuers. But I doubted I'd elude them for long. The cut on my back leg, which I desperately needed to clean, was still dripping blood.

Questions ran through my mind. Why was the school so empty? Perhaps I'd been lost, or stuck somehow in that tunnel, for longer than I'd realized, and everyone had gone home. But if that were true, then how did all this dust get here? Had I slipped into some sort of alternate reality? And who were the two people, or whatever they were, pursuing me, and what did they want?

A "thud" drew my attention as a book from the shelf that bordered my hiding spot fell and landed on the nearby floor, sending up a small cloud of dust. Its cover displayed in bright red letters, *The Story of Lydia*. It didn't list an author.

I picked it up. The cover, binding, and typeface were all extremely old. The table of contents, meanwhile, consisted of a list of people – all of whom, at various points in my life, had mistreated me.

I flipped through the rest of the book. It described incident after incident when someone insulted or bullied me. The girl who'd ripped open my stuffed animal at summer camp. The girl who'd shoved me to the ground on the playground. The girl who told me that nobody liked me, and that even my father was just pretending. The teacher who'd falsely accused me of cheating. And, over and over again, the following words appeared after each description: *Lydia did not fight back.*

The last section recounted everything Carmen and Michelle had done to me, from routine snubs and put-downs to outright violence. Once again, the chapter closed with the words *Lydia did not fight back.*

By the time I reached the end, I was steaming with rage. Both at the many people who'd mistreated me, and also at myself for not standing up for myself and, in a way, sometimes enabling it to happen. Again and again, I'd let people walk all over me.

When I closed the book, I saw three numbers, *211*, written on its back cover followed by a phrase handwritten in red ink, "*Only if you have what it takes.*"

~

I instantly knew what 211 meant. It was my locker number, located on the second floor. When I reached it, my usual combination worked.

Inside, at the bottom of the locker, was a dagger identical to those I'd seen both members of the duo wielding earlier. Underneath it was a note in the same handwritten red ink as on the back of the book. It read, "*They want to kill you. Fight like your life depends on it.*"

~

I resolved to return to the tunnel. It struck me as my best ticket back to reality. Once in it, I'd crawl back to the juncture and, if no exit was apparent, I'd cut through the canvas.

As I walked, I half-expected an ambush by the two phantoms. But I didn't care. I was done hiding. If they tried something like that, I'd try to fight them off. I'd defend myself, or die trying.

Of course, this raised the obvious question: who dropped the book next to me in the library (or created it, for that matter), and who led me to the dagger? Was someone here looking out for me and, if so, why?

As I neared the corridor containing the entrance to the music room and the exit from the tunnel that had brought me here, I noticed a figure in the distance. She was pacing and covered in dust. I dived for cover, successfully managing to avoid alerting her to my presence.

I dropped to a crouch and, once I could tell that she was facing the opposite direction, quietly crept towards her. The air in the corridor was thick, and the light was so dim that the figure was little more than a dusty silhouette. She's one of them, I told myself. *This is my chance to catch her by surprise. My life depends on pulling this off.*

As I narrowed the gap between her and me, a rage inside of me began to fume and boil over. I wasn't seeing a person; I was only seeing the target of years of pent-up hatred. The figure was entirely masked in grey dust, and as I got closer, the smell of mildew and decay that clung to it blocked out all other thought. These two undead women were only the latest in a long line of people who'd never gotten their comeuppance for what they'd done to me. That was going to change, starting now. I raised the dagger and pounced.

~

The events that followed passed in a blur. I remember cries of shock and pain. Dust flying in the air, followed by spurts of blood. A body crashing against the floor.

I remember dropping my dagger as I dove into the tunnel, crawling, *racing* toward a distant light. The sounds of cackling close behind me, then further away, then faintly fading.

I remember emerging into the haunted music room at the end of the school day; bursting into the hallway outside, too frantic to notice, or care, who was there to see me; and running through a door and into a downpour outside. I didn't care about the rain, or the thickets that scratched me as I rushed through them. By the time I got home, I was drenched and exhausted, and there were cuts on my clothes and skin.

~

I knew that telling the truth wouldn't get me anywhere with my dad. So, by the time he got home from work, I'd showered and thrown my filthy clothes into the laundry, and I had an explanation for the cuts that involved slipping in the mud and falling into a thick shrub.

I avoided any Halloween festivities that night. Instead, I lay on my bed trying to make sense of what had happened. Eventually, I considered the possibility that it had all been an anxiety-induced hallucination. I recalled how I'd grown dizzy and nearly lost consciousness while in the tunnel. In that moment, had my mind just combined my worries about Michelle and Carmen with the local legend about witches that I'd been reminded of only a few minutes prior? Yes, I had a gash on the back of one leg, but couldn't that be a scratch left from the thorny plants I'd gone through during my frenzied journey home? My mind slowly settled on this explanation as making more sense than any alternative.

That all changed when I got to school the next morning and learned that Michelle was missing. Worst of all, she'd seemingly disappeared while on school grounds the previous afternoon, which contributed to dozens of uniformed police officers prowling the building throughout the day.

Two of them spoke to me privately. Apparently, Michelle had gone into the haunted room after me. According to the officers, she was 'concerned for my safety' after realizing I'd been in there for quite some time. I knew that this was something Carmen had told them, and that Michelle's motivations had more to do with finding an excuse to further humiliate me, but I kept that to myself. I answered their questions coldly and succinctly, offering nothing about the bizarre journey I'd gone on or the two apparitions who'd chased me in some parallel world. Eventually, they let me go.

"What did you do to Michelle, you freak?" Carmen screamed at me during lunch that day. To the shock of everyone else in the cafeteria, I gave her a bloody nose with an abrupt blow to the face.

~

I didn't care about the detention that followed, my subsequent grounding for three weeks, or my father's stern lectures and disappointed looks. What I *did* care about was that Carmen never messed with me again.

I'm no longer the same person I once was. That person ceased to exist when I realized that the dust-covered figure outside the tunnel was no ghastly witch. When I took out years of frustration and anger not on the entities I believed wanted to kill me, but, rather, on a school bully who merely wanted to pester and embarrass me. Who'd followed me through the tunnel for that very purpose. Who two witches had let pass into their realm to be sacrificed not by them, but by me.

That person, my old self, died along with Michelle as I stabbed her again and again before leaving her body in a distant place where I knew that it would never be discovered.

I wasn't even surprised when, several days later, another book appeared in my locker. After all, I'd caught on to why these spirits, these witches of the distant past, had taken such an interest in me, and I finally had a good idea of the purpose behind their actions. Namely, they had been testing me, and I'd passed with flying colors. I was eager to claim my reward and to finally become part of something greater than myself.

This book was filled with spells and incantations. I'd read spellbooks before, but this one was different. *This*, I knew instantly from the authentic feel of its ancient, grimy pages and the ominous aura I sensed in it, was the real deal. It detailed the steps necessary to carry out many forms of dangerous, dark magic. It was the kind of book people had good reasons to burn. And yet, this particular book had survived, and even made its way to me.

Familiar handwriting inside its front cover read, *Welcome to the coven. You'll be hearing from us again, soon enough, dearest Lydia.*

13

———

LIFE OF LILY: PART 2

The breakthrough came when Mae and I hammered the point that Lily had no recollection of an entire five-day period.

"There *has* to be another explanation. You two are sick." Before we could react, Lily hurried outside, slamming the door behind her.

"Olivia, stay some distance behind me," said Mae as she hurried after Lily. "I've got a hunch about something."

I did as she asked as I followed them outside. Up the street, I could see Lily hurrying away. Then, she slowed, stopped, and dropped to her knees.

Mae caught up to her, and I stood about ten feet back as she'd requested. I could tell that Mae was talking, but I couldn't make out the words. Lily, meanwhile, had her head in her hands. Under the streetlight, I noticed the shade of her skin changing, fading until it was noticeably paler.

"Olivia, come over now," instructed Mae. I crept closer, unsure of what to make of what was happening.

Lily looked up at me with wet, teary eyes. She looked weak, famished even.

"What's wrong, Lily?" I inquired.

"I don't know," she whimpered in a hoarse voice. "But, I feel a little better now that you're here." I tried to grip her arm, only to find that it was outright *missing* past her elbow. Unsure if she had noticed this, I gripped her around the waist and helped her rise to her feet.

"Let's go back to my place, okay?" I asked. She nodded.

I held her and supported her as we made the short walk. Meanwhile, Mae observed us from a few steps away.

As my arms held her around the shoulder, I felt her flesh return and reappear where it had gone missing. At first, the restored portions were cold, then warm. She gradually grew less pale, as well. She seemed to be steadily regaining her strength, such that, by the time we returned to the house, she could climb the front stairs unassisted.

~

Mae left us alone for a few minutes while she flipped through a box of dusty books in the basement where she and Casey stayed. "I'll be up as soon as I confirm a few things," she stated. "In the meantime, Lily, whatever you do, don't take off that necklace."

"So, you're friend's into...magic?" Lily asked, skeptically, as I scooted next to her such that we were sharing a sit-up pillow on my carpeted bedroom floor.

"I know it sounds crazy, but the stuff she's into...we've had some insane experiences in the past, enough to know that some of it's real," I assured. "If anyone can figure out what's happening to you, it's her. Just give her a minute."

"I just want to know what's happening. I can't really be *dead*, can I? That sort of thing isn't possible. If what you're saying is true, then how am I here, and what body did my parents bury?"

"Like I said, just give Mae a minute."

"I need to get back to my family. I need to see my sister. I need to tell them I'm alright."

"I'm not sure you *are* alright," I responded. "This...whatever's happening, it may be temporary. And you saw what happened when you tried to leave."

She gripped my hand. "I'm choosing to trust you on this. But I also don't even know what else to do."

We sat silently for a few moments, listening only to the faint ticking of my *Twilight* Zone-themed wall-clock, before she spoke up again. "Part of why this is so confusing is that I don't remember dying, or anything leading up to it."

"You wouldn't remember. Based on the reports, you were the first, um..." I hesitated to say the next word.

"Victim?"

"Yeah. Out of nowhere. Pulls a gun, you're not even looking. Just doing your job minding your own business. And...yeah."

She sniffled, then cried. I brought her a tissue which she used to pad her wet face. "Just like that," she croaked. "Everything I'd ever done, everything I was ever going to do, just snuffed out."

"I know. I'm sorry."

"Jesus Christ. And you said it was random?"

"He didn't know you, or any of the other victims."

"But the *bar* wasn't random, was it?"

I shook my head, feeling my own eyes tear up.

"Jesus Christ," she repeated, this time in a more bitter, despondent tone. "I spent my whole life terrified of becoming a statistic. And it turns out, there was never anything I could have done to prevent that. Who else died?"

"Just the shooter. Took his own life. The other two are going to make it."

"Who *was* this guy?"

"Some idiot. I can tell you if you want to know, but do you really want to spend whatever time you have left thinking about him?"

She thought about that for a moment before answering, "No, you're right. This second chance...whatever *this* is...your friend thinks it's, like, tied to the necklace somehow?"

"Yeah. Some of the items this guy collected – again, I know this sounds ludicrous, but please trust me – were charmed in some way. I know from experience. This necklace was from a box that wasn't supposed to have anything like that, but well, it looks like it did."

~

"I'm pretty sure I found a match," said Mae, as she carried an old, dusty book into my room. She placed it on my bed and flipped to about a third of the way through it. "According to this, 12 necklaces just like the one Olivia gave to you, Lily, were crafted and infused with a particular charm in the 1300s. A Bohemian merchant appears to have obtained them and, hoping to profit from the power they contained, had them shipped to a major port where they could be sold or traded to wealthy aristocrats. Only, on the way, a fierce storm struck the vessel carrying them. In the ensuing shipwreck, they were lost. At least, presumably. I went back through Jean's notes, and it very much looks like he managed to find one."

"And, what kind of magic does it hold?" I asked, as I sensed Lily's wrestling with a natural sense of incredulity.

Mae expounded, "Dark magic. Such that the storm likely was not mere coincidence. The giver – in this case, you, Olivia – technically passes on a curse to the recipient – that would be you, Lily – once the recipient wears it. The curse operates in such a way that, once it becomes active, it tethers the giver to the receiver."

"But didn't Emma give it to you? And Jean to her?"

"Yes," replied Mae. "But neither of us wore it, and what matters is that Lily had it on when she died. That's what caused it to go into effect."

"So, a 'curse' saved me from death?" Lily inquired, her tone skeptical. "Aren't curses supposed to be, you know, bad in some way?"

"So, the thing about dark magic," said Mae, "is that people can use it to achieve forbidden ends. Like, as you've probably inferred, escaping death itself. But, it always comes at a cost."

Lily and I glanced at each other. "Let me guess," she snarked, trying to make light of the situation. "Something to do with my soul."

Mae shook her head. "Death is inevitable. You can postpone it, but you can't beat it. What the curse is doing – keeping you alive, in a body identical to the one that now lies six feet under – takes an incredible amount of energy. It's the giver – the person who gave you the necklace – who pays the price necessary to sustain you."

I shot up from my slouched position next to Lily. As invested as I'd been in *Lily*'s predicament, I hadn't prepared myself for the possibility of it directly impacting me. "What kind of price?" I asked.

"You're not going to like it," said Mae.

"Please, tell us," demanded Lily.

A sense of dread fell over me as she took a long, deep breath before responding. "Let's say, Olivia, that your natural life is set to last until you're 100. Well, every moment Lily remains alive like this, the curse chips away at that future. And it's hardly a 1-to-1 ratio. Death *wants* Lily, and it's not easily appeased. It takes a lot to protect her from its grip. It may be that, now, your natural life is set to end a few days earlier. And, it's only going to get worse. The longer Lily remains, the faster it eats up Olivia's future. Days in Lily's life will consume weeks of Olivia's. And it'll only get crueler from there, to the point that death catches up to you, too, Olivia. Of course, by then, the curse won't be able to keep Lily around, either, because it won't have anyone to feed on."

I felt myself go pale. I could live with some cuts to the tail end of my lifespan, but what she was suggesting meant that I could soon be churning through years, even decades of my life.

"Th-there has to be some way to get around that," stuttered Lily. "Something else we can do."

"I wish there was," said Mae, her voice cracking slightly. "But there isn't. Getting someone else to regift it you won't work either. You'd have to take it off for that to happen, and, well, if you did that..."

"I'd die again."

"Yep. Immediately."

I was too stunned to respond. I quivered under the weight of a decision we were going to have to make. A decision that involved weighing my life against the life of a woman I loved. The obviousness of the answer did nothing to detract from the painfulness of making it.

"One more thing," added Mae. "Another reason the whole regifting thing won't work is that the curse relies on the bond between the two of you. That's why Lily returned when and where she did – outside our house, for a date with Olivia. Its ability to keep Lily alive will remain strong as long as the feelings you have for each other remain strong. You two stop caring about each other, it stops working."

We sat there silently for a few moments. Then, Lily asked, "Olivia, what are we going to do?"

~

For hours, Lily and I succeeded in losing ourselves to the day. It wasn't until the evening that we began to strain under the weight of the choices we knew we'd imminently have to make.

"My advice," Mae had said, when we balked at making a decision, "is to see this as a temporary blessing. Spend a day together doing whatever you want. It won't tax you too much, Olivia. Then deal with this, and deal with it for good."

Some of Lily's choices surprised me. They were a mix of pragmatic and strangely aspirational. She ruled out contacting her family, even Abigail, on the ground that it would accomplish little more than giving them false hope and, ultimately, retraumatizing them.

"Nothing extravagant," she'd told me. "No skydiving, balloon rides, or dangerous stunts. I don't want to be under the influence of any substances either. After we complete a couple tasks this morning...I just want to spend time with you, the way you'd choose to spend it if you had a day to spend with me."

Lily dressed herself in a set of my clothes, which landed slightly on the large size but mostly fit her, and we then set out for her old workplace. There, we arranged Lily's former co-workers to stumble upon an envelope, set up to appear to have slipped out of Lily's work locker, containing a signed and backdated last will and testament awarding her belongings, as meagre as they were, to her sister.

After that, Lily led me to a Rescue Mission where we spent two hours assisting in preparing lunches for those who couldn't otherwise afford food. "I'd always promised myself that I'd do this regularly," she confided, "But I only went once, right when I moved here."

"It's an awfully selfless thing to do now, given the circumstances."

She shrugged. I wondered how much she was motivated over guilt of what her continued existence was doing to my distant future. Maybe Lily wanted to be better positioned if a creator was set to soon pass judgment on her, insofar as she may still believe in that sort of thing, given her absence of any memories from the prior week. Or, maybe, it was just something she wanted to do, and she'd never had anybody to do it with before today.

"Your turn," she told me, as we left.

"Honestly, I don't really *do* much of anything outside of work. I've gotten reclusive. And the things I used to do are quite mild-mannered."

"I won't be disappointed. As long as it's what you want, I'm all for it."

~

We held hands as we walked together through Centennial Park. It was a pleasant day – hot, but not too much so, and with a nice breeze.

As we circled Lake Watauga, Lily asked several guests if she could pet the dogs they were walking. Most granted her request, and Lily lit up as she knelt to give them pleasant scratches on their necks, backs, and ears.

I took her to an indie bookstore, then two record shops I used to frequent. "They might have all forty of his albums here," I said as we observed the massive selection of Bob Dylan music at one of them.

"*Forty*?" Lily replied. "Who has time to make that many?"

"He's been releasing music forever," I said. "This one," I added, removing *Knocked Out Loaded*, "might just be the worst of all of them, but it has the only song of his on it that Mae likes. It's, like, eleven minutes long, one of my favorites, too."

"You don't have it already, do you?"

"Not on vinyl."

"Well, let's get it, and listen to it when we get back to your place."

~

We arrived back home after picking up some clothes for Lily for the night's event. We soon lay next to each other on my bed. We kissed softly and gently at first, then deeply and passionately.

When we made love, it wasn't like before. Lily had quickly internalized what she'd picked up from me before. This time, we were in complete unison, and the experience was kinetic and immersive in a way that left every part of me shaken and brimming with abundant sensation.

Lily kept the necklace on throughout, and also when we showered afterwards. We dried off and laid out the clothes we were going to wear that night. As Lily put on the dark purple dress we'd picked out together, I removed the record player from where Mae kept it amidst a sea of small cacti. I carried it up to my room, where I set it to play side B of the record we'd picked up.

Lily watched and listened, amused, as "Brownsville Girl" played. I drew her attention to all my favorite lines: *"The memory of you keeps callin' after me like a rollin' train;" "Even the swap meets around here are getting pretty corrupt;" "We're going all the way 'til the wheels fall off and burn, 'til the sun peels the paint and the seat covers fade and the water moccasin dies;" "Now I've always been the kind of person that doesn't like to trespass, but sometimes you just find yourself over the line."*

When it ended, I asked her if she'd liked it. She nodded. "It made me feel like you and I were off on some grand adventure."

~

Our last stop was at an art museum that was hosting a formal dance night as a special occasion. It had a hefty entrance fee, but I paid it unhesitatingly. As the evening progressed, several important looking people made announcements regarding some kind of fundraiser, but Lily and I didn't pay attention. Instead, we kept our focus fully on each other.

Lily held me more and more tightly as the evening progressed. By the end, I could sense her trembling.

We were ultimately among the last couples to leave. As the last song began to play, she leaned into me and whispered. "Wanna know something?"

"That you love me? Well, I love you too."

That seemed to make her happy.

When we stepped back outside, it was dark and eerily quiet. "This way," she said, as she led me through the nighttime cityscape. Before long, we ended up outside the venue where we'd first met.

We sat together for several minutes on the same cobblestone wall, our legs dangling over the asphalt below. "I've had a great day, Olivia," said Lily, breaking the silence.

"Me too," I replied.

"You're never going to forget me, are you?"

"Of course not."

She took a long, deep breath. A moment later, I heard a light shuffling sound, followed by a *"plat"* as something hit the ground.

"Oh, sorry," she mumbled. She motioned towards one of her shoes, which had slipped off and hit the ground. "Do you mind getting it for me?"

"Sure," I said, hopping down. When I climbed back up with her shoe, I found Lily curled into a ball.

"Lily, what happened? What's wrong?"

She looked up at me. Her face was a deep red, and she was sobbing. "I – I thought I could do it. I thought I could take it off. I didn't want you to be here when I did it."

"Lily-"

She cut me off. "Olivia, I don't want to die. I don't want to be selfish either. I don't want to hurt you. But I don't want to die. Not now. I don't deserve it. It's not fair."

I held her against me as she cried. Her tears and, soon, my own soaked through my dress.

"You don't deserve it," I assured her. "And no, it's not fair. I'm so sorry."

With great effort, she spoke again. "I need you to do it for me."

"*What?*"

"Take off the necklace, Olivia. That's the only way this ends."

On some level, I knew that she was correct, but I wasn't willing to admit it. "We can wait longer, Lily. At least a few days."

"Oh God, Olivia, you have no idea how much I want that. But this has to end before I do even more damage to you. Please, I don't have it in me to do it myself. I'll just sit here and look up at the stars while you remove it. I won't move, and it'll all be over soon."

I should have seen this coming, or at least anticipated it as a possibility. But I'd been deeper in denial than I'd realized.

I can do this, I told myself. *I have to.*

I reminded myself that I was always the one to pull through at the end. I may have needed help to get there, but I'd been the one who'd eviscerated my workplace harasser; I'd been the one who'd evaded death and injected myself with an antidote at the last possible moment; and I'd been the one to finally slay the last manifestation of the demon that had tormented April for months. Of course, Lily was the furthest thing from any of those monsters, which made what I needed to do all the more difficult. But, I resolved to rise to the occasion and to do what needed to be done.

Tears ran down Lily's face as she gazed upwards into the sky. I slowly positioned myself behind her. I placed my hands against her neck. Her body quivered as I carefully gripped the clasp on the back of the necklace.

~

When I left Lily alone in my bed, she seemed deeply asleep. She'd needed most of a bottle of wine to get there. In a few hours, I expected a hangover to assert itself, fragmenting her dreams and settling her into a weak, fitful state. But, for the moment, she was at peace.

I went downstairs to find Mae sifting through several books on the living room sofa. "Shouldn't you be in bed?" I asked.

"I cancelled class tomorrow," she replied. "Said I was sick. Given the circumstances, I figured I should make absolutely certain that I'm right about all this."

"And are you?"

"Unfortunately, yes. There's no way around this. I thought you all would take care of it tonight, but it seems like you didn't."

"No, she couldn't bring herself to remove the necklace," I recounted. "And neither could I."

She nodded. "I know you're in a horrible situation, Olivia." She thought for a second, before asking, "Is she asleep?"

"Yeah."

"Deeply?"

"I think so."

"Then you know what the merciful thing to do is. I can do it if you can't."

I wrestled with a hot anger that coursed through me. For the first time in my life, I wanted to scream at my best friend. I wanted to be violent – to *break* something. But I knew, also, that she was absolutely *correct* from any rational perspective. Pouting about it or lashing out at her wouldn't do any good. I sat down on a soft black chair adjacent to the sofa and simply told her, "I don't want you to do that."

"Then what's your plan? It's one thing if you want another day with her. But the longer this goes, the less of your life remains. When I spoke the other day, I used 100 years as an example, but you know that's not necessarily the case. Most people don't live that long. God forbid this turns out to be true, but what if the next rounds of tests confirms that you have it, too? Your mom lived to what, 60?"

"61."

"61. So, if that's the case for you, too, then we're talking about rapidly chipping away at a life that ends at 61. Do you see my point?"

I nodded. "I told Lily about the tests. How they may or may not mean what we fear."

"And she still wants to live, knowing that?"

"She..." Up on the wall, she'd begrudgingly accepted that I couldn't do it. We'd returned home, where I'd told her about my possible condition. She'd begged me to go through with it and remove the necklace. When I still wouldn't do it, she'd thrown up her arms and asked if we had any wine. "Mae, look, when she wakes up, I'm going to have one final conversation with her. We'll decide then."

"I hope she wakes up soon, then. And what 'decision' even is there for you two to make? Isn't it obvious? You had your extra day together. It was a gift. And now your time together is over."

"No, I'm not so sure it is."

Mae shot me a look of disbelief. "You're not really saying what I think you're saying, are you, Olivia?"

"In the years we've spent together, Mae, you've *constantly* pushed me to think with my heart instead of always thinking with my brain. I know how I feel, and I know what I want. If Lily agrees-"

Mae cut me off. "This isn't about relationship or workplace drama, Olivia. You know where what you're suggesting leads: you, my best friend, *dying*. And for what? Spending a few weeks, give or take, with a crush?"

"She's not just a crush. I'm in love with her, Mae."

"You *just* met her."

"I've never felt this way towards anyone before. I don't think I'll ever feel this way again. If I let this go, I won't be able to live with myself."

"*I'll* still be here, you know. Isn't that worth something to you?"

"It is," I said, feeling myself turn red. "You're been my best friend for so long. I've thought about that – about you – a lot. It pains me. I just don't see another option. I'm really sorry."

"And there's Casey, Emma, and April. Heck, even little Harper loves you. You're really willing to give *all* that up?"

"I've thought really hard about it, Mae, and yes, I am, if Lily is onboard with it. None of them depend on me. They'll be okay."

Mae abruptly stood up and marched to the basement. "Olivia, you're being an idiot, and I'm not talking to you any more about this."

~

When Lily stirred, I asked her how she was feeling. "Hungover," she moaned.

At her request, I brought her some Advil, a glass of cold water, and a cup of hot coffee. "Want anything to eat?" I asked.

"Not right now," she said weakly. She sat up, took the pills, and chugged the rest of the water. She then put the glass down on a side table and felt the necklace around her neck, which dangled above the loose nightshirt I'd given her to sleep in. "You didn't remove it."

"The necklace?"

"Yeah. I thought you would've, while I was asleep. You probably should've." She began sipping the black coffee.

"I have some thoughts about that. The whole situation."

"What, another day?" she asked, finally perking up from the caffeine. "Olivia, it's only going to make things worse. I was prepared to go last night. Well...you know what I mean. I don't want to take any more of your life. I don't want you to die because of me."

"And I don't want to live without you."

She made a disgruntled frown. "Well, you're going to have to learn how to."

"Maybe. Look, Lily, I'm not going to force a decision on you. I know that you're a good person, and I know that you don't want to take anything more from me than you have already. It's your choice. But I want you to know that what *I* want is for us to both keep living, for as long as we can."

This clearly stunned her. She put down the mug and took a long, deep look at me as her face turned white. "Why..." Her voice trembled and cut off. I waited. "Why would you ever want that? We both die that way."

"Because I love you. And because you deserve a chance at living your life. *Really* living it."

A long silence fell upon us. Again, I waited as Lily processed what I was saying. "You'd be giving up so much."

"And I'd be gaining even more."

"We're talking about...what, weeks?"

"I don't know. That was Mae's estimate, but she isn't sure. Could be more, could be less."

"And, what, we'd just be hanging out around here?"

"No," I replied. "I thought, maybe, we could go on a trip to see the places you always wanted to see. Just drive off in my car, and keep going as long as we can."

This drew a smile from her even as she brushed a tear from her eye. "I like that idea." She got up, walked over to me, and held me in a hug. "You know what I think?" she whispered into my ear.

"No."

She pulled herself back such that her face was mere inches from mine. "I think your friend's wrong. I think we can beat it. I think, what we feel for each other is capable of breaking all the rules."

"Well, um, I don't know about that." *This wasn't the kind of thing Mae would be wrong about.*

"Drop that," she snapped. "Don't think like that. If it gets us, it gets us. But let's do everything we can to put up a fight. And let's live the time we have together to the absolute fullest."

I looked over at her, this girl I'd so recently discovered, yet with whom I had fallen so profoundly in love. My feelings for her overwhelmed me, shattering every barrier they came across as they flowed through my body. "Okay," I said, smiling with joy. "Okay."

~

I made a brief visit to Emma and April's townhouse, which was adjacent to the one I shared with Casey and Mae. "I doubt this short of a distance will affect you," I'd told Lily, "And I'll be right back, regardless."

When I knocked, Emma let me inside. "Look," she said, proudly. As she held infant Harper in her arms, April had Tessa sit in her designated "place" next to the sofa in the living room of their neighboring townhouse. Harper, upon spotting her family's pet dog, exclaimed, "It's Tessa!"

"Her first full sentence," giggled April. "She said it around Casey, first, while he was over here helping care for her the other day, and we've gotten her to repeat it since then."

"I'm very impressed," I said. "You did a wonderful job, Harper." She smiled at me before Emma returned her to her playpen.

"So, what brings you over here?" Emma asked.

"I just, um, I wanted to tell you that I might be gone for a little while."

"Oh," responded April. "Work trip?"

"No, I...it's not like that. More leisure."

"How long?" probed Emma.

"I can't say for sure. It's just, um...I just wanted to say, before I go, that I really appreciate you guys. You're great friends, and you're raising a perfect daughter."

Harper let out a cry, prompting April to rush over to her. While trying to stand against the end of her playpen, she'd placed her foot on a toy that shifted under her weight, causing her to fall. "It's okay, Harper," April comforted while picking her up and patting her gently.

Emma, upon confirming that Harper was alright, returned to me. "Something serious is happening with you, isn't it?"

"Just...know that I value you, and I'll miss you. All of you."

"Honey, could you fetch me a box of wipes from downstairs?" asked April. "I want to check her diaper, so we may need one, but we're all out up here."

"Sure," said Emma.

"I'm gonna get going," I announced, sensing I was intruding. "See you guys."

"Olivia," called Emma, pausing at the top of the staircase. "Just look out for yourself, okay?"

"Will do." I removed a large treat from my pocket, tossed it to Tessa, and went back outside.

~

Casey and Lily were out front loading packed bags into the trunk of my car.

"We'll miss you, Olivia," said Casey. He gave me a firm hug.

"Thank you," I responded. "How is she?"

"Not wanting to speak to you," said Casey. "I don't disagree with how she feels. But you've clearly made up your mind, so I figured I'd at least help out."

"Well, thanks again. You know I'll miss you. Harper's really coming right along. You should be proud."

"Yes, she is, and I am."

"Take this," I said, handing him a rolled-up set of papers I'd printed the previous night. "It'll make it clear what to do with, well, everything of mine that isn't packed in here, if, you know..."

"Understood," said Casey as he shoved a gym bag full of clothes into the backseat. "And I think that's the last of it." He headed inside.

I sat in the driver's seat while Lily sat in the passenger's seat. For a few moments, I stared longingly at the townhouse. "Everything alright?" asked Lily.

"Yeah. Just, wait here a moment, okay? I owe her one more try at a goodbye."

~

Mae opened the front door just as I reached it. She had a dour, pale appearance. I assumed she hadn't slept all night.

"Mae, I came back to-"

"I know, I saw." She gazed past me, towards the car and the road ahead. "Casey told me you're planning on driving quite a distance."

"Yeah."

For a few long seconds, we stood frozen there, the only sounds being the rustling of tree branches in the wind.

Finally, she made eye contact with me. I was tempted to look away, but I held firm and returned her gaze. "Olivia," she said, "you're doing something really stupid. I don't know if I can forgive you for it. But I'm going to try, and I'm never going to stop loving you." She buried her sobbing face in my shirt as I held her.

"Thank you, Mae, for being my friend all these years. Thank you for keeping me sane, and for always being there when I needed you."

She wiped tears from her eyes and hair from her face as she looked up at me. "You really *are* a fool, Olivia. You should know by now that it was always the other way around."

We held each other again, for quite a while this time. "How far do you think we're going to drive, Mae?" I asked as we broke off.

A smile crept onto her face. "All the way, until the wheels fall off and burn."

~

When I returned to the car, Lily was reviewing a list she'd jotted down in a notebook.

"You got it all figured out?" I asked.

"Not all of it, no, but I've got a list of over 30 sites. But that's just for starters. We'll see many, many more places than that."

"West coast first, right?"

"Yep," she replied. "Then all the way to the east."

"And after that?"

"We start over again."

I gripped her hand and gazed so lovingly at her that I made her blush. "You stop that," she giggled. "You'll have plenty of time to admire me. Now, you need to focus on the road."

"I love you too, Lily," I chuckled. "Let's get this started."

We rolled out of the cul-de-sac and embarked on what we both knew would be the final journey of our lives. We were infected, over-run, by a madness that cut to the very essence of our souls, that defied constraints of space or time.

We began our journey out west with little more than the love we felt for each other, and the knowledge that this, alone, was more than enough.

14

AN OFFICE OF ONE'S OWN

When I reported for my first day of work, the office looked nothing like I expected. The route was a desolate series of winding, narrow dirt roads. In the pre-dawn gloom, my headlights strained to illuminate the otherwise unlit path that stretched through scenery that probably looked gorgeous in daylight.

The installation ahead of me appeared out of place, like a standard low-rise office building had been lifted from a city center and dropped into the middle of a national park dozens of miles from the nearest major highway. It had an uninspired, angular appearance. It looked remarkably clean and untouched by the surrounding nature, especially in contrast to the vines and ivy that extended from the dense woods to cover patches of the dilapidated walls of the security station and old-timey cabins I'd passed on my journey.

The parking lot had only one car, a dusty sedan by the main entrance. I took the spot next to it and, carrying my work bag, approached the glass door.

In the reflection, I saw my long, curly hair and the sharp black skirt suit I'd donned. My face, despite my best efforts, betrayed the exhaustion from the long, early commute. I was just grateful to have a job after months of unanswered applications and stressful dead ends.

I entered an empty security station. It had everything you'd expect - monitors, metal detectors, scanners - but no employees.

"Hello?" I called, when nobody emerged to greet me.

I called again. A gravely voice answered, "Coming!" At the far end of the room, a middle-aged woman with unkempt black and gray hair and a dark blue jacket appeared. She held an ID card to a reader. A green light flashed. The doors opened.

As she neared me, she rolled a wheeled suitcase behind her. "You must be Amanda," she said, extending her hand.

"Nice to meet you," I replied, shaking it. "And you are?"

She ignored me as she fished through the pockets of her jacket, her suitcase dropping to the floor with a 'clang.' "Just a moment," she mumbled before removing a second ID card, which she handed to me. I took it. It displayed my name and picture. "You'll be needing this," she said. "Don't lose it. Can't open the door without your badge."

"Understood."

"The payroll system automatically records when you swipe it to enter and exit. So, if you want your paycheck, make sure to swipe in by your start time, and to not swipe out until your end time. Anyway, I have to get going."

This made me a little confused. "Um, I guess I'll go inside and meet the rest of the team."

This prompted a single, sardonic laugh from her. "You haven't heard?"

"Haven't heard what?"

"Everyone else is laid off. Whole building. I'm here to grab my last few personals, and to give you your card."

"*What*?" I exclaimed, shocked.

"Yep," she nodded. "You're the lucky one. The morons carrying out these reductions missed you because your materials were in administrative limbo during the security check. Those behind you in the onboarding process had their offers rescinded. Those already onboarded were let go. But you slipped through the cracks. Don't worry, I didn't tell anyone. Now, you've got the building to yourself."

"I...huh? The whole building?"

"Yep." She picked up her suitcase and dragged it past me. As she reached the door to the outside, she added, "My advice: keep your head down. Don't cause any trouble. With any luck, nobody of any importance will notice that you're working here. Best of luck, Amanda." With that, she loaded her belongings into the sedan and departed.

~

Dumbfounded, I placed my purse and briefcase by a desk in the corner of a large room full of open offices. It was a sunny spot, with long windows on two sides that provided a pleasant view of the surrounding woods, and it had the same type of computer as all the others. I considered taking an enclosed supervisor's office, but that somehow felt even more isolating.

As I booted up the computer and entered the login credentials, I sat back in my chair and tried to comprehend what was happening. I never could have imagined that *everyone* else in my building would be laid off. I thought about just how devastating the news must have been to the many people who would otherwise be my co-workers.

And where did that leave me? I still had a job, but, from what the woman had told me, that was only due to a fluke. One peep about me to the wrong members of leadership, and I'd get canned, too.

I tried to process the insanity of this situation. All my expectations of gaining experience and making connections would go unrealized while I would be stuck in an isolated, empty office.

This is a blessing in disguise, I told myself. *Think about all the people who wish they had a bigger office, or freedom from deadlines and supervisors.*

I opened my email to find form messages from HR about several mandatory training courses. Putting my concerns aside, I set about completing them.

When I finished the trainings, I had nothing else to do. No assignments, no emails. Was this what every day would be like?

~

I set about exploring the building. The main level had a marble central corridor that connected the entrance door to a series of private offices, two bathrooms, a kitchen, two fire exits, and several openings that led to the open main work area.

A sheet of paper displaying several emergency numbers for fire, electrical, and security services hung next to the entrance. The women's bathroom was in relatively good shape, though it looked like it hadn't been recently cleaned. The kitchen was cramped and gloomy, with a flickering overhead light. A stack of paper birthday plates sat sadly on a large table. From the lunchboxes, canned drinks, and frozen meals in the refrigerator, I inferred everyone had been let go with little warning. The crumbs on the floor and empty plastic bottles in a bin meant no custodian would visit soon.

I took the elevator upstairs, where a walkway overlooking the main floor stretched from end to end. It connected to a series of individual offices that were nicer and larger than the ones below, though just as empty.

The elevator displayed three "B" levels, where I assumed the labs were located, but it wouldn't travel to any. I found a door near my desk marked "Basement Main Access," which opened to a barren concrete staircase. A sickly yellow bulb cast gloomy light over the windowless stairwell, giving it a spooky appearance that compounded my isolation. I decided exploring the basement could wait.

~

As the afternoon stretched on, I called my friend Winona. We'd been close since high school, and we'd even kept in touch during the years she'd spent deployed overseas in the military. She presently teleworked a part-time tutoring job from the apartment she shared with her boyfriend Tommy, and she tended to not mind calls from me during the day.

When I explained my situation to her, she was as astonished about it as I was. "It's so weird being alone here," I confided. "I keep thinking about all the conversation and meetings and laughter that used to fill this place. Now it's all gone, and I'm all that's left."

"I'd be *so* freaked out if I were you," she replied. "Especially with how far you are from, like, everything."

"I know," I said. "But a job's a job. If I don't get work, maybe I'll take online courses or apply to other jobs as a fallback if I'm discovered.

"You should try to relax," Winona said. "At least for now. *So* many people would kill for a situation like yours. Embrace it. Bring books to read, or find a way to watch something you like. Or, better yet, set up a profile on a dating app like I've been saying. With this much time on your hands, you're officially out of excuses."

I chuckled. Winona always said I hadn't dated since Michael broke up with me two years ago, and I used to say I was too busy. Now, I had all the time I needed.

~

For two weeks, I drove the same lengthy route, swiped my card at the front door, and logged into my computer. Time and again, I had no assignments or new emails beyond general announcements. When my first paycheck arrived, I was ecstatic.

I spent much of my time following Winona's suggestions. I finessed my resume, applied to new jobs, enrolled in an online accounting course. The remainder of the days I spent reading, listening to audiobooks, setting up dating app profiles, and jogging around the building to stay in shape.

The first strange thing happened during my third week. I'd just set up a date with Alfred, a software engineer I met through an app. We agreed to meet at a restaurant that night. I'd gotten Winona's approval, as she was more savvy about these situations. The whole process of meeting someone through an app made me anxious and uncomfortable, so I decided to settle my nerves with a snack I'd packed for myself and left in the kitchen. Only, when I got there, it was gone. My entire lunchbox, in fact, was empty.

My first thought was that I'd left the food at home. But how absent-minded could I have been to not only forget to pack it, but also take an empty lunchbox?

This bothered me, but I shrugged it off. In my rush to leave for work, I must have left the food at home. Excited for the date, I soon forgot about it and pushed through my hunger.

The date went well. Alfred was a little reserved, but polite, and he seemed not to judge my hungry self for eating a hefty meal. I liked him, and we made plans to meet again.

The next morning, as I packed my food for work, I noticed that there was no extra meal in the fridge. So, what happened to yesterday's lunch?

There has to be a reasonable explanation," Winona told me. "Maybe you forgot to make it. Or you ate it and don't remember. Neither sounds likely, but what's the alternative?"

"I don't know," I said, as I sat back in my office chair and admired the view outside. "This place is just so eerie. It's like, I can sometimes sense all the people who used to occupy it. I feel like they're watching me sometimes."

"I'm *sure* it is eerie, Amanda, but no spirit of a laid-off employee ate your lunch, if that's what you're suggesting," she scoffed. "Don't be ridiculous."

"You're right," I sighed. We shifted our conversation to my second date with Alfred, a carnival that Sunday evening.

~

After carefully laying out the used plastic water bottles from the kitchen recycling bin, I took the spherical "Outstanding Leadership" trophy, which had once been attached to a plastic pedestal, out of one of the upper floor offices. I rolled it across the marble central hallway, delighted when it knocked over eight makeshift pins.

I set everything up again. This time, I took a video when I released the trophy, bowling a strike. I flipped the camera to capture my little cheer and sent the video to Winona.

OMG, she texted me back. *Using your time productively, I see.* I giggled. *Got to pass the hours somehow*, I shot back. *Might as well have some fun :)*

A few minutes later, Winona responded again. *Amanda, is there someone else in your office today?*

What? No. Why do you ask? I typed back.

I waited, perplexed, until my phone buzzed. Winona had sent a screenshot from the end of my video, my victory dance. *Look above your left should, in the distance*, she wrote.

I zoomed into the area she described, which consisted of the glass window on a supervisor's office. At first, I didn't notice anything unusual.

Then it hit me: the glass reflected a blurred, faint image of a *face*. It seemed to subtly shift and waver, almost like a ripple on water, but I blamed the poor lighting and the angle. It was hard to make out, but I could vaguely discern a long nose, a square chin, and a pair of sunken, dark brown eyes.

My pulse instantly quickened. *What the hell?* I texted her back. "Is someone here?" I called out, my voice echoing in the vast, unoccupied space. No one responded.

I grabbed my belongings and headed to the exit. I considered calling the emergency 'security' number or leaving early.

Maybe it's just an illusion? Winona texted me. *Hopefully I'm freaking you out over nothing.*

Hopefully she was correct. If I called security, that could lead to the consequences I feared.

Don't be the horror movie dumbass, I told myself. *Just leave.* But I also wanted to deal with this. What if it was nothing, and I ended up risking my only source of income for no reason?

I turned and faced the main corridor, where I'd just been bowling. Nothing seemed amiss. Taking a deep breath, I called Winona.

"Yeah?" she answered.

"Look, um, I'm going to try to figure out what happened. I want you on the phone with me."

"Of course!"

"Good."

I took a few tepid steps toward the office where we'd spotted the reflection. When I reached it, it was completely empty. Nervously, I turned to the office *across* from it, where whatever had been reflected in the glass would have been located.

I burst out laughing. This office had posters on the wall and pictures on its desk. Someone had left their personals behind. The posters were of scientists - I recognized Albert Einstein - and the pictures were presumably of the former occupant's family.

I explained to Winona the reflection we saw must have been from one of these images. "Sure, but do any of them look like the face in that reflection?" she asked. "Not really," I conceded. "But, the reflection was so blurry I can't tell for sure. Anyway, it makes the most sense compared to any other explanation, right?"

"Yeah," she said, though I sensed skepticism. "I'm sure that's it."

~

Alfred and I's second date was even better. We'd stayed out late doing clichéd things - he won me a stuffed animal, we took a boat ride, and sat on a Ferris wheel. As our compartment ascended, I held my breath, and sure enough, he kissed me! We became 'that' couple kissing passionately as our car rotated. If anyone minded, nobody brought it up. When I got home around midnight, my heart was too full to settle, and it wasn't until hours later I went to sleep.

Naturally, this resulted in me fighting to keep my eyes open at work the next day. Fortunately, I didn't have any major tasks. After swiping into the building and sitting down at my desk, I leaned back, closed my eyes, and let exhaustion consume me.

My phone awoke me sometime later. It was Winona, asking how my date went. I yawned drowsily, took a few sips from the bottle of water on my desk, and called her back.

We talked for a bit as I recapped my evening with Alfred. "You're making me want to puke," teased Winona. "Y'all are too damn cute. So what's next with him?"

"We're meeting at my place on Friday night," I related.

"Oh my gosh!" said Winona. "I'm *so* excited for you. It's about time you spent the night with a crush."

"What is that supposed to mean?" I shot back defensively. "He isn't necessarily-"

She interrupted playfully. "Oh sure, you invited him over for a chaste night of formal conversation and mild flirtation. How indecent of me to imply anything further might occur."

"Oh whatever," I nagged, as I took another sip of water. "We'll see what happens."

Just then, I felt a soft bump against my neck. *What was that?*

Whirling around, I saw something floating slowly before hitting the ground. It was a paper airplane. "Jesus Christ," I muttered, jumping to my feet and, in my panic, dropping the water bottle.

"What's wrong?" asked Winona.

"Someone threw a paper airplane at me."

"But you're all alone, right?"

"Hello?" I called out to the empty room, my voice once again echoing. "This isn't funny! Who are you?"

I glanced everywhere - the upper walkway, the desks, the empty offices - and detected no signs of life.

"No response?" asked Winona.

"Nope." I bent down to pick up the airplane. Made from notebook paper, it had words crudely written in blue ink: *"Bad match."*

As dread coursed through me, I realized something worse: I hadn't brought a water bottle to work.

~

I ended the call with Winona and grabbed my belongings. On my way out, I took the sheet by the door and, once at my car, called the 'security' number.

"Ma'am," the gruff-voiced man answered, "so you're telling me someone threw a paper airplane at you, gave you a bottle of water, and maybe ate your lunch?"

"Yes, but it's not like that."

"These aren't exactly felony offenses, ma'am. Had the water been tampered with?"

"I don't think so. When I opened it, the cap snapped, like it hadn't been opened before. And it tasted normal."

He paused. "So, you're sure you want us to send someone all the way out there over this?"

"**YES**," I stammered. "Someone is stalking me. *Please*, take this seriously."

"Alright. Stay put. We'll have a park ranger there soon."

~

I stayed in my car, eyes focused on the entrance, foot on the accelerator. I was ready to speed off at the first sign of the creep.

Finally, an unmarked car with a siren pulled up. The uniformed officer, bright blue eyes in his mid-thirties, stepped out. He had a gun holstered at his waist. He tapped on my window, which I lowered.

"You Amanda?" he asked in a deep voice.

"Yes."

"Officer Jackson," he replied. "I've been briefed on the situation. Want to let me inside?"

~

"Well?" I asked, when he emerged a half hour later.

He shook his head. "No trace of anyone else."

"You looked everywhere?"

"Yep," he said. "Look, ma'am, I think you're telling the truth. But like I said, I couldn't find anything. Not even the paper airplane you mentioned."

"I can't *believe* this," I muttered, exasperated. "You must have missed it."

"Ma'am, you're welcome to go look yourself. There's not much more I can do right now, but anything else happens, let me know, and I'll come right over. Do you want me to file a formal report?"

"Of course."

"If I do that," he added, "the people who own this place are going to find out. Is that what you want?"

I let out a moan. This was such bullshit. I wasn't ready to alert leadership to me being here, to this whole situation. Not before I found a new job. "Forget about it," I uttered, frustrated.

~

I arrived at work the next day with a can of mace in my purse. Before sitting down, I reversed my corner desk to face the opposite direction, giving me sight of the open office area, anyone heading towards me from the ground level or the nearby basement staircase. When I used the restroom, I took the mace.

I spent the day immersed in my job search, broadening my horizons by submitting applications to positions I previously would have overlooked. All the while, I remained vigilant, regularly scanning my surroundings for any signs of life.

A few days passed without incident, and I started to calm down. Yes, someone had creeped me out, and for all I knew, was still hiding. But the officers had made valid points: my stalker hadn't done anything to harm me. If they'd wanted to, they could have done it already.

I wondered who this person was. A former employee? A vagrant? How long had they been here, and what did they want?

~

"*A little help?*" read the subject line that popped up one morning on my work computer on Thursday morning.

I sat up straight as soon as I saw it. This was the first personalized message I'd received in my workplace account. The sender had a Gmail account: "EdgarG" followed by seven numbers.

The message read, "*Good morning Mandy! Emailing you from my work phone as I left my ID card at home. You mind letting me in? - Edgar.*"

My first thought: who *was* this? Obviously someone who didn't know me well - I didn't let *anyone* call me Mandy.

I gripped the mace as I tried to think through the situation rationally. Maybe this was just some sick game by the person who'd been spying on me. Or, maybe...

I typed back, "*Good morning. As I do not know you, did you intend to send this to someone else with a similar name? Best of luck getting into your office.*"

The response read, "*This isn't funny, Mandy. We've been work buddies forever! I know it's not protocol, but can you please open up for me? I don't want to go all the way back home to get my card. - Your friend Edgar.*"

Shit, I thought. There was something *seriously* wrong with this person. Why would he be pretending to know me?

I walked to the front of the building and peered outside. Nobody seemed to be there. A little spooked, I returned to my desk.

That's when a loud *thud* resounded, causing me to gasp in surprise. It came from the window next to me. Whatever had been thrown had been heavy, as a small dent in the glass marked the point of impact.

I leapt to my feet. For a brief moment, I saw a figure retreat into the treeline outside. I only got a brief glimpse, but it appeared to be the same person as before with a square jaw and those same longing, deep brown eyes. His face seemed to shimmer, an unsettling distortion that I dismissed as a trick of the light or my own fear.

After that, a flurry of emails arrived:

"Just trying to get your attention! You coming?"

"You're being awfully rude Mandy. You know I'd let you in if you forgot your card."

"Mandy - I thought we were friends. What happened?"

"Hello? I'm still out here. You're really going to make me go home?"

"After all we've been through, I thought I meant something to you. I guess not."

"You bitch. This is not okay, and this isn't over."

"I'm going to get back at you for this, Mandy. You just wait."

~

I dialed the same number for security. To my frustration, nobody picked up. I tried again, with the same result this time. I left a frantic message before dialing 911.

"Let me route you to the nearest park rangers' office," said the operator.

"I already *tried* that," I complained.

"They're the ones who can best assist you," she continued, overtalking me. Before I could protest, I heard the call transfer and a familiar ringing. I hung up.

Winona was more helpful, at least once I calmed down enough to clearly explain what was happening.

"The way I see it," she advised, "You need to leave. We already know that this creep has some way of getting inside, so you're not safe there. Make sure the coast is clear and, if it is, get in your car and go."

"What if he's, like, hiding, waiting for me?"

"That's why you'll want to take the pepper spray with you. Don't hesitate to use it."

~

I kept her on the line as I made my way to a second-floor office and peered out a large window overlooking the parking lot. It appeared empty, aside from my car. Seeing no one, I proceeded to the main entrance. "I can do this," I told myself before swiping my card to open the door to the security room.

Immediately, a dark, hulking figure emerged from behind the security station.

"Fuck you!" I roared, activating the spray.

~

Officer Jackson emerged from the bathroom nearly an hour later, face wet and red.

"I'm so sorry," I told him, still wondering what he was doing here.

"I'll be okay," he said. "I'm trained on this. I just need a bit more time to recover." He'd uttered plenty of expletives after I sprayed him. Fortunately, I'd only gotten off a little before he swiped my arm away, sending the bottle to the ground.

"Again, I'm sorry."

"Don't worry about it. You're just looking out for yourself."

I wasn't sure what to say. I didn't expect him to be this polite, especially considering the excruciating pain I'd just forced him to endure.

He explained he'd been returning from an emergency when dispatch informed him of the message I'd left. He was already in the area and decided to check on me, parking in a small lot behind the building. He was heading inside, in the publicly accessible security room, and about to call me when I ran into him.

For my part, I recounted the creepy emails from "Edgar G." Officer Jackson had many follow-up questions, including if I had anyone in my life, like past romantic partners, who might hold a grudge. "No, no," I said. "My only ex, Michael, would never do something like this. And I *saw* the guy, and he's not anyone I know."

He jotted down the physical description I provided. "So, we definitely have a persistent stalker. We're not sure what he wants or if he's a threat. Look, Amanda, how about you stay home tomorrow? I'll devote the day to investigating, okay?"

~

My phone rang around 3 p.m. "I got him," said Officer Jackson.

A wave of relief swept through me as he described what happened. A man named Lucas had been living off the grid in the national park intermittently for years. He occasionally snuck into buildings, including mine. "His point of entry," Officer Jackson explained, "was a fire exit carefully wedged open from the outside. I've secured it. I don't know what he was messing with you about, but my arrival last week spooked him back to the woods."

"And the emails?"

"He stole a cell phone from a hiker. Decided to harass you. Probably held a grudge for you calling me. We've got him booked on trespassing and illegally residing in the park. He won't bother you again anytime soon."

"Thank God," I said.

"It's my job, ma'am. All in a day's work."

"It's okay, I'm just glad it's over. And, sorry for macing you."

"Maybe you can get me a drink sometime," he chuckled. "Look, if you ever need anything, or if anything creepy happens to you again, you know how to reach me."

~

After that, things felt like they were turning around. Alfred and I had a splendid date Friday night. He stayed over, and I slept soundly in his arms. Come Monday, I pulled into work feeling everything was on the upswing. For the first time, I felt secure, even turning my desk back around to face the beautiful view outside.

"*So*, you texted me things went well with Alfred," said Winona, when I called her in the late morning. "But I want more details!"

"Like what?" I jested, knowing exactly what she was fishing for. "I told you: we had a nice dinner, and he made breakfast for me in the morning."

"I'm more curious about what happened between those two activities," Winona retorted.

"We had a pleasant time, and that's all I'm telling you."

"Oh God, you're really going to make me work for it, aren't you?"

I feigned offense. "What? I would never do such a thing."

"I'm assuming you smooched?"

That made me giggle. "You assume correctly."

"And then..."

"I'm not telling! But, I will say he was *very* good at it."

"At *what*?" she pried.

"Winona, don't you have work to do?"

She groaned. "Did you two, you know..."

"I *don't* know!"

"Sleep together?"

I paused, letting the question simmer. Then, abruptly, I giddily blurted out, "Yes, and it was awesome, and I've got to get back to work, bye!" I hung up, a proud smirk on my face.

~

By Tuesday afternoon, my ecstasy had soured slightly. I'd had a challenging job interview that morning and, worst of all, Alfred hadn't responded to me since I'd seen him last weekend.

"I'm fearing the worst," I confided in Winona. "What if it was all an act, and he's gone now that he got what he wanted?"

"I wouldn't worry," Winona assured me. "From what you told me, he's not the kind of guy to sleep with you and then ghost you. I'm sure something came up. You'll probably hear from him tonight or tomorrow."

"I'm sure you're right," I said.

My cell phone buzzed with a new call. "Someone's trying to reach me, Winona. I'll call you back."

~

That night, Winona and I met up to celebrate. I had another job lined up, though it wouldn't start for a month. My current job had upsides: no work or annoying co-workers. But I needed to develop skills and make connections to progress in my career. I also needed to get out of this creepy building and out of a job that could end at any moment if leadership noticed my existence.

When I arrived at work the next morning, I was nursing a slight hangover from drinks with Winona. I drafted emails to HR, explaining I'd accepted a new position and giving them my last day.

My day passed slowly. I read a chapter, took a short nap, and made progress in the accounting course. Near the end of the day, I got up to use the restroom one last time before the long drive home.

When I returned, my phone, ID card, and car keys were missing from my desk. "What the fuck," I whispered to myself. Meanwhile, emails popped up on my screen, from the same "Edgar G." as before.

No, I thought. Wasn't this guy in jail? Regardless, how did he have access to the same account?

The emails were written in the same style - just a sentence or two each:

"This is the last straw, Mandy. Getting a new job without even telling your trusted colleague?"

"Don't worry, Mandy. I didn't do much. Just a friendly prank to even things out."

"Come and get it." This last message included two photos: one of room B315, the other showing my ID card and phone on a small table wedged between a closet door and coat rack in the room's back corner.

"Fuck," I hissed. Officer Jackson must have arrested the wrong person. I was a fool to think I'd be safe here.

Perhaps it was just a prank, at least in the twisted eyes of my tormentor. My stalker hadn't actually harmed me. Maybe if I went to the basement - which I'd avoided - I could retrieve my belongings, leave, and never come back.

But, fuck that. I wasn't eager to march into harm's way. I opened the phone function on my computer.

"Officer Jackson," he answered.

I explained the situation. "Okay," he replied. "Wait where you are. I'm heading over now."

"How far away are you?"

"Not far."

"Should I try to find a way out? The main door won't work, but I'm sure I could use one of the fire exits."

"Negative," he replied. "The fire exits are all locked."

"Wait, what?" I said, flustered. "Why are they locked? And, if you knew that, why didn't you tell me?"

"Let me ask you a question," he said, "do you recall how you got this number?"

"*What?*" I asked, noting his deflection. "I dunno. On the sheet by the door?"

"Well Mandy, what if I told you the same person who's been stalking you put that sheet there? And, what if I told you each number listed on it went to the same phone?"

My jaw dropped as a nauseous feeling fell upon me. He hung up. A moment later, the lights went out.

Before my mind could process, I heard his voice say, "*Told you'd I'd be here soon, Mandy.*" Only, this time, it came from several yards in front of me, from a corridor connecting the main hallway with the central open office area.

My eyes adjusted to the darkness to make out that a figure in a police uniform. I recognized his long nose and sunken, dark eyes.

Then, something strange happened. His face...changed, its skin shifting around and contorting. His hair changed color, his nose shrank, and eyes lightened from dark brown to bright blue. Now he looked like...Officer Jackson?

"I wasn't going to wait down there for you forever, Mandy," he taunted. "I'm tired of you playing hard-to-get. I think it's time I come and take what's mine."

Survival instincts kicked in. Before my thoughts caught up, I leapt over my desk. He nimbly sidestepped, blocking me if I tried to run around him.

But I wasn't trying to get behind him. If I was going to get out, I'd need the items he'd taken - the items supposedly on a desk in room B315. Instead, I shoved open the nearby basement door and scurried downwards.

~

I flew through the air, nearly losing my balance. As I descended, I saw, for the first time, entrances to levels B1 and B2. "Biolab 1" was affixed next to the former, and "Biolab 2" next to the latter. Through each glass door, I glimpsed a clean, well-lit hallway, its walls lined with a mounted fire extinguisher and ominous safety warnings.

B3 was labeled "Storage & Sanitary." I rushed inside. Unlike the two floors above, the lights were off, except for a single flickering bulb at the far end outside a room I recognized from the pictures "Edgar G.," or Officer Jackson, or whoever he was, had sent me.

For a moment, I settled my nerves enough to pause and listen. It occurred to me I hadn't heard my pursuer behind me. Was he even following? Or did he know another way down?

I remained uneager to walk into what I was sure was a trap, especially with no guarantee my phone, keys, and ID would still be there. But, I also knew I was helpless without the items he'd taken - no way out short of breaking a window, no way to drive, and no way to contact authorities. And, it's not like anyone would be looking for me anytime soon. The only alternative was to hide, but I couldn't do that forever. I pressed onwards, hand outstretched ahead in case obstacles awaited in the shadowy corridor.

Finally, I reached room B315. Just as in the picture, my missing items sat on the small table, illuminated by a bright desk lamp.

I scanned the room. It was plain and largely undecorated. A small set of lockers and two wooden crates sat on one side, a closet on the other. As far as I could tell, the coast was clear.

I stepped forward. As I reached for my belongings, my foot hit a small string, which snapped. *Shit*, I thought, realizing I'd activated a tripwire trap.

The closet door, triggered by the broken string, burst open. I screamed as a bulky male form fell out. Its weight sent me tumbling.

At first, I assumed it was Officer Jackson. But a horrifying sensation fell over me: it was worse - it was Alfred, dead.

"Oh God, no," I whimpered, crawling from under his corpse. He had deep gashes throughout his back, as if hacked by a long blade. Taped to his shirt was the paper that had flown into me a week earlier, with "*Bad match*" still displayed.

I didn't have time to mourn. I jumped to my feet, grabbed the items, and scrambled back to the hallway.

"*Mandy!*" called Officer Jackson's voice from the unlit far end of the hallway. "Got you good, didn't I?"

I inferred he'd been pursuing me after all, just not bothering to run. He wanted me to fall victim to his prank.

I weighed my options. I could try to get past him, but I didn't like my chances; he had a gun. Instead, I darted into the room directly across from B315, hoping to find a temporary hiding place until I could sneak past him.

It was a mostly-empty storage room. In its center stood an arched wooden structure covered in flowers. I snuck into the closet behind it.

I gasped. It smelled disgusting, and I quickly realized why: another dead body. It was covered by a plastic bag and propped against the wall. Oh God, I thought, realizing who it was. Jesus Christ, this guy had murdered fucking Michael, of all people. What the fuck? Why?

I slipped behind Michael's body, continuing to fight against the urge to puke as I did so. I heard the door open as Officer Jackson stepped inside. "Mandy! You in here? Come on out already. Like I said, I'm sick of playing games with you. We were just getting started." I listened to him pace about the room.

I held my breath as he opened the closet door and peered inside. "Big mistake," he said, my heart dropping. "Breaking up with her. I may be upset with her for the moment. But she's a quality lady. Shouldn't have let her go, Michael." He closed the closet door, and I felt as much relief as someone in my situation possibly could.

Officer Jackson opened the door back to the hallway. "No more hiding in the dark, Mandy."

Brightness beamed as he flipped on the lights. It took my eyes moments to adjust. I continued to listen, hearing footsteps, then a closed door. The sounds became muffled and distant.

Recognizing the opportunity, I shoved Michael's corpse aside, sprinted out of the storage room, and re-entered the hallway. As I hurried back toward the staircase, I realized, to my shock, that the walls were *covered* in photographs of me.

Me working, stretching, reading, napping. *Lots* of me napping, with the camera right in my face. It was as if, every day since I arrived, he discreetly shot a new photo album of me.

I didn't have time to feel even more horrified. I just kept running.

"Like my work?" he called, just as I pushed open the stairwell door. A rumbling followed - the sounds of his heavy form dashing after me.

~

I didn't trust myself to keep ahead of him. This man was a schemer, having thought ahead enough not to let me win easily. So, when he finally opened the main level door, I was waiting with a fire extinguisher from B1.

I slammed it, as hard as I could, into his face. It was a perfect hit. Blood flew as the blow sent him sprawling.

I didn't wait to see how badly I'd hurt him. Instead, I dropped the extinguisher and frantically hurried to the main entrance. My card worked, the door opened. I flew outside, hopped into my car, turned on the engine, and zoomed away into the night.

~

Winona and Tommy let me move in with them for the next several weeks. I couldn't be alone.

I met many times with police officers who confirmed I'd been hoodwinked into calling a fake security number. They quickly identified the likely culprit as an Edgar Garrison, who'd briefly worked at the facility as a test subject. Records showed that one of his trials had lingering, long-term effects on his appearance, sparking a lawsuit from him that was ultimately dismissed.

During that time, Edgar developed an attraction to a female lab technician. When she didn't reciprocate his feelings, he turned to stalking. He was eventually fired for it. After that, he'd gotten a gig as a local park ranger but was quickly fired for attempting to use his authority to continue stalking her. The uniform I'd seen him wearing was one he'd failed to return upon his removal from the job.

"He continued to spy on her even after losing both jobs," an officer explained. "There was a defective back door that he'd use to sneak in and out. When she, along with everyone else, got hit by the latest layoffs, he seems to have shifted his obsession from her to you."

The police also discovered diaries he'd kept in the basement, which established he'd developed a fantasy about winning me over by protecting me from men who wanted to hurt me. "I'll be her knight in shining armor," he wrote. "I'll keep her safe from those unworthy, and she'll love me for it." He created some of the very problems from which he then 'rescued' me. When he learned I got a new job elsewhere, he snapped and decided to make his move before I departed from his hunting grounds. His plan…I don't want to go into it in detail, but it involved drugged food, a 'wedding' under the altar I'd stumbled upon, and a room secured by multiple locks.

Edgar hadn't been seen since that night. "Don't worry," the officer told me. "We'll catch him."

~

Winona and I arranged a week-long backpacking trip, aiming to escape the grief and guilt I felt regarding Alfred and Michael, as well as the endless police visits. We both posted our hiking route on social media, along with images of sites visited during our drive to the trailhead.

That first night, we camped close to the road. After setting up our tents, we discreetly snuck out to the designated lookout point where we unpacked the equipment.

Through night vision goggles, we waited patiently for hours. Sure enough, the skulking figure of my nemesis eventually appeared. He had a knife in one hand, a flashlight in the other, and a pistol holstered at his waist.

"Time to end this?" Winona whispered, handing me the loaded gun she'd been training me with.

"I think it is," I whispered back as he slowly unzipped the tent door. We only had moments before he discovered the figures we'd left in the sleeping bags were mere props.

"You know I've got your back if anything goes wrong," Winona assured me. I nodded and gave her hand, which gripped her rifle's barrel, an affectionate squeeze.

Taking a deep breath, I emerged, stood tall, and walked confidently. The last thing he saw, as he spun around and went for his gun, was the laser sight aimed at his bandaged forehead, followed by two quick flashes of light.

15

THE ULTIMATE WEAPON

0,459

Conjure up the most dangerous weapon you can imagine. Think about it, hard.

What have you arrived at? If your mind moved past swords, clubs, and firearms, and towards more creative answers – hazardous chemicals, gases, and bombs – you're heading in the right direction.

80,460

I never dwelt on what my less-than-legitimate clients did with the weapons I sold them. I only cared about what they paid me in exchange. Indeed, when Ralph first convinced me that he was *for real* - that his idea actually *worked* - all I could imagine were suitcases filled with banded stacks of hundred-dollar bills.

You see, Ralph invented something remarkable, something every client of mine would bend over backwards to purchase: the most intimidating, terrifying weapon ever created.

80,461

When Ralph first showed me the "Temporal Distortion Projector," as he called it, I wasn't impressed. The rifle's exposed wire and frail frame made it look fragile and unfinished.

I remained skeptical as he led me to a greenhouse adjacent to his lab and aimed his shoddy contraption at dense, brightly-colored flower patch. When he pulled the trigger, the weapon emitted in a brief flash several thin circles of cobalt blue.

The flowers didn't just wilt. They shriveled inward with violent speed, decaying into a thin, colorless heap until they were nothing but food for fungi and worms.

80,462

You see, among other effects, the weapon stagnates its targets' temporal properties. What Ralph and I observed over seconds, the flowers spent years experiencing. Over five-hundred years, Ralph estimated.

Now, just imagine this weapon used against a living being, against *you*. The first thing you notice is the nerve paralysis. The world around you doesn't stop, it just moves at a rate your perception can't register. The dust in the air hangs like stars in the sky. A single drop of sweat from your brow takes what feels like a geological era to travel to your cheek.

Then, the nightmare sets in, and there's no escaping it. All you can do is think. And believe me, you have a *long* time to think.

The world around you freezes. As roughly three seconds pass to everyone in it, your alert mind and immobile body experience the same duration that separates Joan of Arc from fighter jets. The sheer, deafening silence is the first thing that breaks you. You replay every mistake, every fear, every embarrassing memory you ever had until the structure of your mind begins to fracture. You try to count, to sing, to remember every single word of every book you ever read, just to keep the endless, echoing void of your mind from collapsing into static. Your only salvation lies in death, by pre-existing disease if you're lucky, old age if you're not. Then, observers see your shriveled, aged body crumple to the floor, having experienced centuries of conscious time in what outsiders observe as fleeting seconds.

80,463

I grasped the monetary value quickly. Ralph caught on only after he signed a contract granting me most of the profits.

I was admiring the first complete TDP – the one we'd present at the armament show – when a process-server informed me of Ralph's lawsuit.

I'd had enough of him by this point. His pathetic greed was directly interfering with my ability to earn what I deserved. I knew what I had to do.

I arrived at the office the next morning with a poetic plan. Only, as it turns out, Ralph had the same idea. When I whipped out the TDP, he was already raising his old prototype. Our trigger fingers pulled simultaneously.

Decades for us, one second for you. I've had nothing to do but count the hairs atop Ralph's ugly, stupid head.

80,464, 80,465. My count concludes.

Two fewer hairs than last time. At least an end to this purgatory approaches, ever-so-slowly.

16

——————

BANDAGES

Chelsie and I took turns hugging Erica. I picked up Erica's travel bag while Chelsie led her to the makeshift bed we'd made for her on the living room couch.

The three of us had been close friends during college. In the two years since we graduated, Erica had stayed behind to complete a Master's program, whereas Chelsie and I had found work in a suburb an hour's drive away.

Chelsie and I were roommates, a setup that was still working out well for us despite our differences in personality, and this was Erica's first visit in nearly a year.

In other times, we'd use the occasion to go out on the town, but the pandemic kept us in. Chelsie sipped a plain club soda while I fixed drinks for Erica and me.

At one point, Erica complimented our apartment. In my slight inebriation, I'd let slip a comment about how I hoped we'd continue to be able to afford it.

Chelsie retired early. Erica and I retreated to my bedroom to avoid bothering her.

"You're having money problems, aren't you?" she asked bluntly.

"Being furloughed hasn't been easy," I said. "But a lot of people have it worse. My parents have been chipping in a bit to help me with rent. I'm grateful for that."

"The loans were killing me," said Erica. "Even with my scholarship, just finding a remotely affordable place to live near campus was tough. At least you have a roommate to split the rent with."

I sighed. "Chelsie's been pulling her weight without any problem. I've coughed up my portion late a couple months in a row now."

Erica laid back against my pillow. "What if I told you I knew of a way that would put a great deal of extra income in your pocket?"

"Erica, if this is an MLM-pitch-"

She chuckled. "No, no, nothing like that. As a friend, I just wanted to share something that helped me stay afloat, in case it also helps you."

"Let me guess," I responded. "It involves you selling me something that I then sell to two other people-"

"Enough!" said Erica. "Do you want to hear it or not?"

"Sure," I said.

"Remember that feminism class we took together, where you gave a presentation on stigmatization of sex workers?"

"Erica!" I exclaimed. "This had better not be going where I think it's going. I'm not getting on OnlyFans to pay the bills."

Erica sat upright, her face taking on a serious affect I wasn't used to seeing. "I remember what you said. You talked about how it was a respectable, unfairly-stigmatized profession, one that would benefit from being legal-"

"That doesn't mean I want to do it!"

"Hey, I get it," said Erica. "Really, I do. I used to feel that way, and for good reason."

Used to feel? Had Erica already resorted to what she was pitching to me? I couldn't imagine her doing that.

"There are all sorts of problems with it," she continued. "Terrible social stigmas, pregnancy and STD concerns, and, of course, you almost inevitably find abusive, creepy, or violent clients."

"Plus, you have your personal dignity to think about," I said.

"Well, wasn't your whole argument that it's a perfectly dignified profession?" asked Erica. "You weren't lying about that, were you?"

I shrugged. "Erica, in theory, I'm a fan of sex work being an option for women – for any consenting adult, really – and it not being stigmatized. But we don't live in that world, and even if we did, that doesn't mean that I would want to do it."

"Sure, sure," said Erica. "But, what if I told you that there was a way to get money – a lot of it, enough to not have to worry about your rent for some time - through sex work, and I could guarantee that none of those other issues applied. No one knows about it other than you and your client, your client is polite and good looking – well, at least not bad looking – and it's done safely, with both parties tested in advance. No one else finds out about it. And you only have to do it once, and nothing degrading or violent happens during it. What would you say to that?"

"I'd say that's too good to be true," I responded. "And I wouldn't want to do it anyway."

"Well," said Erica, "We live in a miserable time. To get by, a lot of people have to do something they wouldn't otherwise want to do. All I'm saying, is that if you really meant what you said, and you're also willing to do something you don't want to do to get by, then let me know, okay? You're a dear friend, and I want to help you out."

"Is this something you have personal experience with?" I asked.

Erica gave me a firm look. She didn't need to nod.

"You really did it?" I asked, incredulous.

"Abby, it's just like I said. It was a year ago, and I've suffered no consequences whatsoever."

"How many times did you do it?"

"Just once. That's all he'll hire you for. No repeats."

"And how much did you sell yourself for?"

"Sell myself?" repeated Erica. "You realize that it's men who create the idea that a woman 'sells herself' in some derogatory way by-"

"Okay, okay," I said. "Sorry. But...how much was it?"

She whispered into my ear, "$25,000."

We spent the day as adventurously as we could, given the circumstances. We walked through a local park in the morning and early afternoon before retreating back to Chelsie and I's apartment for the evening. We ordered takeout, watched an old mummy movie, chatted, and played classic video games to pass the time.

Ever present in my mind was the thought of my friend doing what she had for money. I knew better than to judge her or blame her, but it made me uncomfortable.

I thought about things like dignity and self-worth; weren't those violated by what Erica had put herself through? I'd always thought those constructs were meaningless, but I realized that I didn't feel that way. The Erica staying at my apartment was the same Erica I'd always known; the experience hadn't diminished her. Yet, I felt deeply apprehensive.

An email appeared on my phone. The subject line read "Rent". While Erica and Chelsie chatted and laughed, I drafted a new email, putting my parents' names in the "To" line.

"You alright over there?" asked Erica.

"Yeah, I'm fine," I said. I hit the "trash" button on the draft.

Chelsie went to sleep early. "Got to be up for morning Mass!" she explained.

Erica and I again retreated to my room. I took out my small stash of weed. Erica added something to the joints we rolled, mentioning the word "rainbow".

"Be careful with it," she said. "It'll take you places."

I relaxed a bit as recent memories swirled together – the movie we'd watched, our trip to the park, shortfalls in my checking account, and the arrangement Erica had described.

Eventually, Erica initiated the conversation we needed to have. "Do you want more information about what we talked about last night?"

At first, I couldn't bring myself to respond.

"Hey, look, Abby, for what it's worth, I swear to you that I'm not getting anything out of this. No payback or bonus for pushing it. And I vouch for it. One hundred percent. You can trust me."

"Okay," I said. It was all Erica needed to begin explaining.

"His name's Michael Davis," she said. "Boring name, boring guy. Trust fund kid. I heard about him through a TA at school."

"Trust fund kid?" I repeated.

"You know," said Erica, "someone born into vast wealth managed by a third party so he doesn't blow it all at once. He gets massive deposits from his dad's estate every month. Never had to work a day in his life. Oh, and, obviously, he's an adult now. Probably about thirty."

"A lot of people in those circumstances," she continued, "grow up to be entitled assholes. Brats. Bullies. But not all of them. Some of them are just...nice and friendly, partially because they've never had to learn to act differently."

"So you're setting me up with a 'nice guy'," I said. "Great."

She explained further. Michael had a lot of standards: he only arranged this with people who'd never been involved in sex work before and who sent certified clean STD results in advance.

"I hope none of that's an issue for you?" she asked.

"Just keep going," I said. "And, no, I don't think so."

He'd, in turn, provide similar documentation regarding his own health, he'd use protection during the act, and he'd require the woman to use or be on some second form of protection to be extra safe. He'd have someone run a discrete background check on candidates as well, to verify their claims and also to confirm that they weren't mentally unwell or impoverished.

"He doesn't want to exploit someone with emotional issues, or who's struggling to get by," explained Erica. "You fit the bill perfectly, because, while you have some worries, you're not exactly on the brink of starvation. You're doing okay."

"And, about 'the act' itself..."

"Fifteen minutes," said Erica. "Maximum."

"Well, there's more to it than the length of time."

"Sure," said Erica. "Let me tell you: it's vanilla. It's like he learned about sex from movies where married couples slept in different beds. I mean, he has a basic understanding of things, but nothing more."

I should my head in bewilderment. "Why is he willing to go to all this trouble, when he could, I dunno, just get on a hookup app, or hire a prostitute if that's what he's into?"

"I have no idea," said Erica. "I didn't ask."

She reached into her purse and removed a business card containing nothing more than a neatly-written number.

"Did you enjoy it?" I asked.

Erica shrugged. "Not really, no, but it wasn't terrible either. I almost felt like I was robbing him, given how much he paid me for how little I lost."

~

Three weeks later, I knocked at the door to a condominium. It was on the seventeenth floor of an eighteen-story building in a good location within easy walk distance of a historical district and the city center.

I wore a red dress and a nice pair of shoes. My purse contained a box cutter and a small canister of pepper spray. Erica expected to hear from me in an hour; I'd made her agree that if she didn't, she'd tell Chelsie that I might be in trouble.

Michael led me in. He wore a loose black t-shirt that contrasted with his pasty white skin. He smiled a lot. His place was compact and well-organized. He wasn't handsome, but he wasn't bad-looking either. He didn't seem to have any muscle, but he was in decent shape, and his face was freshly-shaven.

I handed him a folder. He reviewed the test results inside. "Good, good. Here's mine." He passed me a stuffed envelope. "It's got all the tests, plus a certification that there's no video surveillance equipment or recording devices. You can keep it."

I examined the condominium. It was fairly clean and well-kept. One corner contained a treadmill and a jump rope. He had two huge televisions, one in the living room surrounded by bean bag chairs and one in his bedroom connected to several video game consoles.

"Would you like something to drink?" he asked, motioning to the kitchen.

"Sure, water," I said. I followed him as he poured me a glass. A closet door to my right was wedged shut. A strange smell emanated from it.

"Don't go in there!" he said. "It's private."

He handed me a full glass. It tasted sterile. Before I knew it, I gulped it all down.

"Well, this way," he said, stepping into the bedroom. Aside from the television and the large bed, it contained several dressers and a desk built of matching oak.

"Can I ask you a few questions?"

"Sure," he said, "but it won't count against the fifteen minutes."

"I'm just wondering-"

"Why I do this? It's an understandable question. I could just go on dates, like everyone else, right?"

"Sure," I said.

"I tried that once. I got rejected. I didn't like that. So, I didn't do it again." He began untying his sneakers.

"If you're going to pay for it," I said, "you could, you know-"

"Hire a professional? Yeah, I thought of that. But it just sounds dirty, and artificial too. With women like you, who've never done something like this for payment before, I can suspend my disbelief, and for a moment feel like there's some sort of bond there. Of course, I know there isn't one. But it's what I want, and I have the money to pay for it. Everyone comes out a winner. Now, why don't you get comfortable?"

I figured this was my cue to undress, which I started to do.

"By the way, if you've changed your mind, you can leave right now," he said. "In fact, I'll give you $100 cash for your trouble. I want to make absolutely sure that you're okay with this arrangement."

I considered the offer. But I wanted more than $100, and I'd come this far already. "It's fine," I said.

"Okay. Well, please confirm that you consent."

"I do."

"Okay, but do it again, this time enthusiastically."

"I do," I said, at an ever-so-slightly louder volume.

"Good enough," he said.

Erica's description of 'the act' was accurate. He got on top. I only put in a minimal effort, but he seemed to enjoy himself all the same. He moved at his own speed, paying no attention to what I wanted. I didn't mind. At least he wasn't demanding that I act like I was enjoying it. I focused on a clock above the bed, counting down the time for it to be over.

After about nine minutes, he asked to switch places, which I agreed to do. He finished soon after. Thirteen minutes had passed when I rolled off of him.

"That was great," he said between heavy sighs. "How was it for you?"

I told him I'd enjoyed it.

He gave a quick laugh. "There's a good sport!"

He cleaned up in the bathroom, and then I did the same. When I emerged, a cloth bag stuffed with cash waited for me. He wrote in a notebook on his desk. "I'd say that was a strong seven-and-a-half out of ten," he said.

"Are you *grading* me?" I asked.

"Not you, specifically, but the act of having sex with you," he said. He flipped through the pages of the notebook. "All twenty-nine times I've done this are in here! The worst score I ever gave was a six, and that was mostly my fault."

His beaming expression faded a bit as he registered my disapproval.

"Does this bother you? I only have you listed in here by first name."

"It does bother me."

"If you want, I can rip out your page. I can throw it away, or give it to you to dispose of if you prefer. Do you want that?"

"Whatever," I said. I just wanted to leave.

"Well," Michael said, gesturing to a Nintendo console, "if you want to stick around a bit, I'm doing a 101% *Donkey Kong 64* speed run this evening. There are so many collectibles in that one – it's quite exciting to watch someone gather them all, I think. I may order a pizza, too, and you're welcome to have a piece or two if you stay."

"I think I'll go."

"Sure thing," he said. He loaded up the game and started playing. "Just close the door on the way out."

The hallway outside his condo was eerily quiet, and several lights appeared broken at the far end of it. For a brief moment, I thought I saw a pair of yellow eyes peering through the shadows.

When I made it home, I naturally didn't share a word of the afternoon's events with Chelsie.

"How was it?" texted Erica.

"Like you said," I responded.

I spent a long time looking at my reflection in the bathroom mirror. What had I just done, and what did doing it make me? I scrubbed hard at my body in the shower. I didn't want a single skin cell of Michael's to remain on me.

I deposited the cash gradually over several weeks. The new funds allowed me to pay money back to my parents, and I ended up with enough in my account to hold myself over for a little while longer.

Life moved on. I landed a part-time tutoring gig online. Nothing strange happened until two weeks later.

I was carrying a bag of trash down an alley to the curbside can when I thought I heard a second pair of footsteps. They stopped and started with my own, but when I looked around, I didn't see anyone else. The same thing happened a few days later. I asked Chelsie if she'd encountered anything similar, and she hadn't.

Another time, I got up to pee in the early morning. When I left the bathroom, I noticed the door to the apartment slowly swing open, even though nobody was there. I figured that it may not have been shut properly. I used the chain lock from then on.

I started having terrible dreams. In one, a video of my encounter with Michael emerged and went viral, and people kept sending stills from it to my parents.

In another, I was back with my ex-boyfriend. We were happy, but he angrily broke off an engagement when news of what I'd done spread through social media.

In a third, I heard a knock at the door. I looked through the peephole, finding Erica, of all people. "Hurry!" she yelled.

I let her in. She bled from a knife wound. "Close the door!" she whimpered. "It's right behind me!"

"What's behind you?" I asked.

A figure hobbled in. Hardly an inch of skin was visible amidst its loose blue clothes and layers of bandages. It wielded a long, sharp blade, which it jabbed into me. I woke up screaming.

The next morning, I tutored a seventh grader by video. He kept getting distracted. When I asked about it, he insisted that someone was behind me. Eventually, I had to turn off my camera to keep him focused.

That evening, Chelsie and I carted up groceries from the building garage to our apartment. As I brought the foldable cart back down to my car, footsteps again trailed me. I dropped and peered underneath a truck, where I noticed a bandaged foot shuffling against the ground on its other side. But, when I ran around the vehicle, no one was there.

The sense of unease continued as I returned. I looked around frantically as I waited for the elevator to arrive. When the doors opened, I rushed inside, only to find myself staring face-to-face with the bandaged figure from my dreams.

It swung its knife at my face, scratching the hand I raised to protect myself. I fell out of the elevator. The doors shut a moment later.

Chelsie helped bandage my hand. I filed a report with the police. The officer raised an eyebrow when I described how dozens of bandages obscured its face.

"Did he or she try to follow you after cutting you?" the officer asked. I shook my head. "No, it didn't follow."

Building management claimed the relevant security cameras were inoperable and needed to be replaced.

I began to feel afraid to leave the apartment. Chelsie noticed that I was letting her run most of the errands, but she didn't complain.

The next Sunday morning, I asked her to take me with her to

Mass. In my closet, I shoved aside the red dress I'd worn to Michael's as I selected something more formal.

I'd read about how these churches presented troublesome messages on sexuality, especially towards women. As I sat a few feet apart from Chelsie, I hoped the pastor would excoriate promiscuity and prostitution. I wanted to be chided. But, instead, he gave a square sermon about overcoming hatred even against an enemy, referencing the World War One Christmas truce.

"Does he do confessions?" I asked.

Chelsie nodded. She didn't pry. I liked that about her.

In the confession booth, I told the shorthand version of what I'd done with Michael. I expected the pastor to insult and demean me. Instead, he told me to say a few prayers and talked about forgiving myself if I thought I'd done something wrong.

Knocks at the apartment door startled me that evening. Through the peephole, to my surprise, stood Erica. "Abby? Chelsie? Anyone home?" she called.

I froze, remembering the dream. Chelsie opened the door, and I calmed down enough to show excitement at seeing my friend.

Erica explained that she'd started seeing someone who lived halfway between her and us, and that after leaving his place earlier, she'd decided to stop by to deliver an early birthday gift to me in person. I'd forgotten my 25th was only a few days away.

I kept my eye on the door for a while, but eventually I calmed down. It was just a weird dream, after all.

I was glad Erica had thought of me. Talking to her made me feel better. When she left, I walked with her down to her car. I'd been avoiding the garage, but I felt safe with her around.

"You seem worried. I don't blame you, given what happened by the elevator. I'm so sorry about that. I hope that creep gets caught. How's your hand healing?"

I still wore a bandage, but I explained that it was getting better. "I'm feeling better, too, since you visited," I told her.

"I'm always happy to house you, too, if you need a break from things here," said Erica.

I waved at her as she pulled out of guest parking.

When I turned around, I spotted the bandaged figure waiting for me several yards away amidst flickering lights. It stood still, as if waiting for me to make the first move.

Fuck, no, I thought. I'd left the pepper spray and box cutter in my apartment.

The standoff ended when I reached for my phone, which prompted the figure to sprint towards me. I barely had time to scream before it was on me. I tumbled. It struck with its knife, barely missing me as I rolled to the side. I climbed to my feet, only to scream as the blade pierced my foot.

I found the panic button on my car keys. It fled in the resulting noise.

Chelsie sat for hours in the ER waiting room as my foot was treated. The police officer took notes and gave me the contact information for a psychiatrist.

"You think I'm crazy, don't you?"

"Look," said the officer, "you've called us twice for reports of a bandaged stalker that has evaded all security cameras. How would you feel, in our place?"

"How, exactly, do you think I managed to maim my own foot?"

"With the box cutter we found on you," said the officer.

"What?"

"It was right there in your jacket pocket," he said, motioning to a report describing this.

I returned home from the psychiatrist with several bottles of pills and elaborate instructions on when to take them.

"I'm so sorry to be putting you through this," I told Chelsie. "I don't know what's wrong with me."

She told me she just hoped I got better.

The next day, I knocked again at the door to Michael Davis' apartment. He wore an exercise shirt and a pair of gym shorts. "Oh, hello again...Ally?"

"What the hell did you do to me?" I asked.

"Woah there," he said. "Calm down. Now, take a deep breath-"

"Ever since…ever since that day, I've been seeing weird shit, and I know you had something to do with it!"

"Look, Ally-"

"Abby."

"Abby, I don't know what you're talking about – woah, watch out there." He backed away as I held out the box cutter.

"That – that closet by the kitchen," I stammered. "Take me to it."

"W-what? Why?"

"Just do it."

Reluctantly, he opened the door to it. Inside, I found shelfs upon shelfs jam-packed not with victim's body parts, but instead with pristinely-preserved Star Wars action figures.

"What were you expecting?" he asked. "Forgive me for not wanting women I'm about to sleep with to see my toy collection."

"But…but…the smell-s"

"I probably just sprayed some cleaning solution on the shelves when you were last here."

I lowered box cutter. Tears welled in my eyes. "I'm sorry. I-I just wanted answers for what's been happening. I feel like I'm losing my mind."

"Hey, it's alright," said Michael. "I won't call the police. I don't particularly want them clued into what I'm doing; it's technically illegal to, you know…"

"Yeah, I know."

"You can stay for a bit if you want," said Michael. "It's an exciting time for me. Did you hear the big news?"

I shook my head.

"Just last week, someone discovered a previously unknown rainbow coin in *Donkey Kong 64*. It disqualifies all the perfect completion records from the last 17 years. This is a rare opportunity, no pun intended, for me to burst into the speed-running scene with the first legitimate record! You could be here to witness it."

I left. He locked the door behind me.

As I waited for the elevator, I noticed that the hallway had grown even darker than before. More lights were out.

"Leave me alone," I said to the shadows, expecting no one to hear me.

"No," a voice barked back.

All at once, the bandaged figure lunged out of the shadows. I tumbled to the ground as its knife punctured my shirt and grazed the side of my chest. I banged on Michael's door and begged him for help.

"Sorry, I've started the speed run, please come back later!" he called.

The figure jabbed its knife into my back and then removed it to strike again. I stumbled into the elevator, frantically hitting 'Garage' and then the 'Door Close' buttons. The figure leapt inside at the last moment.

We struggled as the elevator descended. I shrieked as it dug the knife into my shoulder. I kneed the figure in the chest, throwing it off me. I pulled out the knife and dived onto it. I put my body weight on one of its arms as I repeatedly slashed its face. The blade penetrated the bandages. Blood from each incision spilled onto the marble elevator floor.

The figure emitted a high-pitched, animalistic scream. It threw me off of it and proceeded to dig razor-sharp nails across my cheek.

The doors opened. I shoved the figure back and hobbled across the garage. If the injured figure wanted to find me, it could have easily followed the thick trail of crimson I left behind.

I climbed into my car. My pursuer was nowhere in sight. I drove woozily back to my apartment building. I wanted to go home. I didn't want to talk to cops who dismissed me or doctors who told me I was delusional.

I ignored the other residents gawking at me as I made my way to my apartment. The door was locked and Chelsie didn't answer. As I fumbled with my keys, the door to the stairs opened at the end of the hallway. Had it followed me?

I slipped inside and applied the chain lock. Several loud bangs against the door followed.

I felt dizzy. I sensed I was about to pass out from blood loss.

The knocks continued. "Enough," I whispered to myself. I drew the knife, threw open the door, and punctured the neck of the figure outside. A wrapped gift flew into the air.

My last memory, before losing consciousness, was of the shocked, wide eyes of my roommate as she bled out.

~

I wake up later in a hospital. I'm now in a loose blue gown and handcuffed to my bed. For hours, I answer questions from a hostile detective. When I mention the confrontation with my stalker on the elevator of Michael's building, he shakes his head. "We've seen the footage, ma'am. You were all alone."

Erica, who's been waiting outside, is finally allowed to visit me. Through tears, I beg her to hold up a mirror. She resists, but eventually relents. I recognize the bandaged face that looks back at me.

At first, I lay there quietly as the truth of what occurred rushes through me. It's too much – what I've done to others, what I've done to myself. The pain and guilt boil over. I scream and attempt, in vain, to escape my restraints. Erica is escorted away. I watch as a nurse holds me down and prepares a syringe with the longest needle I've ever seen.

A calmness settles upon me as the ceiling fractures and dissolves. The blinding white light of the hospital room fades into the dim, familiar shadows of my bedroom. My arms and legs are, at last, both free and in my full control, and the faint scent of stale smoke and old carpet replaces the clinical odor of the hospital.

My head throbs, my mouth is cotton dry. Recent memories slam into me: Erica's casual confession of how she turned twenty-five grand; the foreboding, bandaged figure at the center of the mummy movie we'd watched; Chelsie's mention of morning mass.

Has whatever Erica added to the joint finally relinquished its hold, freeing me from a self-induced nightmare? Or is *this* the illusion - a temporary, false reprieve as I lie sedated on a hospital bed?

I stand up and stumble against the couch, where Erica is curled up in a deep, peaceful sleep.

I make my way to the bathroom, leaning heavily against the

counter as I reach for the light switch. I barely recognize the desperate, sweat-drenched creature that looks back at me. My face is pale, my eyes wide and red-rimmed, but there are no lacerations, no stitches, no bandages.

I seize a heavy porcelain mug from the counter. With a guttural cry, I smash it into my reflection in the bathroom mirror and watch as the glass shatters into pieces.

THE ROGUE TRAIL

Growing up in Dickenson County in the southwest corner of Virginia, Breaks Interstate Park was always a part of my life. My parents brought me here for everything from seasonal festivals to camping trips. Even though it's been a constant for me and for everyone in this corner of Virginia, I'm still surprised by how little-known it is outside our little piece of the world.

Its name, credited to Daniel Boone, derives from the Russell Fork of the Big Sandy River, which stretches along the borders of Kentucky, Virginia, and West Virginia. Over time (a *long* time, mind you), the water dug a long, deep canyon through the Blue Ridge Mountains - Pine Mountain, specifically. The resulting chasm, through which rapids run, is the distinctive feature of the park, which occupies the Virginia side of the state line with Kentucky. It's only a little ways from West Virginia, and about a two-hour drive from northern Tennessee.

For the last nine years, I've worked there as a park ranger. Naturally, by now, I know the park like the back of my hand, from its many interlocking trails to its camping sites, rafting routes, lake, and family-friendly water park. It has cabins, traditional lodge rooms, and a place to eat (the Rhododendron Restaurant at the Chafin Lodge).

The primary attractions, in my view at least, are the incredible views that can be found at various overlooks and, if you book the right rooms, out the windows of many of the guest lodges. Words can hardly do justice to the astonishing sight of miles of rugged, heavily-forested hills, punctuated by rivers and streams, and their sky-high, rocky peaks.

It's always a pleasure seeing the tiny dots of distant hikers and climbers as they trek the park's many routes to reach its towering summits. Some are positioned just off the road, allowing for easy access; others can only be reached through trails that, due to their steep, winding layout, take much longer to hike than their length, alone, would suggest. A few, such as arguably the park's most prominent feature, 1,000-foot sandstone cliff known as "The Towers," are inaccessible, though views of them can be enjoyed from the many scenic overlooks.

My role as a park ranger is typically limited to dealing with campers violating basic park rules regarding subjects like littering or avoiding the modest park entrance fee. Intermittently, I get involved in resolving more serious issues like domestic violence, drug use, or guests experiencing medical emergencies.

The most interesting cases, and those I want to expound upon a bit here, involve lost hikers. Now, you wouldn't expect this to be a major issue, so long as guests stay on the trails and follow the rules. The trails are clearly marked, after all, and nobody's supposed to be on them after dark. But, inevitably, some people nonetheless decide to embark on midnight strolls through thick foliage, trusting themselves to find their way back. Alcohol often plays a role in these decisions. By the time I get to them, they're usually sobered-up, apologetic, and thankful enough at being found not to mind the scolding I invariably give them.

I want to focus more on another subset of lost hikers: those who *did* follow all the rules, but nevertheless, inexplicably found themselves where they shouldn't be. You see, there's a legend about a rogue trail - yes, you read that correctly, a *rogue trail* - that predates the park itself.

To be clear, the rogue trail is not quite what you may think from that description, as it lacks the first quality you'd expect it to have: a fixed location. Rather, it appears in different places, temporarily clearing out a path of no more than two or three miles. To those who don't have the park trails system memorized, it looks wholly inauspicious and indistinguishable from the other, permanent trails. Once the moment has passed, the trail fades away, receding back into the dense woods from which it came.

Word's never really gotten out about the rogue trail. This is, in part, because it appears so sporadically, with months or even years passing between reported encounters. It also lacks a consistent name or location, and plenty of people who traverse it exit never realizing they encountered something supernatural. Some hikers have reported seeing signposts identifying it as the "Hemlock Trail," "Pincushion Moss Trail," or "Dogwood Trail" - none of which, naturally, are the names of trails that actually appear in the park. Others have described it as marked only by rectangular silver blazes with a phosphorescent quality.

There are old legends about it, passed down by locals with ties to early settlers in the region. They may well be apocryphal, but I've seen enough strange things not to fully dismiss them.

The first relates to a prospector in the late 1800s. He didn't know what we know now - that, for all the rich natural resources in the region (including bountiful amounts of coal), it lacks any deposits of gemstones like gold, silver, or rubies. Lacking this foresight, he spent weeks fruitlessly searching for minerals that could get him rich. Obviously, at this point, Breaks Interstate Park didn't exist - it wouldn't be founded for another 70 years - and neither did the vast majority of its trails. So, it certainly stood out to the prospector when an inviting, well-maintained path appeared before him.

He followed it down a steady incline until he found himself at the water's edge by a cave entrance. Inside the cave, he stumbled upon a large deposit of quartz veins packed with nuggets of gold. Only, when he attempted to return later, he never found the cave or the path that led to it again.

For years, he searched the area, including the shores of every nearby riverbed. He even spent the last of his savings hiring others to join in the effort, to no avail. His health steadily deteriorated as he obsessively sought out the ticket to prosperity that so cruelly made itself known to him, only to abruptly slip away. One day, he rolled out of a hospital and hobbled several miles to the Breaks woods for one final search. He was never seen again, though some claim to have witnessed a brittle man in tattered, antiquated clothing hobbling through the woods at night.

Another set of stories involves criminals fleeing the authorities. Some of these occur around the same time as the prospector legend, but more recent variations exist as well. They typically involve criminals responsible for some heinous act fleeing custody and attempting to hide in the woods, only to find themselves back where they started thanks to the rogue trail.

The most well-known of these tales involves a man named Isaiah…I'll leave his last name out for the moment. In the 1930s, Isaiah performed as a tramp clown in a traveling circus that came through the area. One night, several men from a few counties over accused him of having abused several small children at the carnival's previous stop. The exchange grew heated, and one of the men - the father of an alleged victim - drew a shotgun. This sent Isaiah, in full costume and makeup, scrambling away. He fled into the woods when his colleagues, likely intimidated by the growing mob and perhaps suspecting the allegations to be true, refused to protect him. Before long, found himself in the vicinity of what had just been deemed part of the Jefferson National Forest and, twenty years later, would mark the official outskirts of the Breaks Interstate Park.

With his pursuers close behind, Isaiah sprinted up a rocky trail that appeared before him. Only, when he reached the incline's peak, he found himself face-to-face with his pursuers. Of course, this made no logical sense, as the trail had taken him in a straight line. Yet, there he was, as if he'd somehow traveled in a perfect loop. He turned and ran back the way he came, only to stumble upon the riled-up mob once more. This time, they subdued him and, well, let's just say things didn't turn out well for Isaiah.

The final rendition of this type of story - the last I'll relate before refocusing on a few more recent occurrences - is the earliest of all, and occurred in the aftermath of George Stoneman's 1864 raid through the region. Stoneman was a Union general during the Civil War, and his goal was to disrupt Confederate supply lines and infrastructure in the region. His mission was largely successful, with his forces damaging lead mines in Marion and saltworks in the fittingly-named Saltville, located about 60 miles south of what would become the Breaks park. His goals largely accomplished, he split his forces so as to return by separate routes to Union-controlled areas in southern Kentucky and eastern Tennessee.

Confederates hounded the returning Unionists during their return to friendly territory. The Union soldiers were in a precarious position, as they were divided into small groups while traveling through unfamiliar, hostile territory. Worse, they were well-aware that their pursuers were not keen on taking prisoners. After all, following a battle at Saltville the previous year, the victorious Confederates had massacred many of the captured and wounded Union soldiers, most of them from a Colored cavalry unit. One leader of this atrocity, Champ Ferguson, would be tried and executed for the crime after the war.

A handful of stragglers amongst Stoneman's men soon found themselves approaching Pine Mountain, with several dozen Confederate guerrillas and regular soldiers steadily closing the distance behind them. We know what happened next primarily through the diary of Private William Hunt, an 18-year-old Confederate conscripted out of North Carolina.

As recounted by Hunt, the pursuing Confederates stumbled unexpectedly upon a path through the woods that appeared to cut through a prominent, rocky ridge. Taking it would enable them to get ahead of their prey and prepare an ambush while the Union soldiers progressed slowly through difficult mountainous terrain. The commanding officer, Colonel Anderson, ordered Hunt and a few others - mostly younger, less experienced soldiers - to stay behind as the rear guard. Anderson, a veteran of the prior year's engagement in Saltville, proceeded to lead twenty men into the woods.

What happened next shocked those who witnessed it. Mere moments after Anderson and his men disappeared from sight, six figures suddenly emerged from the trail. They collapsed before the rear guard and desperately demanded food and water. Noting their tattered grey uniforms, Hunt and his comrades provided them the requested sustenance.

The men claimed, and very much appeared to be, members of Colonel Anderson's contingent who'd departed mere moments earlier. Perplexingly, however, all insisted that they had been gone for weeks. Those who had left clean-shaven, or close to it, now had considerable facial hair. Their supplies, including all rations, were missing.

The path, as they described it, simply kept going in a short, endless loop, and when they'd attempted to leave it, they found themselves impossibly approaching it once again. Slowly, it had dawned on them that there was simply no way out. The forest, for whatever reason, was keeping them as its prisoners.

Over time, the hopelessness of their situation slowly dawned on them. They attempted to ration food and water, but both steadily depleted. The survivors attempted to hunt for food. In time, however, the supply of animals and edible plants ran out, and it fell on the men that they had no choice but to take more drastic measures to survive.

"I wish not to recount the details of the incidents described," Hunt wrote. "Other than to state that a cruel and impossible predicament drove my comrades to resort to the most base and inhumane of methods for obtaining the nourishment necessary to live. It is for this reason that only six of the men returned, and not the others. The ghastly acts taken by those who survived will undoubtedly haunt them for the rest of their existence. Clearly, something truly hostile to our presence occupies these woods. It wants us gone. I shall oblige, and never return."

The stragglers, meanwhile, made it safely back to Union lines in southern Kentucky.

~

Since starting this job, I've never directly encountered the rogue trail. But, on three occasions, I've had experiences involving guests who, I believe, did so.

The most recent case began with a late-night knock at my door. I knew the face immediately: Laura. I hadn't seen her in a while, but she was hard to forget. We grew up a few streets apart, and I was best friends with her older brother, Daniel, until we all went our separate ways after high school. She was only 25, if that; yet, her dim hazel eyes betrayed a jaded, world-weary perspective befitting of someone whose family had seemingly been cursed by misfortune.

Painkiller addiction had destroyed Daniel's life, and he'd been presumed dead after disappearing a few years ago. Laura's mother had died in a freak environmental accident shortly after giving birth to Laura, when the dam containing waste produced by a chemical factory broke down and engulfed the surrounding town in waves of toxic sludge. Laura's father, meanwhile, was struggling with poor health and required regular assistance.

"Can I come in?" she asked. I nodded. As she stepped inside, she asked if I had any beer.

"Sure. You okay?" I asked, noticing a few small cuts on her face.

"Yeah. I fell. It's a long story." I went to the fridge as she took a seat on my living room couch. Sensing her mood, I brought her a pint of Steel Reserve instead of the standard can of Bud Light I'd normally offer.

She snapped it open and took several deep gulps. She closed her eyes and leaned back for several moments while I took a seat across from her.

"That feels better," she said. She took a deep breath. "Roy, a few things. First, I'm really sorry for being such a jerk. Showing up here unannounced, demanding beer, and all that. Thank you for being kind. Second, if you can impose on you even more, I really want to vent to you about something. Can I?"

"Sure," I said. "I just don't know why you'd come to me, of all people. But don't get me wrong - I'm happy to listen, and to help as much as I can."

She took another few sips before placing the can on a coffee table. "I'm already feeling it. This is my first drink since I gave up this stuff years ago."

"Then drink it slowly," I cautioned, as I started to worry that I'd assisted her in breaking a sobriety that may have been hard-earned.

"Will do," she affirmed. "And, to answer your question, it's because it, what happened, it was all at your workplace. At the park. You've talked about...odd things happening there. Let's just say, I saw some, and you're pretty much the only person I know who I think might fully believe me."

I've compiled what she related to me below.

~

For nearly two years, I'd been seeing Elliott. He was charming. He provided for himself. He was clean, in the sense that mattered to me. He was also the first man I truly fell for. We'd talk for hours, and when he looked at me, I felt like the weight of it all - Daniel, my mom, my dad's poor health - would just disappear. He filled me with warmth and affection.

My love for him was so powerful it turned my head from all the red flags. My friend Addie saw them all, and I shut her out for it. I regret that now. The warnings started about a year into our relationship, a few months after we moved in together. He'd have these mysterious absences, coming home late and going straight to sleep with barely a word to me. He'd claim his phone signal was always too poor to reply to my texts. When I asked him simple questions, his entire body would tense up in defense. I would tell myself I was being paranoid, that he was just stressed from work, but his mind always seemed to be somewhere else.

I know I sound oblivious. It's a story as old as time, and I wished so hard that my situation was different. He swept me off my feet, to the point that I truly thought we'd spend the rest of our lives together.

Which brings me to the park. He planned our long weekend there, and I ensured my father would be cared for in my absence. We drove up with another couple, Jose and Addie. Jose's a close friend of his and Addie's a close friend of mine.

Our first full day there, Elliott insisted we split up by sex. He and Jose ventured off to a shooting range, or at least that's what they claimed to be doing, while Addie and I stayed around the park. We spent the late morning relaxing at the water park.

Addie and I agreed that Elliott was going to propose to me that week-end. We'd talked about it - getting married - a lot, and everything about this occasion felt ripe for it. "He and Jose are probably setting something up," Addie told me. "I guarantee you he's going to ask you tonight or tomorrow."

"Oh God, I hope so," I said yearningly.

The silence that followed annoyed me. I sighed, peeved that Addie still had reservations about me marrying Elliott. Reservations that she knew, based on the scalding she'd received the last time she'd voiced them, to keep to herself. It's not like anything she said could dissuade me at this point. I was madly in love, after all.

As we dried ourselves off, I saw that I had a new message on my phone from Elliott. He wanted me to meet him, alone, in a few hours at a place called "Lake Caldicott."

I showed the message to Addie. She knew the location - she'd hiked to it before with Jose. According to her, it was a scenic spot by a small lake reach-able by a mile-long trail that stretched downwards along the southside of a rocky hill. It's not usually listed on maps, though I'm sure you've heard of it.

I took a deep breath as a satisfied smile spread across my face. This was "it."

We grabbed our belongings and returned to our rooms. I hurriedly showered and changed clothes. When I stepped back outside, Addie was waiting for me. With forced enthusiasm, she wished me luck as I headed out to the trail.

Naturally, I felt butterflies in my stomach as I strolled toward the beginning of the trail. It was an easy enough hike - the weather was nice, and the path, though a bit narrow, was at a gentle decline.

Then everything changed as a large hickory tree swayed, then abruptly collapsed. My instincts kicked in just as its shadow fell over me. I sprang off the trail, tumbling down a steep incline into the valley below. With a 'thud,' the tree crashed where I'd just been standing. (Sidenote here from Roy - I note that, the morning of Laura's visit, I was involved in removing a fallen tree from the path Laura was describing.)

I remember tumbling, sharp pain, and dull, aching sensations all over me. Now you know where I got these cuts from. There's a bruise on my side, too. But, all things considered, I was just lucky not to be hurt more.

Anyway, the next thing I remember, I lay amidst thick foliage. My phone was busted - that's why I didn't call you in advance - and I was lost. There were hills on both sides of me and, as embarrassed as I am to admit it, I didn't know which one was which.

I figured I couldn't be far from a trail. I was still in the park, after all. Surely I'd find someone before too long. So, I walked.

And walked. This went on for a while, until I grew tired and a bit panicked. I didn't feel like I was making any progress, and it occurred to me that I could just be making the same mistake so many people make by wandering even farther from the trail.

I sat down on a stump, caught my breath, and tried to think of what to do. Maybe, if I squinted hard enough at the surrounding wilderness, I'd find a landmark that I remembered, or a sign of a road or trail, or a hiker or park employee who could help me. It was at that moment, as I scanned my surroundings, that I first spotted the bright red balloons.

The balloons were held by a clown, *Roy. An old-timey, sad-faced clown. Maybe 300 yards from me. In full makeup. He stood at the start of what looked like a trail, and he was staring in my direction.* (Roy here with another side note - there is no trail, to my knowledge, in the area Laura is describing. Also, at around this point, Laura began drinking a second pint of beer.)

What was I supposed to do? Wander deeper into the woods, away from the only path I'd identified? Maybe he wanted to help me. I wouldn't have noticed the trail but his balloons drawing my attention to it, after all. Regardless of where the trail led, it was my best bet for getting back to civi-lization.

When I got within earshot of him, I called out asking what he was doing there. He didn't reply. He just raised a white-gloved hand and slowly curled his index finger toward him.

You can imagine how thoroughly creeped out this made me feel. As I approached the trail, which was marked by glowing silver blazes, I kept my distance from the clown, maintaining several car-lengths between us as I cut through a patch of woods to get onto the trail. As I passed him, he rotated such that he continued to face me, but he otherwise did not move.

As I hiked up the trail, an unnatural, thick fog fell upon me, and I felt the temperature drop. I got the distinct impression that I was in some kind of artificial environment - like, a simulation of what a patch of woods in the park ought to look like, rather than the real thing, if that makes any sense. I began hearing the faint whispers of voices, many of which I recognized, calling out to me from just out of sight. Worst of all was Daniel's, which repeated the last words he ever said to me - that I...Sorry, I'm keeping that to myself.

Before long, I came to a fork where signposts pointed in both directions. "Park Entrance," read the one to the left. "Lake Caldicott - 0.5 mile," read the one to the right. As I tried to decide what to do, I heard laughter resonate from behind me. Through the mist, I discerned the outline of two figures holding hands: a tall, burly man, and the same clown as before, recognizable by the two licks of bright orange hair that jutted out on both sides of his miniature tophat. The man looked happy, but the clown's face had formed into a self-pitying pout. They were closing in on me.

I didn't want them to catch up to me. Who would? Without putting any conscious thought into the decision, I took the right fork and continued up the path. I scurried along as fast as I could, desperate to escape. The path, meanwhile, leveled out, then angled downward.

I jogged as fast as I could manage while avoiding tripping on any loose rocks or tree roots until I came upon another fork. The signpost to the left read, again, "Park Entrance," while the signpost to the right was updated to display, "Lake Caldicott - 0.1 mile."

Bright lights disrupted the fog to my left, revealing a roadway. An engine hummed, and I briefly glimpsed a car passing by. A young woman - who I vaguely recognized, though I wasn't sure where from - appeared to be driving it, and I caught the frame of a larger figure in the passenger seat before it zoomed out of sight.

As I hurried to the right, I started to feel...different. My movements became awkward and uncoordinated, and it became difficult to maintain my balance. I looked down and saw, to my shock, that my light hiking boots had somehow...changed. My shoes were clunky and oversized, with bright red and yellow patterns.

As my mind struggled to process this, my feet slipped over a long root. For the second time, I felt myself tumble and roll.

When I finally came to a stop, I found myself in a distinctly different environment. Everything looked normal, from the gently swaying trees to the small nearby lake. The fog had entirely faded, my shoes had reverted to normal, and there was no clown behind me.

I heard Elliott's voice calling my name. When I spotted him waving at me, senses of comfort and safety spread through me. Even better, he was dressed handsomely in a nice button-down shirt.

As I approached, he asked what took me so long and, noting my appearance, if I was hurt. "I'm fine," I answered, not wanting to ruin this moment by babbling about a bizarre forest clown. "I slipped, and I got a little lost for a bit. But, I'm okay now. I'm so sorry for keeping you waiting."

He nodded. "It's gorgeous here, isn't it?" he said.

Everything from the distant, mountainous scenery to the clear, crystalline water of the lake prompted me to agree. The spot he'd chosen, in a grassy clearing at the water's edge, was perfect for the occasion.

That's when he knelt and held out the diamond ring. I gasped at the sight of it and proceeded to hold my hand against my heart as he asked to marry me.

That's when I noticed something unusual in the reflection in the lake beside us. The water perfectly reflected Elliott's tall, chiseled frame. But my own reflection was something else entirely. It was a circus clown. A grotesque, smiling figure with a pained look in its painted-on eyes. My skin crawled as I stared at the grotesque image, its red smile a mockery of my feelings, its white-painted face a lie hiding a mess of emotions. I wasn't just looking at my reflection; I was looking at what I had become. The realization hit me like a physical blow: I had been a fool, blind to the lies and so lost in my performance that I couldn't see the truth even when it was reflected back at me.

I stepped backwards as a sense of revulsion pulsated through my brain.

It took a few moments for my conscious thoughts to catch up to what I was feeling: disgust at myself, disgust at Elliott, and disgust at the prospect of marrying him.

I said no, firmly, and left him there dumbfounded.

As I hurried up the hill, all the signs piled up. The park, in its own weird way, had shown me what I was, what I'd let myself become. All the excuses, all the oversights. He hadn't been honest with me in a long time, and I'd just closed my eyes to it. Our relationship wasn't built around trust or respect. It was built on lies, a joke at my expense.

I didn't look back as I rushed back to the lodge, where I knocked on the door to Addie's room.

We talked for a long time. I asked her to open up and tell me everything she knew about Elliott. Sure enough, Addie had learned through Jose that Elliott had been cheating on me for a long time. "I know of two other women," she told me, "though I suspect there have been others. Lately, he's been seeing Joanna regularly."

It all made sense now. He'd hired Joanna about a year ago. They must have started the affair, which apparently wasn't even his first, right away. Then it hit me: Joanna had been the girl driving the car I'd spotted in the mist. And Elliott had been the passenger. It was like I'd glimpsed them on their way to a discreet rendezvous.

Addie apologized for not telling me sooner, insisting that she had wanted to do so. I told her not to worry about it. She'd tried to warn me, but I'd made it clear that I was too infatuated with him to listen.

~

"Everyone else left town this morning," she said, as she finished the second drink. "Elliott drove himself home. Addie had her friend Maria pick up her and Jose. And here I am, rattling on about things that can't happen, that don't make any sense, getting drunk on two cheap beers like the lightweight I am. I know I sound crazy."

"Don't worry about it," I assured her. "You don't sound crazy. I believe you."

From the look she gave me, I could tell she appreciated that. "I was afraid to tell anyone else. I knew they wouldn't believe me."

"You're probably right. I barely believe it myself sometimes. But, on some level, I know that it's real, even though I've never encountered it directly. It makes itself known to who it wants, when it wants."

"I won't ever find it again, will I?"

I shrugged. "Maybe, maybe not. What matters is that you've gotten the message it was sending."

"I just don't understand any of this. How, how could, how could..." Her voice trailed off as she made a wide yawn. "Mind if I stay here tonight?"

"Not at all. I'd assumed as much."

We talked for some time, at first about park legends and then about more lighthearted subjects. By the end, she was happy and giggly. Before going to sleep under the blankets I'd draped over the couch, she insisted on looking at herself in the bathroom mirror. Having just finished her third drink, she stumbled a bit on her way there, such that I took it upon myself to provide her a little physical support as she walked.

When we got to the bathroom, she stopped and gazed into the mirror. I could see the cuts on her face and the smudge of dirt on her cheek. But as she looked at her reflection, a sense of peace settled over her face that hadn't been there before. She turned to me, and her eyes were no longer weary, but clear. "I look a mess," she said, her voice soft but with a sense of certitude. "But I finally left that clown back in the woods."

~

The second occasion occurred last April. My older sister went out of town for the weekend to be with her husband's father, who was having a medical emergency, leaving me to look after her two daughters, Lucy and Maggie.

It was Easter weekend, and the air at Breaks Interstate Park was crisp and filled with the promise of spring. Lucy, all of seven years old, buzzed with excitement for the egg hunt happening at Potter's Knoll. Maggie, at twelve, fancied herself too old to participate, but she enjoyed watching just as much as I did. We stood together, sharing a quiet laugh as we watched Lucy zip and dart across the field, her basket growing heavier with each colorful egg she found.

A staff member in a festive Easter vest then rang a large brass bell, signaling that time was up. Lucy immediately held up her basket, beaming at all the colorful eggs and candy she had collected. With the hunt now complete, we made our way to the Rhododendron Restaurant, where the next event on our Easter itinerary awaited: breakfast and a meet and greet with the Easter bunny.

When we arrived, a small line of parents and children had already formed. As we waited, Maggie nudged me and subtly motioned toward a nearby table. A group of five people - one woman and four men - were finishing their breakfast. They looked like out-of-towners, and their backpacks were spilling over with professional video cameras, tripods, and even a boom microphone.

"Do you recognize that guy?" Maggie whispered, her eyes fixed on one of the men with a slightly receding hairline and a wide smile that seemed just a little too practiced. I shook my head, but Maggie was sure she'd seen him somewhere before. It was Lucy's turn next, and all thoughts of the strange group vanished as her face lit up with pure delight while she hugged the fluffy bunny. After getting a photo and a hug, we found an open table and settled down to enjoy a well-deserved breakfast.

After finding a table, we dug into a classic Southern breakfast of pancakes, biscuits, and eggs. As we ate, Maggie suddenly froze, her fork halfway to her mouth. "I know who that is!" she exclaimed, a slow grin spreading across her face. "He was Lucian on *Lucian and the Lilicrank!*" I vaguely remembered the children's show she had watched religiously a few years back. She explained that even though her friends had long moved on from the show, she still loved it and had even kept her Lilicrank plushie, a stuffed animal she had held onto even after giving most of her others to Lucy.

I offered to go over and introduce her, but she immediately shrank back, her cheeks flushing. "No way!" she muttered, shaking her head. "I'm not going to bother him."

I gave her an encouraging look. "Maggie," I said, "if you want to say hi, you should. You shouldn't be afraid to just go for it."

Her resistance faded, replaced by a spark of courage. "Okay," she said, her voice barely a whisper. "Let's do it." With a shared glance of encouragement, we all got up from the table and headed toward the man.

As we approached their table, I cleared my throat to get his attention. He looked up, and I smiled at him, gesturing to Maggie. My niece, for her part, looked like she might bolt at any second, but she gathered herself and managed to speak in a firm voice.

"Excuse me," she asked. "Did you used to be on a kids' TV show?"

A few of the other people at his table exchanged smirks and some let out a quiet chuckle. The man, however, smiled warmly and nodded. "I did," he said, and then added with a theatrical flair, "The danger is real, this is not a prank!"

Maggie's face lit up. "We need your help, Lilicrank!" she finished, her voice full of genuine excitement. The man's smile widened as he shook his head. "Wow," he said, a genuine laugh escaping him. "It's been a little while since anyone remembered that. Thanks."

The other people at his table began to stand, announcing that they were heading out to set up their equipment for the day. "You go ahead," he said, waving them off. "I'm going to stay behind and enjoy a cup of coffee with my biggest fan."

~

The man, who revealed his real name as Jason, invited Maggie, Lucy, and I to sit with him while he slowly sipped a cup of coffee. He listened attentively as Maggie gushed about her favorite episodes. He seemed to genuinely enjoy hearing that someone still cared about the show.

After a few minutes, I asked him what brought him and his crew to the park. Jason's smile faded slightly as he explained that he'd moved on from trying to live off his childhood fame. "A few things happened," he said with a vague wave of his hand, "that convinced me it was time to move on from that part of my life for good."

He explained that he and his crew were paranormal investigators, filming a new ghost-hunting show. "The market's a little saturated," he said with a chuckle, "and we're still a small operation, but I'm hoping to make a name for myself again - this time, on my own terms."

"Anything in particular you're looking into here at the park?" I inquired.

He shrugged. "We're still trying to come up with something. The park's not what brought us here. We were in the area to check out an old mansion nearby. The owner, an old guy, invited us to film there." He sighed and ran a hand through his hair. "He seemed...off. He had all these historical flags - the kind you really *don't* want to see, if you catch my drift - and corresponding memorabilia. Paintings of Robert E. Lee, J.E.B. Stuart, that kind of thing. He told us this long, rambling story about fighting off 'dark demons' trying to kidnap his wife. He led us to a clearing on his property that he referred to as an old slave graveyard, claiming that was where they came from."

Jason leaned in a little, his voice dropping. "It became pretty clear we had stumbled into some kind of racist fantasy. We made up a quick excuse and got out of there as fast as we could." He gestured around the restaurant. "We'd heard this was one of the few major historical spots in the area, so we decided to check it out on a whim. Got in here two nights ago hoping to find something here to make a good episode about instead."

"Any luck so far?" I asked. As we spoke, Maggie, the caring sister she was, temporarily shifted her focus from her idol to Lucy, who was visibly becoming bored. Out of the corner of my eye, I watched as Maggie used two blueberries and a bent strip of bacon to make Lucy's pancake, to Lucy's delight, into an edible face.

Jason sighed, looking a little defeated. "Not yet. We filmed around this historical marker for a Civil War soldier. Some guy was killed right there on his way home from duty, and no one ever figured out who did it. We thought for sure there'd be some local rumor or legend about his ghost, but everyone we talked to said they'd never seen anything like that." I knew just the marker he was talking about and, indeed, I'd never heard of any reports of ghost sightings connected to it.

"We did come across this one old guy walking along the trail. He was really pale, with ragged clothes, and hobbling along with a pickaxe. We asked him if he'd ever seen the soldier's ghost, or any paranormal activity around here at all." Jason shook his head, a small smile playing on his lips. "He just looked at us with a blank stare and asked, 'Gold?' I guess he was hoping we'd pay him to make something up, but we're trying to be legit with this show. A lot of other shows do that, but we'd rather not. No ghosts so far, but at least we're not faking anything."

"Well," I said, keeping the irony to myself, "I wish you better luck today. I've worked and lived around here my whole life, and I can tell you that plenty of people have seen strange things. The woods have a mind of their own."

As he gulped down the last of his coffee, his eyes narrowed as he appeared to ponder the meaning of my words. "You know," he said, "If you're from around here, could you help us with something? There's a gorgeous looking peak in the center of the park. We'd love to get some footage from up there."

"The Towers Overlook, you mean?" I asked, referencing one of the better sites for viewing the location he was describing.

"No, no, the Towers themselves."

I shook my head vigorously. "No, no, no, there's no way up there. Completely inaccessible."

His face took on a skeptical expression. "Is that so? Cause we saw two people up there today."

"You must be mistaken," I assured him. "There's simply no way to get there."

Jason motioned me to approach him. He lifted a small backpack from the floor, removed a fancy camera, and turned on its LCD screen. "I had my 600 millimeter lens on it at the time, hence being able to get a pretty good shot of them." Sure enough, the image he produced showed two women, both probably in their mid-to-late 20s, sitting casually on the precipice of the Towers summit. They wore light, comfortable hiking attire, though one of them also had on a striking, ornate necklace. There was no equipment in sight. Certainly, nothing about them screamed "trespassing thrill-seekers."

"I don't understand," I mumbled, at a loss to explain how the couple had gotten up there.

Jason put the camera away and zipped up his backpack. "What can I say?" he retorted. "Strange things, like you said." He turned to Maggie as he stood up. "It was *such* a pleasure meeting you, Maggie."

She blushed again. "I'll never get rid of my Lilicrank doll," she promised.

"That's wonderful," assured Jason. "I'm so honored to have you as a fan. But, Maggie, if you ever feel yourself growing out of it...that's okay too. I won't be hurt if you choose to leave it behind."

Maggie glanced up at me, not sure what to make of Jason's statement, as he exited the building.

~

My sister picked up Maggie and Lucy the next morning, and I headed into work soon after.

Upon arriving, I stopped by the main lodge where I asked Emily, one of the desk agents, if she'd encountered a pair of women fitting the description of those I'd seen in Jason's image. "I have reason to believe they've gone to an off-limits area," I told her. "If they're still here, I need to warn them that they can't pull a stunt like that again."

"I know just who you're talking about," Emily replied, her eyes lighting up. "I was only around them briefly to give them the key to the room they reserved, and again when they returned it upon check-out this morning, but I remember them clearly. Let me tell you, even in as little time as I saw them, I could sense that they were *madly* in love. It was obvious, just from the way they looked at each other and held each other at every opportunity, like there was no divide or personal space between them. It honestly touched my heart. Would've given them a room for free if I could."

"Did they tell you anything else about who they were, or what they were doing here?"

"Yep. I try to do some friendly chit chat with visitors, especially those clearly not from around here. Said something about seeing sights all around the country. They'd started in Tennessee, hit the east coast, and had just started making their way out west. I told them they'd made a good choice stopping here."

"Well, if they're already gone, then I suppose that's that. You know, I saw them at the top of Towers, of all places. No idea how they got there."

Emily's jaw dropped a bit. "You mean they actually went up there, for real? They told me about that, but I assumed they were confused because their description made no sense."

"What about it didn't make sense?"

"They said they took a trail with an unfamiliar name, and that it led them all the way to the precipice of the Towers formation. You know as well as I do that there's no trail that leads there."

"What did they say the name was?"

Emily's brow furrowed as she struggled to remember. "Oh, um..." Then, it came to her. "Lover's End, that was it. Lover's End."

~

All that happened a year ago. It's a windy morning, and the sun has yet to rise. The crews setting up the Easter celebrations cause my mind to drift back to that delightful weekend when Lucy and Maggie were in my care. They're with their parents now. In a few hours, they'll slip on their Easter sweaters, and my sister will undoubtedly text me a few adorable photos of them hunting for eggs - well, in all likelihood, Maggie encouraging Lucy to hunt for eggs - in their backyard.

I think about how little my own life has changed since then. I dated a woman for a while, but it wasn't a good fit, and we eventually drifted apart. The park, with all its stunning views and scenic trails, has remained the constant in my life. It's odd to me that, despite how often I visit, I never have a direct supernatural experience like the ones I've heard about, but I don't mind.

I remember meeting Jason and his crew last year and have since caught his show a few times on TV. He had his big breakthrough episode at the park, filmed the day we met. The whole episode was centered on a video in which Jason's crew was surrounded by what looked to be a contingent of Confederate soldiers on a hidden trail.

They were starving and desperate, and the crew barely got away. The episode blew up online, but plenty of people called it a hoax, pointing out that no such trail existed and arguing that the zombie soldiers were just actors in heavy makeup. Still, enough people believed it, and Jason's show now has a sizable audience. I sense that Jason is proud to have made it big doing something other than his kids' show.

Just then, my phone buzzes with a message from Emily: *"Can you come over? I just started my shift, and there's something I want to tell you."*

She greets me when I reach the front desk of the main building. "It's them! The two women you saw up on Towers last year. They must've checked in last night while Amanda was on duty. I don't like tattling on guests. But I thought you might want to know. When they checked out a little while ago, I warned them not to go off-trail, or into restricted areas. They looked surprised and said they had no intention of doing that. So hopefully they won't be any trouble. Still, I figured I'd at least let you know."

I nod. "Thanks. I hope they won't be any trouble either."

"There were a few funny things about them," Emily continues. "First, they seemed, well, tired. But not in the sense of it being so early. Like, they were still all over each other, still clearly in love, but they moved and talked kinda slowly, like it was a significant exertion. It was odd. They still looked on the young side, but they acted like they'd aged decades since I last saw them. Anyhow, I told them I remembered them, and how they were traveling the country, and I asked them if they were still doin' that. And, well, one of them - she had this fancy necklace with a big jewel on it - said they'd never stopped. Just kept traveling and traveling, livin' the life, seeing new things together. But, about a week ago, this big wave of exhaustion had fallen over both of them, like they knew it was almost over. This had been one of their favorite stops, and it was nearby, so they'd decided to come back here, to the same trail and the same peak as before."

"I'm guessing that's where they said they were going? Back to Towers?"

"Yep," Emily responds. "I figured I should bring that to your attention. One last thing: the other woman asked me for a favor." She motioned to a medium-sized package. "She left me this package. Asked me to mail it for them. Left me some money to cover the expense and an address to use. It's in Nashville, someone named Mae. Said it was filled with photos, letters, mementos they'd picked up. I don't see any problem with me just mailing it like they asked."

"Neither do I," I reply. "Go ahead, when you get the chance. I'll keep an eye on Towers."

~

When folks decide to go into the off-limits areas and get themselves into trouble, it's not just a risk to them. It's a risk to the people who have to go out and get them. A rescue operation eats up a lot of time and resources that could be used for other things.

Thus, the ordinary procedure in a situation like this - where I had good reason to believe these women were going to return, somehow, to the Towers summit - is to act quickly to put a stop to it. Heck, even calling in a helicopter wouldn't be unmerited.

But these are not ordinary circumstances. I don't understand what these two women are up to, but the park does. If the park created a path for them up to the Towers peak before, then it may do so again.

So, instead of spreading the word amongst the other rangers of a possible situation involving off-trail hikers getting themselves into danger, I head out to the Towers overlook, taking a pair of binoculars with me. By the time I arrive at the fence that marks the overlook's perimeter, pink hues of the approaching sun are beginning to spread across the soft blue sky. Bracing myself against the heavy breeze, I raise the binoculars.

Sure enough, I spot them together in the same location, though this time they're standing by, instead of sitting on, the edge of a rocky precipice. There's no logical way for them to have reached the peak of the Towers at all, much less as quickly as they did, but something tells me that the park has provided them a shortcut through the same impossible trail as before.

One, who looks slightly older, wears a classic outfit of a denim jacket and black jeans. The second woman, younger with light jeans and a flannel button-down open to reveal a t-shirt underneath, has an ornate necklace that I recognize.

They stand side-by-side, their arms wrapped around one another. They kiss, then turn to face the rising sun.

The sun finally crests the horizon, spilling daylight across the valley. And, all at once, they're simply...gone. I gasp as I realize that their bodies have, in an instant, vanished.

The necklace and most of their clothes sink to the ground. Their jackets and t-shirts, however, are propelled by a strong gust of wind into the air. They drift away, off the peak and above the river below. As they fall, they intermingle until they are wrapped tightly around each other. Like a ghost chased by Jason's crew, the resulting formation takes on a vaguely human form as it floats across the sky, flapping with the wind as it steadily drops.

For a moment, as the makeshift figure, a tangle of denim and cotton, sinks into the valley, I think about these two women becoming a part of the park, endlessly wandering it in some form that exists beyond the boundaries of life and death, to be spotted on occasion by those to whom the park chooses to grant access to its secrets.

Perhaps that will happen. But perhaps not. As the shape appears to embark on its last descent, a burst of wind sends it soaring. It regains the height that it's lost, floating above the Towers, then higher, and higher, almost impossibly so. It continues to ascend, farther than any natural force could propel it to reach, until it disappears amidst a distant sea of grey, welcoming clouds.

BONUS CONTENT

Night in the Haunted Library

Who can resist a sleepover party in a haunted library? Not you, Cassandra or Sebastian, who emerge from hiding as the janitor exits and locks the front door. Before you can plug in the speakers or open the vodka, a pale figure emerges from the shadows. Do you approach it (**M**) or hide (**F**)?

A. You join Sebastian under a decorative tree. As you spot a loose window nearby, Sebastian sniffles. He's about to sneeze! Do you stay (**I**) or abandon him (**H**)?

B. *Method one: sacrifice a virgin while chanting "Occidit Omnes Librarios". Try this on* **K.** *Method two: make an extremely loud noise. Try this on* **D.**

C. As you open it, your hand sticks to the pages. You feel sick. Your body dissipates into a mushy pulp that the book hungrily absorbs. Congrats, you found the worst ending!

D. You power up the speakers you brought. Your dance music angers the ghost, but isn't loud enough! Run for the nearby entrance (**L**) or find Sebastian (**G**) – maybe he can help!

E. You've wasted too much time! The ghost librarian finds you. Go to **J**.

F. Hiding's a good idea! Follow Cassandra to the paranormal section (**O**), or follow Sebastian to the children's section (**A**).

G. Good thinking – Sebastian shows you and Cassandra a loose window. The ghost watches as you all flee. Your joy at escaping is tempered only by your knowledge that the library remains haunted.

H. As Sebastian sneezes, you run for the window. Only, your foot slips on a carpet displaying a world map. You fall. A shadow looms over you. Go to **J**.

I. Sebastian's 'achoo' attracts your pursuer, who croaks "SILENCE IN THE LIBRARY". "Take them instead of me!" yells Sebastian as he shoves you to the ground. Sebastian, then Cassandra, climb out the window as the ghost's cold hands restrain you. They suck, but at least they survived. Go to **J**.

J. She swings long, knife-like nails. A sharp pain runs through your neck. Your head detaches. On the bright side, you can keep the library party going forever as a ghost.

K. "I can't help with that," says Cassandra. She narrows her eyes at you. "What about you?" If you qualify, go to line **N**. Otherwise, go to **E**.

L. You rush towards the front entrance, adrenaline overriding your logic. You rattle the door handle, only remembering the click of the janitor's lock a moment too late. Go to **J**!

M. It's probably friendly, right? You approach the pale woman with wispy white hair. She extends a bony hand. Go to **J**.

N. "Well, I've never 'done it', but let's think about-" Cassandra swings her knife while repeating the phrase. As you die, you take some satisfaction in watching the ghost cry out and disappear. At least she won't haunt anyone else.

O. You decide to stick with Cassandra – she's ex-military, after all, and carries a knife. As you crouch behind a shelf, you decide to check out one of two books with interesting titles: *Two Methods of Defeating Librarian Ghosts* (**B**) and *Dionaea Muscipula* (**C**).

Dead Man's Deck

"There's a morgue down on deck 1, and it's rarely occupied," says Zach, the deckhand who's been flirting with you all night, to the annoyance of your best friend Anju. "It's a perfect spot for restricted activities...like those between employees and guests." Follow Zach (**J**) or reject his advances (**D**).

A. You grip the cold, rotting skin of the attacker and pry him off Zach. Suddenly, a strong force from behind sends you hurtling to the ground. As Zach flees, you realize, despondently, that he left you behind as a distraction. Go to (**E**).

B. You and Anju giggle as the pile of empty drink containers around your poolside lounge chairs grows steadily larger. "I think she likes you," slurs your tipsy friend, gesturing to a woman staggering in your direction. Go to (**E**).

C. The lifeboat drifts in the water. You and Anju ignore the moans emanating from below as you wait on its roof for help. You embrace when a rescue helicopter descends to your position.

D. Zach storms off angrily. "Good call," quips Anju as she hands you a third tequila sunrise. Soon, you hear excited screams. Are they coming from the casino? Investigate (**I**) or keep relaxing (**B**).

E. There's no escape. The zombie's grip is strong. Your last sight is of hungry eyes and chomping teeth.

F. A familiar voice – Zach's? – rings out on the intercom. "Anyone alive, go to the port-side lifeboats!" Head straight there (**H**) or find Anju first (**L**).

G. You notice an enclosed lifeboat slowly descending to the ocean. As a mob of zombies approaches, you and Anju jump onto its roof. Go to (**C**).

H. You spot the lowering lifeboat, but the deck is swarming. You can try to hop aboard immediately (**M**) or jump over the railing to try and swim for a derelict inflatable dinghy you spot drifting nearby. (**N**).

I. "Jesus," you mutter, observing the gore and stray limbs strewn about the room. Aside from one guest – who operates a slot machine even as the undead tear into her – the casino's inhabitants are no longer among the living. Go to (**F**).

J. Eying his intoxicating biceps, you follow Zach below. The door he leads you to is already open. "What the-" exclaims Zach as he steps over puddles of crimson liquid. A pale figure cuts him off, emerging from the shadows to dig its teeth into Zach's neck. Help Zach (**A**) or run (**K**).

K. You sprint away, eventually reaching the casino. Before you can raise the alarm, a horde of undead guests and crewman burst inside. Go to (**F**).

L. You can't leave Anju! Her shrieks lead you to the putt-putt course, where several decrepit figures surround her. Using a golf club, you swing your way through them and reach your friend. Head to (**G**).

M. The lifeboat launches successfully. Before you can ask Zach why he didn't wait for anyone else or about the teeth marks on his neck, he coughs up blood, collapses, and turns. Go to (**E**).

N. You barely clear the railing and hit the cold, dark water. The ship is moving fast, and the current immediately pulls you under the massive hull. You manage one gasp of air before the churning propellers of the cruise ship chop any hope of survival into bloody mist.

CONTINUITY REFRESH

Below, you can find a list of characters and events from my prior compilation, *Friends, Lovers, & Other Gaslighters* ("*FLOG*"), that are referenced or otherwise relevant to this compilation.

FLOG featured a 'recurring' story centered around a group of friends. One series of events within this overarching story followed April, her wife Emma, their baby Harper, and their dog Tessa. Another followed their friends Olivia, Mae, and Casey. Casey is Mae's boyfriend, and Olivia is Mae's best friend. *FLOG* ended with Olivia, Mae, and Casey moving into a townhouse next door to April, Emma, Harper, and Tessa.

Several stories in *FLOG* involved a company called "Abernathy Industries," which engaged in various disreputable practices, including unethical experimentation on its own employees. One story, "*The Perfect Job*," focused on a young woman named Monica as she began to ascend the corporate ladder at Abernathy Industries.

One story ("*Transformations*") followed a man who used to star in a children's television show called "Lucian and the Lilicrank" who encountered a peculiar set of fans.

One story ("*Muck*") followed a woman named Laura as she traveled to a deserted town in southwest Virginia at the request of her drug-addicted brother Daniel.

One story ("*Purity Pledge*") involved a group of friends consisting of two couples: Maria and Aaron and Addie and Jose.

Most of these characters and events (all but Olivia and Mae) only appear briefly in this compilation, such that rereading their respective stories is likely unnecessary to fully enjoy it.

ACKNOWLEDGMENTS, ADAPTATIONS, & THE AUTHOR

Acknowledgments

Thank you to Fran for doing so much to promote my prior book, and to her daughter Christina for test reading two stories in this one.

I remain extraordinarily grateful toward Laura & Izzy for their enthusiastic support and outstanding craftsmanship. Their meticulously detailed miniatures, which form the main attraction of my book fair display tables, do an astounding job of bringing many of my stories to life.

Past Audio Adaptations

Return to Office: Adapted on *The Antiquarium of Sinister Happenings* on April 9, 2025.

The Visitor: Accepted for adaptation by *The NoSleep Podcast* to air in Season 22. (Not yet released as of finalizing this book.)

Phantom Train of Roanoke Valley: Narrated by YouTuber Mr. Creeps on November 22, 2020. (This story was heavily rewritten for this compilation.)

A Better Sibling: Adapted on *The NoSleep Podcast*, Season 15 Episode 4 on September 19, 2020. (This story was heavily rewritten for this compilation.)

A Perfect Ten: Adapted by YouTuber DodgeTheGrave on March 14, 2021.

The Initiation: Adapted by YouTuber CreepyStoriesJR on October 13, 2025.

About the Author

B.A. Ries resides in Alexandria, Virginia with a perfect and brilliant wife and a somehow even more perfect and brilliant daughter. All three take orders from a dog who believes she can climb trees.

Please feel free to take a minute to complete this short survey about this book (and, if you read it, my prior book): https://forms.gle/5rNs AKndSj4phuEX8